BELOVED
GOMORRAH

Acclaim for Justine Saracen's Novels

"*Mephisto Aria* could well stand as a classic among gay and lesbian readers."—*ForeWord Reviews*

"Justine Saracen's *Sistine Heresy* is a well-written and surprisingly poignant romp through Renaissance Rome in the age of Michelangelo. ...The novel entertains and titillates while it challenges, warning of the mortal dangers of trespass in any theocracy (past or present) that polices same-sex desire."—Professor Frederick Roden, University of Connecticut, Author, *Same-Sex Desire in Victorian Religious Culture*

"...the lesbian equivalent of Indiana Jones. ...Saracen has sprinkled cliffhangers throughout this tale...If you enjoy the History Channel presentations about ancient Egypt, you will love this book. If you haven't ever indulged, it will be a wonderful introduction to the land of the Pharaohs. If you're a *Raiders of the Lost Ark*-type adventure fan, you'll love reading a woman in the hero's role."—*Just About Write*

"Saracen's wonderfully descriptive writing is a joy to the eye and the ear, as scenes play out on the page, and almost audibly as well. The characters are extremely well drawn, with suave villains, and lovely heroines. There are also wonderful romances, a heart-stopping plot, and wonderful love scenes. *Mephisto Aria* is a great read."—*Just About Write*

Sarah, Son of God can lightly be described as the "The Lesbian's *Da Vinci Code*" because of the somewhat common themes. At its roots, it's part mystery and part thriller. *Sarah, Son of God* is an engaging and exciting story about searching for the truth within each of us. Ms. Saracen considers the sacrifices of those who came before us, challenges us to open ourselves to a different reality than what we've been told we can have, and reminds us to be true to ourselves. Her prose and pacing rhythmically rise and fall like the tides in Venice; and her reimagined life and death of Jesus allows thoughtful readers to consider "what if?"—*Rainbow Reader*

"*Mephisto Aria*, brims with delights for every sort of reader. ...At each level of Saracen's deliciously complicated plot, the characters who are capable of self-knowledge and of love evaded their contracts with the devil, rescued by each other's feats of queerly gendered derring-do done in the name of love. Brava! Brava! Brava!"—Suzanne Cusick, Professor of Music, New York University

Visit us at www.boldstrokesbooks.com

By the Author

The 100th Generation

Vulture's Kiss

Sistine Heresy

Mephisto Aria

Sarah, Son of God

Tyger, Tyger, Burning Bright

Beloved Gomorrah

BELOVED GOMORRAH

by

Justine Saracen

2013

ISBN 10: 1-60282-862-8
ISBN 13: 978-1-60282-862-9

THIS TRADE PAPERBACK ORIGINAL IS PUBLISHED BY
BOLD STROKES BOOKS, INC.
P.O. BOX 249
VALLEY FALLS, NY 12185

FIRST EDITION: MARCH 2013

CREDITS
EDITOR: SHELLEY THRASHER
PRODUCTION DESIGN: SUSAN RAMUNDO
COVER DESIGN BY SHERI (GRAPHICARTIST2020@HOTMAIL.COM)
COVER PHOTO BY JEAN-MARIE LEFEBVRE

Acknowledgments

I wish to acknowledge all the divers who have acted as technical advisors for this novel, especially Riccardo Preve, Dawn Williamson, and Yves Leflot, who explained how to kill someone underwater without being caught. (In the event of my sudden and unexpected death while diving, these three should be the first suspects.)

I'd also like to thank Philippe LeDoux, who lured me into diving in the first place, Gilbert Collins, who guided me through the frigid outdoor waters of Belgium, and Charlie (Top Gun) Hernie, who whetted my appetite for shipwreck-diving and then accompanied me down to the magnificent wreck of the *Thistlegorme*. I owe a special salute to Georges Guillaume who organized our diving trips to the Red Sea two years in a row and is far nicer than he is portrayed in this story.

Shelley Thrasher must surely know how valuable she is to me, this being our seventh novel together, but she is also a friend and a scuba diver, and one day I hope to collaborate with her on a dive. Thanks to Sheri for another deliciously dramatic cover (with fire *and* water, this time) and most of all, thanks to Radclyffe for being our Prime Mover and *éminence grise*.

Dedication

To the Wolu Plongée Club

And there came two angels to Sodom at even; and Lot sat in the gate of Sodom: and Lot seeing them rose up to meet them; and he bowed himself with his face toward the ground; And he said, Behold now, my lords, turn in, I pray you, into your servant's house, and tarry all night, and wash your feet, and ye shall rise up early, and go on your ways. ...And they entered into his house; and he made them a feast, and did bake unleavened bread, and they did eat. But before they lay down, the men of the city, the men of Sodom, compassed the house round, both old and young, all the people from every quarter: And they called unto Lot, and said unto him, Where are the men which came in to thee this night? bring them out unto us, that we may know them. And Lot went out at the door. ...And said, I pray you, brethren, do not so wickedly. Behold now, I have two daughters which have not known man; let me, I pray you, bring them out unto you, and do ye to them as is good in your eyes: only unto these men do nothing; for therefore came they under the shadow of my roof. And they said, Stand back. ...And they pressed sore upon the man, even Lot, and came near to break the door. But the men put forth their hand, and pulled Lot into the house to them, and shut to the door. And they smote the men that were at the door of the house with blindness, both small and great: so that they wearied themselves to find the door.

Genesis 19: 1-11 King James Version, 1769

Then the LORD rained upon Sodom and upon Gomorrah brimstone and fire from the LORD out of heaven; And he overthrew those cities, and all the plain, and all the inhabitants of the cities, and that which grew upon the ground. But his wife looked back from behind him, and she became a pillar of salt. ...And it came to pass, when God destroyed the cities of the plain, that God remembered Abraham, and sent Lot out of the midst of the overthrow. ...And Lot went up...and dwelt in the mountain, and his two daughters with him; ...and he dwelt in a cave, he and his two daughters. And the firstborn said unto the younger. ...Come, let us make our father drink wine, and we will lie with him, that we may preserve seed of our father. And they made their father drink wine that night: and the firstborn went in, and lay with her father; and he perceived not when she lay down, nor when she arose. And it came to pass on the morrow, that...the younger arose, and lay with him; and he perceived not when she lay down, nor when she arose. Thus were both the daughters of Lot with child by their father.

Genesis 19: 24-36 King James Version, 1769

Prologue

Ezion-Geber, later Aqaba, Jordan

Roused from sleep by the banging at his door, Maneshtu did not have his wits about him when he opened it. And thus he stood perplexed by the sight of two young women cowering in the doorway each carrying an infant.

"Forgive us, sir, for the intrusion and this late hour. We come in secret from our husbands, and no other time is possible."

"In secret?" he repeated, his befuddlement deepening. But for lack of better wisdom, he bade them enter, raising the wick on his lantern the more to see them. Drawing them to his table, he offered water, but they declined. "For what reason, may I ask..." He struggled for a polite way to inquire why they had disturbed the sleep of an old man.

The one who seemed the older of the two spoke first. "Again, we beg forgiveness for this imposition, but our cause is just. We implore you, hear us out."

"Yes, dear lady. I do so willingly." The old scribe leaned forward on his elbows.

"I am Astari." She held her infant close so that he slept. "And this is my sister Aina. We are the daughters of Lot, the son of Haran, who is the brother of Abraham."

"Yes, I have heard of Abraham and of his nephew Lot."

Astari said, "We fled from Gomorrah before it was destroyed and came to live in Zoar. There we met men who revered the One God, and hearing of the destruction of our city, they took us into their households, not knowing of our condition, and shortly we were espoused to them. They are merchants who do business in Ezion-Geber."

He urged her on, trying to draw some wisdom as to how Gomorrah and "our condition" were connected to the secrecy of the visit.

"All was well in our new home, but within a two-month time Lot came unto Zoar with condemnation and forgiveness in one breath. For he gave report of how we were with child with his own seed, but that it was we who forced ourselves upon him. It was an evil tale, and our husbands gathered up stones to bring judgment against us. We were spared the stoning when Lot raised his hands and proclaimed it the will of God. The people took him at his word, for he was the nephew of Abraham, whom they held for righteous above all other men."

She said "righteous" with venom, which stirred his curiosity. Maneshtu was nothing if not a judge of tales and the way they were told. This one had the ring of truth. "Dear ladies, why do you come to me, a stranger, and not to one of your own people?"

"Our own people will not hear us. But it is said that Maneshtu is wise and much trusted in the courts. The tribe of Abraham is growing strong and they proclaim the judgment of Gomorrah, yet we would bear witness here, with you, that the tale is false."

"Gomorrah." Maneshtu scratched under his chin. "Men say it was destroyed, and Sodom too, for the people's iniquity."

"No, teacher. That is a slander as great as the one that taints ourselves. Truly, it was the fairest of cities—a place of sages, shopkeepers, and honest men. Gomorrah was a crossroads. Its caravanserai sheltered merchants passing through from Egypt and Damascus. They haggled in the marketplace and said their prayers in many languages. The city had temples to Dagon, El, Anat, Ba'al, and Moloch, and shrines to all the lesser gods."

"Indeed, that is a rare thing," Maneshtu said, and the young woman shrugged.

"Our father called them idolaters, yet his own wife, our mother who was born in Gomorrah, was a follower of Anat. She renounced the goddess and converted to the True Faith upon her marriage to our father."

"A place of great freedom, then." Maneshtu furrowed his graying brow. "Perhaps too much freedom. I heard talk of depravity as well, of men who lay wantonly with men and women with women."

"Yet more slander, teacher, by those with no understanding of the old ways, where family was more than kith and kin, and one might join by affection alone. Our mother had such a lover, whom she met at the fountain every day. It was a tender and enduring thing, not wanton at all, though it much enraged our father. He called her "daughter of Eve" and beat her for it, but she held fast to her love in spite of him. We too longed to have a companion in this way."

"But then the angels came." The younger woman spoke for the first time and with a certain melancholy. "And they told us this was an abomination in the eyes of the One God."

Astari interrupted gently. "But we would not burden you with tales of our youth. We wish only to leave a true account of Lot and the cities of the plain, so that one day, when the story is widely told, you or another can say, 'No, this tale is false, for here is the word of the maids themselves.'"

Maneshtu scratched his beard, uncertain.

"Teacher, we are prepared to pay. Our husbands prosper, and we have saved money from our allowances." The young woman untied a small cloth from her waist and poured out four pieces of silver. "We need only a few hours of your time."

The silver pieces glimmered in the candlelight, and Maneshtu made up his mind. "Let me fetch some clay and cut a new stylus."

While he gathered his tools, the child of Astari began to whimper, and she stood up. "Forgive me, teacher, but my son Moab cries for hunger. With your permission, I will go into the other room to let him suckle. My sister can tell her tale, and when she is finished, I will tell mine."

❖

At the end of two hours, the tales were told. Maneshtu took his payment, led the two young women to the door, and bade them farewell. Mechanically, he threw the bolt into the lock and returned to his worktable, shaking his head in amazement. Fifty years he had carried on his craft, and thirty of those years he'd kept a library, but he had never been called upon for a task such as this.

He raised the wick on the lantern a second time, for his eyes were weary. Then, careful to protect the still-damp clay, he reread the cuneiform texts he had so carefully incised. The tale seemed fanciful, yet both the women's voices held a somber conviction. He himself was a follower of Marduk and cared not a whit about the desert tribes and their ways, yet it troubled him that any man should be called righteous who had acted thusly. He might indeed have good reason to save the two testimonies.

He slid the four damp clay tablets onto wooden planks and took them to his kiln. Once the fire hardened them, he would cement them back-to-back, making two double-sided documents. Then all that remained was to keep them in his library and await the day that someone asked for them.

He rubbed his neck, and glanced up through the window. The position of the moon told him it was nearer the morning than the night. But just as he returned to his bed and was about to extinguish the lantern, another knock sounded at his door.

The night had already proved remarkable, so he was not perturbed to open to another stranger. But this one hunched forward, his face concealed under a cloak, as if fearing to be seen. Maneshtu waited quietly for explanation.

"Master," the man said in muted tones. "This night, you have received the daughters of Lot and they have surely told you their story. But another part to the tale wants telling, which is unknown to them, and so I beg you to hear me as well."

Maneshtu sighed. "Come in," he said, and went to fetch a new clay tablet.

❖

Maneshtu waited long for someone to inquire about the tablets of Gomorrah, but no one ever did. They languished in a corner of his library until his death, when his house passed to his son, and then to his descendants, unto the tenth generation. Finally, none could read the scrolls and tablets, and the library was given over to store grain in.

When the family line died out, the house, which was on the outskirts of the town, fell into such disrepair that it was pillaged of its furnishings and abandoned. The land around it became a scrap heap that rose ever higher with broken crockery and objects that did not weather or rot. Desert creatures took up residence and rats scampered in the pitch-dark chambers, consuming whatever was of parchment or of wood. Asps and scorpions made their colonies around it, discouraging interest in the bit of wall that jutted out of the pile of rubble.

❖

The desert is discreet. Its sands blow equally over mankind's feats and follies covering them for centuries or millennia. But men are curious, and they penetrate the darkest places in search of things. And so it was, fifteen hundred years later, when Ezion-Geber returned to life as the city of Aqaba, that an Egyptian merchant named Ibn Yunus al Qasim arrived. Ever watchful for opportunity, he sent his men into the rubble field outside the town and they came upon the crushed remains of a house. The roof had long disintegrated into powder, and only fragments of the stone walls stood. But under the sand they uncovered a cache of tablets, in hieroglyphic, hieratic, Greek, and in cuneiform.

Al Qasim could read none of it but believed he had a treasure and resolved to ship the tablets back to Luxor. It made no difference that their contents were a mystery. They were documents of an ancient time and would surely have value. Many scholars dwelt in Luxor, and even more in Cairo, who would pay well for such antiquities.

In good time, he packed his treasures in a crate and set sail on an Egyptian dhow, bound for Safaga. It was the month of May and the Red Sea was calm. Al Qasim stood each evening with a Persian scholar who also made the passage, and they talked of weighty things: of faith and reason, of God and science, and of the stars by which they navigated.

The scholar pointed toward a band of three stars low in the sky. "There hovers *al jabbar*, the giant whom the Hebrews call Kesil, the fool, and the Greeks have named Orion. See how he raises his arm and menaces? He swings the mace, rigid and arrogant in his strength. Some say that he aims to kill all animals who, in their variety, somehow offend him. Others say it is the Pleiades, the daughters of Atlas, that he pursues, but perhaps, in his brutishness, he does both. Giant that he may be, the tiniest of creatures, the scorpion, fells him."

"Do you mean to read a lesson of justice in that?" Al Qasim chuckled.

"Perhaps only that the prideful and the cruel look not at their feet, and the smallest of things can bring them down."

"So you think the stars are there to instruct us." Al Qasim twirled the hair at the tip of his beard. "I think they are indifferent. In any case, I leave the stars to the pilot for navigation and my fate to Allah."

Having amicably disagreed, the two men curled up in their blankets under the gunwales for the night and sought to sleep.

But before the dawn, storm winds drove the dhow against a reef just off the coast of Egypt, near a tiny fishing settlement that one day would be called El Gouna. Within minutes, the ship foundered. All hands went down, and the cargo of salt, incense, hammered gold, and al Qasim's tablets was given to the sea.

CHAPTER ONE

A shiver of pleasure went through Joanna Boleyn as she plunged into the warm water of the Red Sea. It was her two hundred-something dive, but she never ceased to experience a sense of wonderment at the first undersea moment. She allowed herself the leisure of turning once on her own axis, like an ice-skater, absorbing the bright-blue world that surrounded her and Charlie. The sense of three-dimensionality was so completely different from the horizontal experience of solid ground. She no longer stood across from things, detached and analytical, but was suspended in a sphere, in the primordial element, and wherever she looked she saw life.

The fish, some in such gaudy colors they seemed a cartoon, swam by indifferently, and a few hovered teasingly within reach. A shoal of silvery sweepers engulfed her, like a shower of coins, surrounding but never touching her, as if magnetically repelled, then swept away.

They descended farther, and for a brief moment she missed the chattering of the surface world and the ease of communication. The rasp of her inhalations through the regulator and the gurgle of the exhale-bubbles that rose in a column over her head did nothing to dispel the sense of silence.

Soon the concrete structures came into sight, dull gray-green walls and arches and domes, like a ghost city. Lone groupers darted in and out of the low doorways, and an eel snaked through without stopping, as if in a hurry. This was the audacious project that the Ministry of Culture had officially named the International Egyptian Underwater Exhibit of Ecological Art, but the local Egyptians simply called *al medina*, the city.

At an average depth of thirteen meters, and stretching over nearly a hectare of dead coral, the joint UNESCO/Egyptian art project had reached its final stages. When completed, it would be an underwater sculpture museum. Eventually, however, a new reef would form over it, while the public that had contributed to its original destruction would witness and help pay for its regeneration. Even now, when only a few of the art works had been installed, the surfaces of the buildings had a soft velvet growth. Three small gray reef sharks glided toward her from the side. They approached with animal curiosity, and when they were close, Joanna could see that the largest one had a badly torn dorsal fin, perhaps from a fight with another male. The sharks circled once and then swam off over her head, indifferent.

Charlie looked back over his shoulder, his trim beard flashing white against the black of his diving suit, and she quickened her pace. In a few moments they spotted the steel rod and signpost that identified Site 13, which had been assigned to her on the outer edge of the coral plain. They paddled closer and she reached for the measuring tape in her net bag, preparing to fix the optimum position of her fountain. But something was wrong.

The rod identifying Site 13 tilted at a forty-five-degree angle with scarcely a square meter of ground beneath it. Beyond that, the coral dropped away immediately at a steep angle into the abyss.

Baffled and annoyed, she swept in closer. Charlie paddled to her side and, through his mask, she could see his expression of *What the hell?!*

Where there was supposed to be ground she saw only a crevice. It appeared the designers had located Site 13 too far toward the edge of the coral shelf, and some blow, perhaps something as simple as driving in the identification rod, had broken away a porous section of coral. More astonishing was the size of the damage.

She followed the crevice downward as it widened and darkened increasingly with the depth. Damn. The site was useless for her sculpture. She would surely be assigned another spot, but that would mean delay, maddening delay, which she was already familiar with. For starters, she and Charlie would have to write a report of the damage to the committee in charge of the project, explaining how it precluded the installation of a fountain. Damn! Damn! Damn! She groused inwardly as she descended farther, fanning the ever-widening walls with her torch beam.

At thirty meters, she checked her tank pressure. No hurry. She still had plenty of air to allow time for the safety stop, provided they didn't stay long at a great depth. She continued downward and Charlie followed. At thirty-eight meters the crevice flattened out to a shallow slope.

She made a sweep with the torch, trying to memorize what she saw so she could file a report to the project committee and request another site. Just gray, dead coral, split to a width that could encompass a car. Then something below caught her eye. *Fish*, she thought, their scales catching the light. But no. They didn't move.

She dropped down another meter and peered, intrigued. Charlie swept in close to her and tapped on his wrist computer. They were pretty far down now and this part of the dive was unplanned, so they'd have to ascend soon. She signaled agreement, then pointed toward the shining objects jutting up out of the white grit of the slope. She poked at them with her finger and almost jumped when she saw what they were. Cups, a plate, other more mysterious objects, and, farther along, what looked like clay tablets, both broken and intact.

After a moment of disbelief, realization hit. If the objects had been embedded in the coral until the catastrophic split, they might well be artifacts from a shipwreck. Since she detected no sign of a rusting vessel, it would have to be a very old one.

Charlie was already reaching for one of the cups. Joanna signaled *don't touch* but he ignored her, dropping the cup into the net bag hooked to his vest. Then he tapped on his wrist computer again. It was time to go. She agreed, and as they turned to ascend, Charlie snatched up two more objects from the sand.

They hovered at twelve meters, to decompress, and then again, for safety, at six. Joanna had time to shine her torch on the objects he had pilfered. A metal cup, possibly gold, with a simple geometric ornament around the rim, and two clay tablets. Through the net, she could see they were covered with writing. She tried to make out the lettering and then gasped so hard she almost sucked in water. It was cuneiform.

The artifacts were ancient.

A half dozen thoughts went through her mind. Whatever they had found, it was something big, very big. They'd surrender them to the Egyptian authorities right away, of course, but what would happen then? Presumably the committee would assign her another exhibit space, but would they close off the wreck site to divers? Or would they halt work on the project altogether? She feared that the Egyptian government was not well-enough organized to do anything but delay.

Their safety stop over, she signaled *up*. Overhead a dark form dropped toward her, surrounded by a ring of froth. Something heavy and dead. While she peered upward at it, vaguely irritated, more ominous forms appeared from both sides. Within seconds of the strange object hitting the water, the three reef sharks were back.

As the object, which she could now see was a dead fish, dropped past her, the sharks tore into it, thrashing wildly in a sudden feeding frenzy. She kicked upward, to escape them, but before she could rise more than a meter, something bit through her wetsuit into her lower leg and pulled her downward. She struck out with her torch, trying to dislodge it, then felt a sudden bright pain on the side of her face. Under slashing teeth, the strap of her mask broke, and it fell away, exposing her eyes to the intense salt water. She swung her torch wildly, trying to protect her face and air tube and sensed Charlie struggling next to her. She forced her eyes open to a squint against the scalding water but saw only the red mist of her own blood seeping out from her cheek and enveloping her head.

Oh, my God, she thought. *I'm being eaten alive.*

Chapter Two

With the words "still a knockout at forty-nine" buzzing in her mind, Kaia Kapulani let the review of her last film slide from her lap and began to doze on the sunny upper deck of the yacht *Hina*. The voice of her husband jolted her to wakefulness.

"What the hell is this?!"

She squinted up at him. "What the hell is what?"

"This!" He shook the remains of a very large and no-longer-fresh fish at her. "I told Jibril to dump it this morning, but he said you ordered him not to. You *know* how I hate it when you contradict me. It confuses the help and makes me look foolish. Don't ever do that again."

"You're not allowed to throw garbage into the sea here," she replied softly. "You can dump it when we get back to the dock."

"Are you stupid, or what?" His volume was increasing. "It's not *garbage*. It's a goddamn *fish*. What the hell do you think the sea is already full of?" He heaved the pungent remains over the side and, without even watching it enter the water, stormed off muttering "bloody eco-fanatics."

Kaia stared up into the cloudless blue sky, mentally shrugging as she heard the splash. There was no point in arguing with Bernard once he'd made up his mind. He made the decisions—about nearly every aspect of their lives—and since his decisions had earned them a lot of money, she rarely challenged him.

But now that she was awake, the review began to trouble her. No matter if it was couched in a compliment, forty-nine was a frightening number in Hollywood. They had come to the Red Sea to celebrate her fiftieth birthday in seclusion, away from the media and cameras. But the fact that her age had appeared in the review showed that the press—and the public—were counting. Was it going to be the countdown, or count-up in this case, to the end of her career?

A loud male voice disturbed her once again, this time from the water. She lurched from her chair to the railing and saw a diver waving frantically. He held another person hooked in his arm, and even from a distance, Kaia could see the second diver's face was covered with blood.

At the same time one of the Egyptian crewmen swung a life-ring toward him. It was a good throw, and once the diver grabbed ahold of it, the crewman reeled him in.

Kaia clambered down the stairs to the stern deck and arrived just as Jibril was pulling the injured diver up onto the deck. A woman, but it was impossible to make out her features for all the blood.

She snatched the towel that she'd had around her neck and pressed it against the open wound on the woman's cheek while the other diver hauled himself up the ladder next to her.

"Sharks," he said. "I kept them away from me, but they got to her. In her arm and her leg too." He pointed to the semicircles of punctures on the left sleeve and leg of the wetsuit, from which blood now oozed onto the wooden deck.

"Back to the dock," Kaia shouted toward the crewman standing behind her, though Bernard must have already given the order, because the yacht was turning.

He was standing next to them now as well. "What happened?" he asked. "Are you hurt too?" He pointed to the blood on the diver's beard.

Cradling the delirious woman in his arms, the diver whispered comfort, pressing the towel over the wound. "No, I'm okay. It's *her* blood. We were inspecting a site and saw a few sharks, but nothing unusual. Then, as we came up, some damned fool chummed the water, and they went into a feeding frenzy. We were right in the middle of it. We beat them away but not soon enough."

Bernard held up his cell phone. "I've already contacted the hospital. They'll send an ambulance right away." For once, Kaia was relieved at his ability to take charge. Now all they could do was try to stop the bleeding.

"What's your name? Her name?" Kaia asked, for lack of anything better to say.

"Charlie Hernie. Her name's Joanna. We're with the underwater-museum project."

"Oh, yes. I've heard about that. The underwater City on the Plain, the paper called it. We saw boats putting down a statue a few days ago."

"That's right," Charlie said, but his attention was on the woman, who had begun to moan. "Don't worry, kiddo. We'll have you to a doctor in just a few minutes."

Jibril brought another towel and wrapped it around the bleeding leg, though it did little to halt the flow. In the soaking wetsuit, blood couldn't coagulate.

They were at the dock now and the pilot backed the yacht up against the end of it. Jibril dropped a plank across the short gap between stern and dock, and together he and Charlie lifted the woman off the deck. They had carried her most of the way along the long dock when the ambulance pulled up at the far end of it.

Kaia stood, stunned, on the stern deck of the *Hina*, while the men draped the limp form onto a stretcher and slid it into the ambulance. "What do you think we should do now?" she asked her husband.

"Call the goddamn lawyer," Bernard snarled, and walked away.

Kaia watched him, nonplussed. This vacation wasn't turning out well at all.

Charlie paced nervously in the waiting area, furious that he couldn't find anyone to give him an update on Joanna, furious that he hadn't been able to fend the sharks off her as he'd fended them off himself, furious at whoever had attracted them in the first place.

After arriving at the hospital and seeing her disappear into the emergency room, he had been barred from coming inside in his wetsuit. He had no trouble hitchhiking back to the dock, but then it had taken him nearly half an hour to retrieve their dinghy with the help of Bernard and to change out of the wetsuit into dry clothes. The rented car was parked near another dock, so fetching it and getting back to the hospital ate up another half an hour. By the time he arrived at the hospital with Joanna's clothes, he was frantic with worry.

The emergency-room staff directed him to the waiting area, but nobody could tell him how long it would take. And so he paced.

He scratched his beard, debating whether to telephone someone, but couldn't think of anyone. The committee in charge of the project would want to know if one of their artists was affected, but he had no one, really, to turn to for advice in an emergency. The people back home at the museum would care, of course, but he didn't know yet what to tell them. He patted the bundle of clothing he had brought from the car: blue jeans, hoodie, and sandals. She most likely wouldn't be putting them on right away, but when? He couldn't stop thinking of the blood that kept oozing through her wetsuit. How much had she lost?

The door from surgery swung open and two orderlies wheeled out a gurney with someone on it. It took a second look to ascertain it was Joanna, for one side of her face was covered with gauze, and she was still unconscious. The gurney didn't stop for him but continued along the corridor toward an elevator. He started after it but halted, seeing one of the doctors emerge from the operating room. "How is she? Will she be all right?"

"Please, have a seat." The doctor, a sinuous man whose hair and beard were trimmed to about one centimeter and seemed to grow together in a single white balaclava, directed him to a row of chairs.

"How is she?" Charlie repeated, sitting down. "How bad is it?"

The doctor shook his head. "It took a long time before we could even get to her. We had to cut away the wetsuit, and all that time she was bleeding. But she was lucky. She had only punctures and lacerations and no loss of limb."

"So she's going to be all right?"

"Her heartbeat is good, and we gave her a lot of blood serum, but she's not out of danger yet. We'll keep an eye on her for a few days and see what happens. The punctures on her arm were easy to close, but the muscle damage in her leg will keep her from walking for a while. Then she may need cosmetic surgery on her face."

"Oh my God. It's that bad?"

"The shark's teeth caught her just in front of her left ear, cutting downward, but fortunately missed her eye and critical facial nerves. We have to monitor how well the wound closes. But it looked like the strap on her mask kept the teeth from slicing too deeply. In any case, we'll know a lot more in a day or two. She needs to rest in a clean, quiet place and let her body heal itself."

Charlie rubbed his forehead. Outside of the hospital, there *was* no clean, quiet place. The hostel attached to the workshop where they were staying had no services, and she had a room at the top of a flight of stairs.

"She's going to need someone to take care of her then, right?"

"Yes, of course."

"I see." Charlie's voice dropped. "Can I see her now?"

"There's really no point. She's sedated and will be unconscious for several more hours."

"Right," he said, defeated. "Um. I brought her clothes." He held up the neatly folded pile.

"You can leave them here if you like. She won't need them for a while, but she may find comfort in seeing them. Why don't you come back tomorrow morning when she'll be awake. I'm sure she'll be happy to see you."

"Yes, all right. I'll do that." He handed over the clothing and shook hands with the doctor. Then, dazed, he walked down the hospital corridor and out the door.

Kaia stood on the prow of the *Hina* looking westward, trying to enjoy the sunset, but the red glow in the sky agitated her more than it calmed her. This was supposed to be a vacation, a quiet week at the Red Sea on their boat after the shooting of her last film. Her salary had been considerable, so she should be celebrating, but she wasn't in the mood.

Bernie himself had soured the air. His aggressive take-charge manner made him an invaluable agent but a rotten husband. It had also gotten them into trouble again. He just couldn't accept rules other than his own, and now he had endangered the life of a young woman. God, the poor thing was covered in blood. Would she die? Or be maimed or crippled? Kaia rested her elbows on the railing and stared at the darkening sea.

Bernard came up beside her. "I've called Landau."

"What did he say?"

"That we're in deep shit if she decides to sue."

"You mean because of the fish you threw overboard?"

"Yeah, apparently signs were posted all over the dock saying, NO GARBAGE DISPOSAL IN THE SEA. And since they're working on that damned underwater-city thing, they're real Nazis about it."

Sued for criminal negligence. Her money for Bernie's aggressive stupidity. She wanted to say, "I told you so, goddamn it," but instead she simply rubbed her face. "So what do we do now?"

"Well, we try to stop her from suing."

"And just how are we supposed to do that?" She faced him, turning her back on the spectacle on the horizon.

Unperturbed, he lit a cigar, sucked in its first smoke, and exhaled it from the side of his mouth. He puffed again in short bursts and, in the increasing darkness, the burning tip glowed menacingly. She hated his cigars, although they were expensive ones that didn't smell so bad. It was the image he projected. Bad enough when a big man puffed on a stogie, but when a short man did, he looked slightly pathetic, like a child playing grownup.

"Landau suggested we make friends with her, offer to take care of her here on board. Hell, even pay her hospital bill. He thinks it will take her a while to figure out that we were the closest boat and that the dead fish came from us. In the meantime, you'll have won her over with your tender, loving care. After being nursed back to health by you, she won't have a case."

"You're worried about her 'case'? We have no idea how badly hurt she is. What if she dies? That'll be our fault. No, *your* fault."

"Stop being so hysterical. She's not going to die. I already called the hospital and they said she was out of surgery. She's in serious condition, but otherwise she's fine. In a few days she can move out of the hospital and, if we play our cards right, on board the yacht. Then you two can start becoming best friends. You're an actress. It should be a piece of cake, for chrissake."

"Oh, so I'm to be the nursemaid to make up for your criminal act. For a woman I don't even know. Great."

Bernard shrugged. "It has to be you. I've got to fly to New York in a few days. Don't forget, I'm going back to finish up *your* next contract, for a big fat fee. So I don't want to hear any more crap about criminal acts and who's at fault. Just do what I tell you until I come back. Haven't I always managed the business just fine?"

"If by 'business' you mean my career, that's debatable. I'm tired of making so many crap movies. Why can't you find me something with some intellectual quality, instead of these broad-screen spaghetti spectaculars?"

"What an ungrateful bitch you are. Look around you. We're on a frigging million-dollar yacht, for chrissake. We've got two homes and four cars."

"You've got three cars. I've got one."

"That's not the point. Those movies you're looking down your nose at have made us rich, so unless you want to go back to waiting tables in Honolulu, I suggest you shut up and do your job here. And that includes schmoozing the broad who has the power to take us to court for a few million bucks. If you think she wouldn't take advantage of us given the chance, you're even more naïve than I thought."

"You make me sick," Kaia muttered as she walked away from him toward the stairs. She was relieved to know that the woman—what was her name again, oh, right, Joanna—would recover, but she resented being ordered to spend the next week, or longer, waiting on her.

The sun had set but the stars were not yet visible, and the sky was a somber gray-brown. It mirrored the way she felt as she made her way toward the stairs down to her cabin. Bernie could be such a bastard.

CHAPTER THREE

As Kaia reached the front entrance of the El Gouna Hospital, the door swung open. She stepped out of the way and two staff members in white coats rushed by in animated conversation. A third man followed them, and in the impatient moment she waited for him to pass, she recognized him.

"Mr. Hernie," she said, stopping him. "Have you seen her? How is she?"

He blinked for a moment, then recognized her in return. "Oh, it's you. Miss Kapulani."

"Please, let's get past the formalities. It's Kaia, and you're Charlie, right? Is she okay?"

He nodded. "She's awake but a little fuzzy. I'm sure she'll be glad to see you."

"I'm so relieved. Did the doctors say how long she'd have to stay in?"

"They didn't say anything for sure. They're waiting to see how she does. Please, go talk to her. She's in room 27 on the second floor."

"Thank you. Perhaps I'll see you later." Having run out of small talk, Kaia offered her hand and, after a warm handshake, turned and entered the hospital.

Inside the lobby, she looked for a nurses' station where she could have asked but saw only white-jacketed staff hurrying past and other visitors with small children in tow. Fortunately, the stairwell was easy to find and she took the stairs to the second floor. Room 27 was at the far end of the corridor, and after a soft knock for which she heard no answer, she opened the door and peered in.

The room held two beds, but the closest was empty. On the far bed someone huddled, facing away from the door. All that Kaia could see emerging from gray sheets was a head swathed in gauze. "Joanna?" she called softly.

The bandaged head moved slightly in response, then made some sound that could have been "Come here," but Kaia wasn't sure. She moved around to the other side of the room where the patient was facing.

She saw half a face, swollen and pink. The other half was bandaged with a long swath stretching vertically from her crown over her ear and cheek to her chin. Both eyes were closed, but when they opened, the pale-blue light that seemed to beam from them took Kaia by surprise. Then they closed again, as if extinguished.

"Do you remember me?" Kaia asked.

"Mmm, no. Remember…nothing." The bright-blue eyes opened again for a moment, then closed.

"We pulled you from the water yesterday, my husband and I. Well, actually, our crewman did. But we called to shore for an ambulance. You were hardly conscious, so I don't expect you to remember." Kaia felt like she was babbling.

"Yeah, Charlie said…" The woman murmured with difficulty, and Kaia saw why. The bandage was looped under her chin, making it difficult for her to move her jaw, and the swelling of the left cheek must have made talking painful.

"You don't have to say anything. I just wanted to make sure you were all right. We were all so worried yesterday."

"Umm." Joanna opened her eyes again. "Who are you?"

Kaia chuckled softly. She hadn't heard that question in years; everyone knew who she was. "Kaia Kapulani. You were on my boat yesterday."

"Kaia, the actress?"

"Uh, yes. That one."

Joanna's eyelids dropped again, but the right side of her mouth curled up in an awkward smile. "Liked your last movie. Costar was a jerk, though."

Kaia remembered the weeks of working with one of the highest paid and most narcissistic actors in Hollywood. "Yeah, he was," she offered. "But let's talk about you. How are you feeling?"

Joanna licked her lips with obvious effort. "Like crap. Thirsty. Is there water?"

Kaia glanced around. "Yes, there's a bottle and glass right here. Am I allowed to give you this? I don't want to do the wrong thing."

"It's fine."

Kaia poured water into the glass with a plastic straw. It was not the kind that had folds that allowed for bending, so she held the glass as low as she could, tilting it so the tip of the straw reached the swollen lips. Joanna took a few small sips then let her head fall back.

"Can you move your arms? I mean, if I put it close, can you get the water for yourself later?"

"No. Wrong side. Left arm bandaged. Leg too. But the nurse comes by." Joanna appeared to fall asleep again.

"Maybe I should leave and let the doctors take care of you." Kaia started to back away.

"No. Stay. So bored. Rather talk." Joanna paused for breath. "Tell me about the boat." Her voice was barely audible.

"My boat? Oh, well, it's a Princess sporting yacht. Eighty-four feet. Four cabins, two main and two auxiliary."

"Big boat," Joanna murmured.

"Yeah, well, my husband likes to fish, but he also thinks that looking successful brings in more business."

"Business?"

"Bernie's an agent. *My* agent, in fact, though he has some other talent on the roster. But I'm his big moneymaker. So I guess, in the end, the boat is mine."

"Good thing you were there." Joanna licked her lips again.

"Yes, I guess so," Kaia said, and hastened to change the subject. "Charlie said you were working on the underwater art project. That sounds fascinating. I thought only Egyptians were doing it."

Joanna took a few breaths. "Egyptians did the city part. Walls, houses, archways." She paused again. "Then they had a competition for sculptors."

"An international competition? Oh, yes, I think I remember reading about that. So you were one of the artists chosen. That's fantastic. Congratulations. What are you sculpting?"

Joanna's eyes stayed closed. "Fountain. Some people."

"I see." Kaia didn't see. An underwater water fountain made no sense at all. "So how do you do that? You chisel a statue and drop it down there?"

"Supposed to. Dunno what I'll do now." Joanna's lips seemed to tremble, as if she was about to cry.

Kaia started to lay a comforting hand on her, then withdrew. So much was bandaged, she didn't know what to touch. Finally, she gently grasped Joanna's bare wrist.

"Things will be all right, I'm sure. If the Egyptians chose you to come here, they can't possibly object to waiting a few weeks until you get better. Please, don't let it upset you."

Joanna inhaled through her mouth a few times. "Not just that. How can I go back? Can't even walk. Charlie can't take care of me. He has his own work."

"Listen." Kaia gripped Joanna's wrist more firmly and bent over her. "You don't have to worry about a place to stay. That's one reason I came today. We have this big yacht with four cabins. You'd have your own private space with a little bathroom. The crew prepares our meals so you don't have to shop or cook. You can't ask for anything better."

Joanna sniffed like a child who was all cried out. "Are you sure? What will your husband say?" The half-bandaged face looked almost pitiful.

"Oh, you mustn't worry about him. It was his idea."

"Thank you. Thank him. It'll only be a few days. Just until I can walk."

"Don't worry, dear. You'll be no trouble at all. And I'll enjoy the company."

Joanna looked up at her with eyes the color of the Egyptian sky. "You are so good. I don't know how to thank you."

With a twinge of guilt, Kaia clasped her hand again. "Just get better, that's all."

❖

An actress! Joanna would have laughed out loud if it wasn't for the pain in her face. Her mother would turn over in her grave, after all the years she had worked to keep her away from actors lest they drag her back into the mire. As if she feared her daughter had a genetic disposition to the fantastical.

Well, perhaps she did, having an actor for a father, an alcoholic one at that. Though she had lost him at the age of ten, her memories of Charles Boleyn were the theatrical ones—of the times she visited him in his dressing room after a performance. She recalled the exuberant, late-night fantasy world of laughter, of musty-smelling costumes and over-expressive stage-painted faces. Her father seemed to live in two realities, and the play-acting one was by far the more fun.

But, as she was to learn later in her life, he was a philanderer, a lousy husband, and a drunk. Well, she already knew about the drinking, because it had ended his life in a stupid drunken accident when she was ten. The accident was no doubt the reason her mother broke ties with the theater, or tried to. Her own brother had stayed in the life, as a manager and administrator, but she'd kept the family contact cordial and distant. Henceforth shielded from the fairy-tale world, Joanna received a solid education in reality. And what was more real than being a scientist, Joanna assured herself. Her mother was justly proud, until she herself died twenty years later.

But now the world of her father appeared like a haunting. Exhausted, she fell asleep again and dreamed of him dressed as Prospero, holding her unbandaged hand.

Joanna laid her good arm over the shoulder of the nurse who slid her up to a sitting position, and she thanked her, using some of the few Arabic words she knew. She was regaining strength and, by the next day, was sure she'd be able to stagger with help to the toilet. No matter what, she refused to use the bedpan for another day.

From her elevated position, Joanna watched the departing nurse halt in the doorway and then pass Charlie and two of the other artists. She smiled sideways to avoid using the muscles on the injured side of her face.

"Hey, old girl!" Charlie advanced to the bed in three steps and bent over to kiss her on her forehead. "Look who I brought! Marion and Gil wanted to see for themselves that you were still in one piece."

Her two friends kissed her in turn and she felt a wave of comfort. Disabled and in a foreign country, she needed to know she had friends. Charlie she'd known for years and was certain she could trust him with her life, had in fact. But Marion and Gil had also proved themselves good comrades in the short week they'd worked together on the project.

Red-haired Marion Zimmerman, a German from Dresden whose English left much to be desired, had created a huge model of the most important image of the ancient religion, the Great Balance weighing the heart in the underworld. Joanna had found it curious that a quintessentially Egyptian work should come from a German, but perhaps the Egyptians thought themselves above all that. Too bad for them. Joanna had seen some of the sculptures and was impressed.

The taciturn Irishman Gilbert Collins was worlds apart from the forceful Marion. Avuncular, gray-haired, and of a comfortable girth, he projected such natural cheer she could easily imagine him with a cluster of grandchildren at his knee. Gil didn't talk much, but when he smiled, she thought of Santa Claus. In keeping with this image, his contribution to the underwater city was a railroad, complete with a scaled-down steel locomotive, cars, and a miniature concrete station. As if to suggest one could make a rail tour of the exhibit, the tracks emerged from the station, curved around the southern half of the plain, and disappeared over the edge of the coral shelf.

Marion poked Joanna's good shoulder. "Crazy woman." She pronounced the *r* in *crazy* somewhere deep in her throat, and *woman* with a *v*. "They call you now Dances vit Sharks."

Behind her, Gil frowned. "Don't tease her, Marion. It must have been a nightmare."

Joanna smiled sideways again. "In fact, I don't remember a thing. Just diving with Charlie and seeing a hole in the ground. After that, it's a blank."

From the other side of the bed, Charlie took her hand. "Really? You don't remember coming up, the decompression stop, the sharks? Nothing?"

"No, only the broken sign for Site 13. Then I woke up here in the hospital. Just as well. I don't want to remember sharks attacking me."

Charlie nodded to himself. "Well, good. But we have to talk about how you're going to get around in the hostel, not to mention the workshop. I can assist you of course, but maybe we need to hire

someone to help you dress and, um, you know, do the personal things."
Charlie's cheeks showed pink over his trim white beard.

Joanna raised her good hand. "Don't worry, Charlie. Kaia Kapulani
was here right after you left yesterday and offered to let me stay on her
boat. They even have a cook."

"Kaia Kapulani? The actress?" Gil whistled softly.

"Yes, apparently several boats were close by, but her crewman
saw us first. She and her husband were the ones who pulled us out and
brought us back to shore. She's a very sweet person."

"Not to mention beautiful," Gil added. "I saw her in *Samson and
Delilah*. For a woman like that, I'd pull down the temple too."

Marion nodded agreement. "Strange that a Hawaiian woman
looks so perfect as a Philistine. Dark eyes to dive in. She is, how you
say, a knockover."

"Knock*out*," Charlie said. "Yeah, she's a winner. I'm just surprised
by the offer. It can't be a tax write-off."

"Don't be so cynical, old man," Joanna said. "Sometimes people
just do good things."

"I suppose so." Charlie sounded unconvinced. "But listen,
I've contacted the committee about the accident and asked for a
postponement of your deadline. They're meeting tomorrow and will let
you know, but I don't think you have to worry."

"Well, I do, of course. I'm lying here, useless, while the rest of
you are moving along, finishing your work."

"Not everyone is moving along," Charlie said. "Remember
George, the American guy? He's complaining that the site he was
assigned is too small for his piece. So he's on strike for the moment."

"Idiot," Marion grumbled, putting the accent on the last syllable.
"You can't make a strike when someone gives you a prize."

Charlie snorted. "A prize he doesn't deserve. You know the
committee accepted him because his father's a big shot in USAID.

"USAID? What's that?" Marion asked.

"The US Agency for International Development. One of the
groups funding the project. But forget about him. He'll solve his own
problems, or not."

Joanna let herself relax against her pillows and enjoy the banter
passing over her head. The pain from the wound on her temple had
let up, and though the aches in both her left arm and left leg persisted,

she could at least move them, and for now that was enough. It was just a question of time before she would be on her feet and working again. But how much time? A week? A month? How long would Kaia Kapulani and her husband put up with an invalid in their midst?

What nice people they were.

CHAPTER FOUR

Charlie watched from the dock as the barge that had deposited Marion's sculptures chugged back into the harbor. The vessel was an impressive sight, some two hundred meters in length, he guessed, the essence of functionality. Obviously designed primarily for lifting and lowering, it had little cargo space or crew housing. Its main superstructure and tool was the huge crane at its forward end, and he marveled at how it could lift heavy concrete blocks such as those that made up the walls of the City, and not plunge the bow under water.

According to the schedule they'd all received at the hostel complex, the barge would have just deposited Marion's last figure. He'd seen the work in the yard, awaiting delivery to the sea, and had been deeply impressed. A ten-foot-high set of scales, its center post in reinforced concrete, its arms and dishes were made of stainless steel, one holding a sculpted feather and the other a heart. Along with it were several Egyptian gods—one with a jackal head, one with a long curving beak, and a seated god he thought represented Osiris. He couldn't help but feel a twinge of anxiety. Marion's work was done, while Joanna's had scarcely begun.

Joanna was safe; his worst fears of her being killed or crippled were allayed. But he hated the downtime while she recovered. He'd come to Egypt to work, goddamn it. His own project was well on track. The fiberglass skeleton and its platform had arrived and needed only to be cemented. The marble stele was set up and ready for drilling, which would take at most two days. They'd planned for him to finish the whole composition within three or four days and spend the next week assisting Joanna. Now at least a few of those days would simply be a hiatus. Damn. He'd just be spinning his wheels. Well, at least nothing was holding him back from returning to the site where they'd found the tablets.

It had been four days since the accident, so for all he knew, the Egyptians had already investigated the spot and collected the artifacts. If so, fine. But if not, he had as much right as anyone to explore the shipwreck, or whatever it was. He would surrender anything he found; that went without saying. But he'd photograph it first.

The barge pulled past him and he stepped into one of the several inflatable dinghies issued to the project divers and deposited his vest and tank. In just a few moments he was at the exhibit site, carefully marked with a wide ring of bright-red buoys. He tied up to one of them, rigged a rope so he'd be able to drag himself back into the dinghy when he surfaced, then pulled on vest, tank, and regulator. Checking the pressure gauge to make sure he had the full two hundred bars, he dropped backward over the side.

In the crystal-clear water, he had plenty of late afternoon sunlight to guide him to Site 13. Schools of brightly colored fish passed him, but he ignored them. He had to hurry because the twelve-liter tank didn't allow much time for deep-water exploration.

He dove into the drop-off behind the site. Visibility was good until about thirty meters, when he had to click on his torch. He checked his wrist computer as it ticked off the meters of his descent. Finally, at thirty-eight meters, just as he'd remembered, he found the debris trail.

He examined the site more carefully now, noting the layout of the objects. To his dismay, he saw many more broken fragments than he remembered. He began to have second thoughts, recalling that archeologists generally marked out a discovery site with a grid work indicating placement of the objects before removing them. Well, he would disturb things as little as possible, but he was not going back empty-handed.

Finally something metallic caught the light of his torch and sparkled back at him. He brushed away sand to find a plate with the same markings as the cup he'd found four days earlier. Fantastic. Was there even more gold? The Egyptians would love that. He could already imagine the exhibit. He swept the light beam back and forth for several minutes but found no other metal. Other clay fragments were scattered about, however, and brushing away more sand, he uncovered the corner of what seemed to be a chest. It was partially shattered, so he could already see that it contained more clay tablets. Scores of them. He was loath to break open the chest, so he ran his fingers again through the sand, searching for others that had fallen out. He hit upon something, half of a tablet, then close by, a matching piece. Cuneiform again. He slid them carefully into his net bag alongside the plate.

He checked his wrist computer and saw he'd reached his time limit at that depth. He ascended gradually, unconcerned. Soon he was back at the plateau and swam leisurely across the city, keeping at the twelve-meter depth, making it a partial decompression stop.

To his surprise, another diver was still working in the installation, measuring something on the slope with a reel and tape. He couldn't be sure, but it looked like George Guillaume. He recalled that George had especially long, translucent fins. Expensive ones that Charlie had immediately coveted. This was not a welcome encounter, since he couldn't ascend or descend, and he couldn't conceal what he was carrying. He tried to back away and wait out his time at the other end of the plain, but the diver saw him and waved a greeting.

Shit. Charlie gave a small wave back and hovered, turning his back. But the other diver was next to him now, and it was George after all, his expensive fins keeping them exactly level. He mimed that he was measuring, though the measuring reel in his hand made it obvious.

Then George caught sight of the net bag and its contents. He poked at it and signaled an ambiguous "fine." Charlie shrugged with equal ambiguity and tapped his wrist computer to indicate he had a decompression stop. George nodded but remained stuck to him like a remora.

When the time had elapsed, Charlie surfaced, and George emerged close by. "Hey, where'd you get the loot?" George asked.

"It's not loot. It's part of our sculpture." Charlie bluffed. "I was checking to see how visible it was at fifteen meters. It's got to look good or it's not worth using."

"Uh, right," George said, and it was impossible to tell whether he agreed or was skeptical. "You shouldn't be diving alone."

"I have to. Joanna's injured." Charlie paddled toward the dinghy. "What's your excuse?"

"On short notice, I couldn't get anyone to come with me. The committee just took back my display site, and I was measuring what they gave me in exchange. They really fucked me over because it's useless."

"Hey, I'm sorry to hear that, but maybe we can talk about it later. I've got to get back to Joanna."

"Yeah, sure," George said, and paddled back toward his inflatable as Charlie prepared to haul himself back into his own. *Damn,* he thought, unable to shake the feeling that George was going to bring trouble.

❖

Charlie wiggled together the two halves of the clay tablet, anchoring both pieces with blocks of wood to keep them in place. The line of text along the crack was partially obscured, but the Egyptian archeologists would have a fit if he used glue on them, so this was the best he could manage.

Shining the brightest lights in his room on the artifacts, he took a series of close-ups, from top to bottom and then from side to side.

The new tablet seemed to be of the same material, size, and coloring as the two they had already found. Were they a set? Well, he'd soon find out. Maybe they'd salvaged nothing but cargo lists or hymns of praise to the gods of the sea. Whatever they turned out to be, that was fine with him. They'd be worth at least an article in the museum magazine, and the chairman of their department would like that. It would add a layer of value to their month of absence from the museum.

He had invested in a high-quality digital camera, and now he was glad of it. With the new software in his laptop computer, he could send the pictures back immediately to London. Unfortunately, the dial-up from the hostel was tricky and tedious, and he had to do it from the hostel office. Well, with a little luck, he'd manage it again this time.

He finished photographing and downloaded the photos into his computer. Nervously, he glanced at his watch. Almost six o'clock. The office was still open and, if he hurried, he could attempt to send the files before it closed. Grabbing the USB cable from his suitcase, he hurried down the stairs to the office below.

"Hanan, good evening." Charlie tried to charm, knowing the hostel owner was no fool and would guess right away he'd want something. "Ten minutes, I swear. I need only ten minutes." He held up ten fingers, as if to underline his pledge.

She squinted for a moment, apparently judging the degree of inconvenience and deciding it was not great. "Of course, Mr. Hernie. I will clean up the desk for a few minutes. But please don't take long time. I must to cook dinner for my family."

"Yes, ma'am," he said, already plugging in his laptop and attaching it to the telephone line. The random beeps and tones of the dial-up seemed to take ages, but then, praise Zeus, the connection held.

He addressed the message to Judy Zytowski, in Ancient Semitic Collections, and typed a brief note.

Latest tablet. Please translate as soon as possible. Nigel has others. Longer explanatory fax to follow.

When all the photos were loaded in, which took another age, he hit Send.

Chapter Five

Joanna tilted sideways, supporting her weight on her cane and trying to ignore the aches in both arm and leg. In front of her at the administration desk, Kaia Kapulani paid her hospital bill. "You know, I have perfectly good insurance, and once I file the claim, I can reimburse you for every pound."

"Yes, I know, dear," Kaia said over her shoulder. "We'll take care of all that in good time. That's the last thing you need to worry about now." She counted out the proper amount in Egyptian pounds and signed the receipt.

"Can you manage all right?" she asked, turning her attention to Joanna. "Why don't you take my arm?"

"No. My left arm is still sore, and I have to hold the cane with my right hand. I'll be okay this way. Just walk slowly." Joanna hobbled toward the glass doors of the hospital, weakened by five days in bed and by a leg still massively bruised, even if the semicircle of deep slashes had been stitched closed. Still, it was invigorating to step out into the bright, warm air outside.

She had showered for the first time that morning, supporting herself awkwardly against the shower wall. She'd held a plastic bag to the bandage on the side of her face with one hand and shampooed her hair with the other. Her left arm wasn't as badly mauled as her leg but was still swollen and hurt when she used it. Thank God the sharks that had slashed her had been small and their bites not yet strong enough to break bones. Terrified of slipping on the tile floor, she had inched her way along the wall in tiny skips until she could reach her cane.

Drying with the towel while she leaned on the cane had gone fairly well, but dressing had been a battle. She had not realized it took so much musculature to put on a brassiere and panties, let alone cargo pants, and finally had to appeal to the nurse for assistance. By the time Kaia arrived at the door of her room, Joanna was exhausted. It did not bode well for not being a burden on the Kapulani yacht.

"The car's over here." Kaia pointed toward a small cream-colored Mercedes parked outside the hospital entrance.

"Very nice."

"It's just a rental my husband uses to get to and from the airport. We came here for a few weeks for a rest and for the fishing, but Bernie never really stops working, and he has to fly from Hurghada several times during our stay. Here, let me help you in."

Joanna struggled into the seat and then shifted around, finding a comfortable position for her leg. She forced herself to relax as Kaia slid in from the other side and started the car. It was finally dawning on her that she was about to spend several days on a luxury yacht with an internationally famous film star and her agent, and all she had to do was let a few sharks chew her up.

While they made the short trip to the dock, she stole brief glances at the woman driving. Kaia's thick auburn hair was combed back informally and hung loosely down her back. Seen from the front and heavily made up, as she was in all her films, she looked darkly sensual, in a gypsy or Mediterranean sort of way. A perfect femme fatale. But without makeup and in profile she revealed the broad nose and forward cheekbones of the Polynesian. Enormous brown eyes were placed somewhat close together under luxuriant eyelashes. Her teeth were creamy white, with the faint prominence of her incisors filling out the muscles of her lips and lending an authoritative squareness to her mouth. Her chin was wide, firm, and the skin on her cheek and throat was a warm tan, a shade similar to that of most Egyptians.

Joanna let her gaze slide discreetly down Kaia's neck to her pale-blue shirt and noted that her breasts were smaller than they appeared on-screen. Joanna blushed thinking about Kaia's breasts and forced her glance back onto the road.

"I hope I won't be in the way. Really. It's still your vacation, after all."

"You won't be in anyone's way. You'll have the VIP suite on the aft side of the crew's cabins. If you're not claustrophobic, you'll enjoy it, I think. Charlie has already dropped off your clothes and some of your books. Maybe you can work a little."

Joanna winced. "Work? Yes, I suppose so, though all my designs are finished. I really need to begin the actual sculpture, but I can't do that until I can walk and use both arms."

"That will happen soon enough. Before you know it, you'll be up to speed again." Kaia glanced over at her with an unreadable expression. Was it impatience at the thought of being a nursemaid? The whole arrangement was inexplicable.

"Charlie told me your full name is Joanna Boleyn. Do you ever get teased about it?"

"I used to at school. Especially when the class was studying English history. And when I would complain about it, someone would always wisecrack, 'Now, your majesty, don't lose your head over it!' They always thought they were the first to make that joke. But those were kids. Adults aren't usually so boorish."

"Do you suppose you're related to her? The Tudor queen, I mean."

"Well, as you recall, she had only one daughter, Elizabeth, and that daughter had no children. It's true, we might have some very distant connection through her father, but not enough to get me invited to Buckingham Palace for tea."

"Well, you're invited to mine. And…here we are." Kaia swerved to the right and brought the car to a halt.

The *Hina* was beyond what Joanna had expected. The white steel exterior was sleek with a streamlined shape that screamed money, power, and speed. She had always wondered why vacation fishing boats were designed that way. Did they expect to be chased by pirates?

They boarded from the lower stern deck, which was some four by two meters square, with narrow staircases on both sides and a large steel locker fixed against a rear bulkhead. At the forward edge, two swiveling fisherman's chairs were bolted to the deck. They had armrests and seatbelts, suggesting that the owners fished for big game.

Kaia slipped an arm around Joanna's back, helping her up the stairs to the main deck. At the top of the stairs, sliding-glass doors opened to reveal the interior and an immediate change of aesthetic.

They stopped just inside and Kaia said, unnecessarily, "This is the salon."

Joanna suppressed the urge to express the "Oh, wow" she was thinking. The room that stretched out before her was wider than her London apartment, paneled in some pale honey-colored wood, probably teak. Rows of windows ran the length on both sides, illuminating the entire interior. On the left side was a cushioned bench, some four meters long, and covered with brightly colored pillows. On the right side were two tables, one significantly larger than the other, presumably for formal and informal dining, and beyond them a circular staircase led to the upper and lower decks. At the far end, an open door revealed the galley. The floor, of the same hard wood, was inlaid with the image of a giant marlin.

A wiry, dark-skinned Egyptian of about thirty was just coming from the galley. Kaia gestured toward him. "This is Jibril, the one who pulled you out of the water." Joanna offered her hand.

He took it in a cool, quick handshake. "Allah has shown his mercy."

Genuinely grateful to the man, Joanna declined to inquire why Allah in his mercy had not held back the sharks in the first place and saved them all a lot of trouble. "Thank you so much for your help. I hope this goodness comes back to you."

Jibril's slight smile told her she had said the right thing.

"You'll meet Abdullah, our cook, later, but this is Hamad, our pilot and engine man." A portly man with a handlebar mustache bent toward her and shook her hand as well.

"But, poor thing, you look like you'd rather just lie down a bit, so let me take you to your cabin." Kaia led her to the spiral staircase just in front of the galley.

"Can you manage?" Kaia stepped down first and offered a hand, seeming unsure where to take hold. She walked backward and watched while Joanna negotiated each step, first with the cane and then the weaker leg, while supporting her weight on the banister.

"Yes, as long as I pay attention and make every move in the right order. But I won't be up for any fire drills for a couple of days."

Kaia chuckled softly. "No drills of any kind. No calisthenics or morning jogs either. It's a promise." She led her a few steps along a narrow corridor to a door on the left. "The VIP cabin, with its own bathroom, is all yours. We haven't used it in ages, so you can make yourself at home."

Joanna stood in the doorway absorbing the spectacle of a stateroom as large as any bedroom she'd ever slept in. As in the salon they had just passed through, the walls here seemed to be teak. The berth appeared to be queen-size, and its headboard had side panels with bookshelves, though they held only a few magazines. At the center of the bed her battered rucksack looked very much out of place on the pristine linen bedspread. One side of the cabin held lockers and a set of drawers, and the other a mirrored door. Kaia opened it, revealing the bathroom and walk-in shower behind it.

"We hook up to land plumbing when we're at the dock, so you don't have to worry about skimping on hot water. Towels are here, and of course you can ask me or one of the crew for anything else you need."

Joanna entered hesitantly, supporting herself on her cane. "I don't know what to say. It's certainly nothing like the hostel I've been sleeping in."

"I expect it's not. But this cabin's empty most of the time, so I'm glad someone's getting the benefit of it. I'll let you unpack now and rest a little." She glanced through the porthole at the afternoon sky. "It's still early. My husband will be along soon, but we won't have supper until around seven. You can have a nap if you like." Kaia clasped her hands in front of her, looking vaguely like a housekeeper, a drop-dead gorgeous, Polynesian, Academy-Award-winning housekeeper.

"Uh, yes. Thank you. That sounds wonderful. This is my first day on my feet and I'm spent."

Kaia smiled and backed out of the room, closing the door softly in front of her, but Joanna limped over and opened it again. She'd had enough of the stupefying solitude of her hospital room and craved to be around human activity again. If she couldn't stay on the deck above her, she could at least listen to its sounds: Kaia talking to Jibril, the invisible Abdullah clanging pots in the galley, even the seagulls flying overhead.

She glanced at herself in the mirror and was shocked at how battered she looked. The bandage on one side of her face made her look frightful. Was it still necessary? Peeling back one corner, she saw that the slash underneath was bright pink and swollen, but it was fully closed and looked free of infection. The only discoloration was the residue of the Mercurochrome the nurse had painted on her.

Gritting her teeth, she unpeeled the adhesive strips that held the gauze pad against the sensitive skin and removed it. Ah, much better. She still looked like hell but more like a prizefighter now than a war casualty.

Then, weary from the strain of so much walking on uneven ground, she slipped off her sandals and hobbled over to the bed. With a sigh of relief, she let herself drop onto it without removing the bedspread.

Strange where fate had taken her, she brooded, staring at the white ceiling. Exactly a month earlier she had gotten the letter from the Egyptian Ministry of Culture accepting her proposed work for the underwater exhibit.

Having it accepted thrilled her, of course. What person wouldn't be ecstatic to be part of an exhibit of such magnitude? But it also reassured her that in choosing marine biology and a nine-to-five job, she hadn't killed off her creative imagination. Playing at both science and art was a juggling act, to be sure, and was possible in this case only because the British Museum of Natural History had granted her generous leave.

What incredible luck that Charlie's design had also been accepted and that they could travel and work together. His wife Viviane had taken a little convincing, but she'd finally agreed to see him off for two weeks. Charlie was already sixty, knew he would rise no higher in the ranks of museum curators, and had no aspirations to do so. He had enough seniority to take leave time for private diving projects yet not so much that his presence was indispensible to his department. God, what would she have done if he hadn't been by her side when the sharks came?

She wished she could remember what had happened, but nothing came back to her. Only vague flickerings of checking depth and oxygen gauges, of something being wrong with the site, of Charlie carrying something in his net. It tired and frustrated her to attempt to reconstruct the event, like patching together a glass from shards. Better to simply ask Charlie to tell her the details. She was ready to hear them now.

In the meantime, she would enjoy the company of Kaia Kapulani. Joanna had seen most of her films, all big-box-office, general-audience movies: *Carmen of the Factories, Vendetta, Samson and Delilah.* She had always been beautiful, though not in the way that Joanna found interesting, at least in past years.

Then came *Queen of Thebes*, for which she won an Academy Award. Another sprawling wide-screen historical with over-simplified heroes and villains, but playing Hatchepsut, Kaia had delivered her lines with a depth and nuance that the other characters lacked.

Joanna vividly recalled the final scene, as the female king lay on her deathbed, confronting her weasel of a stepson Thutmose III. "Finish, if you can, the evil you've begun, of erasing my name. But I have scattered Egypt with my images and temples, and you'll never efface them all. Karnak itself cries out Hatchepsut from every wall."

Kaia had paused, straining for breath, yet remained upright. "I hear the footfall of Anubis, come to fetch me to the Judgment, yet my heart is light. When the seasons have numbered as the stars, men will still know my name and will say, 'Hatchepsut was pharaoh, and the land did prosper.' Now see to your own name, and get you from my sight."

Damn, the woman could act.

She must be in her forties now, Joanna mused. Age had taken away some of the overstated voluptuousness of the early roles and replaced it with solemnity, had hardened her in the way that fire hardens fine pottery and reveals the final colors of its glaze. The faint crow's-feet around her huge brown eyes made them seem as much wise as seductive, and the demarcation—one could not call it a wrinkle—around her mouth had changed pout to determination. *Yes, it is a very beautiful mouth,* Joanna thought as she drifted off to sleep on her soft new bed.

"Oh, there you are. I was wondering where you'd gone off to." Kaia greeted her husband.

Bernard Allen stood for a moment between the sliding-glass doors of the salon, his diminutive frame making an unimpressive silhouette. "I was talking to the dock master about the docking fee. It's higher than at Sharm el-Sheikh, but he refused to lower it. Bastards."

Kaia frowned at what sounded like another confrontation, but it wasn't worth caring about. "I brought our diver back. She's in the VIP stateroom now."

"The stateroom? Why couldn't you put her in one of the twin cabins? I'm sure it wouldn't make any difference to her."

"Because I wanted her to have the best. We never use the VIP anyhow." Kaia dropped down onto one of the cushioned chairs and tried not to sound defiant. "We want her to be happy, don't we?"

"Did you pay her hospital bill with the company card, as I told you to?" Bernard hiked his belt over his slight paunch and tucked in his shirt. The rings of sweat under his arms told her he'd been arguing. He always sweated when he got angry.

"No, they wouldn't accept it. I had to pay cash. But I got a receipt."

"Cash? What the hell were you thinking!? You know how these Arabs are. You have to haggle over everything. You should have told them no card, no pay. Now how the hell am I going to write off the expense?"

"Lower your voice or she'll hear you," Kaia hissed. "And stop worrying. Your accountant will straighten everything out. He always has."

"And I'll have to pay him for it. Next time, show a little backbone." He glanced down the staircase toward the cabins. "So, our little diver's settled in now, is she? I guess I should meet her and play the host."

"Change your shirt first. There's a clean one folded up over there with the laundry that Jibril brought back. I'll go downstairs and see if she's awake."

"Yeah, do that." Bernie turned away, unbuttoned his soiled shirt, and began to rifle through the pile of clean laundry.

Kaia stopped at the foot of the stairs, surprised to see the door to the VIP stateroom open. Was everything all right? She crept closer until, standing in the doorway, she saw Joanna sleeping, fully dressed, just the way she had left her an hour earlier.

She hesitated, uncertain whether to call from the doorway or intrude in Joanna's private space. Finally she stepped inside to waken the sleeping woman, then stopped, feeling both the shame and the pleasure of the voyeur.

Joanna lay on her back, on her good shoulder, partially tilted toward the door and with her injured leg slightly drawn up. She was still dressed in tan cargo pants and shirt, though the shirt had become untucked. Her injured arm lay across her, below her breasts. Very nice, full breasts, pressed together by the position of her arms.

Kaia stepped closer and studied the face she'd dared not stare at before. Loosely curled hair that was a shade too dark to call blond and in need of cutting was swept back from her face. The new bright-pink scar in front of her ear ran from her hairline almost to her chin. Kaia's guilt was in that scar.

She moved her focus to the rest of the face: the curved brows that seemed almost to frown, even in sleep, the oval lids that covered piercing blue eyes, the long straight nose. Her narrow, rather sharp chin made her appear youthful, but the absence of plumpness in her cheeks and the faint lines around the well-developed muscles of her mouth revealed the mature woman. She guessed her to be about thirty-five.

A French face, Kaia decided, using her personal inventory of national faces. A smart face too. Her too-pale skin, from five days in a hospital bed, starkly contrasted to her otherwise athletic form. Her mouth was slightly open, and her lovely young breasts rose and fell with her breathing. Did she have a boyfriend, someone who was allowed to touch those breasts?

Kaia backed away again through the door, then climbed the stairs back to the salon puzzling over her conflicting emotions: interest in a new person that fate had brought into her home, embarrassment at having violated the woman's privacy, and a sudden urge to protect her.

"So, where's our princess?" Bernie met her at the top of the stairs in a clean shirt.

"She's sleeping. It's her first day out of the hospital, after all. Let's put off the introductions until supper. And don't call her princess. Her name is Joanna Boleyn."

"Boleyn!" Bernie snorted. "That's a good one. I'll have to remind her the next time she's attacked by sharks not to lose her head." He walked away chortling.

CHAPTER SIX

Joanna awoke at some sound, though she was not sure what. She drew herself up, befuddled, trying to recall where she was. She concentrated on the sounds around her, the faint calls of sea birds, the footfall over her head on the main deck, and the soft murmur of voices. Ah, yes. Kaia talking to someone male. But she detected another sound that was harder to place, and it took her a minute to make sense of it.

It was the rhythmic droning in Arabic that she'd heard every day from the local men outside her workshop window. Someone was in the adjoining cabin saying one of the daily prayers. Not wanting to disturb whoever it was, she was careful to make no sound, but the prayer ended in a few moments. The other cabin door creaked and Jibril walked past her open doorway, apparently without seeing her, and ascended the spiral staircase.

His passing by brought home a central question: was she going to stay in her little cabin and be waited on, or should she attempt to struggle up the steps on the first day? *Bedridden guests grow tiresome very quickly*, she decided, and made up her mind.

She glanced at herself in the mirror again and raked her fingers through her disheveled hair. She would have to do something about cutting it soon. Then, grasping the cane propped against the bulkhead, she set about negotiating the stairs.

However, the deed was rather more challenging than the thought. The whole architecture of the staircase required two usable legs, but Joanna's bruised left leg wouldn't support her full weight without causing a jolt of pain. Well, that's what the cane was for, she told herself, and began the ascent.

Right foot…cane…lift, right foot…cane…lift. Gripping the banister, she hauled herself up, step by step, until she arrived at the top, panting.

Kaia rushed to her side. "You poor dear. Why didn't you call me? I'd have helped you."

"It's all right. I have to rebuild those muscles," she said with a strained voice. "You know, use 'em or lose 'em."

"Welcome to the upper world," Bernie said, holding out his hand. Joanna took it and studied her host.

He was a short man in his fifties, well-tanned and attractive, with dark hair thinning slightly at the top and thick, black eyebrows. His eyes were gray, intelligent, but something cold, even calculating in his glance put her off. Perhaps it was just the look of a big Hollywood agent. A rich, successful one.

His handshake was firm, overly firm, in fact, and it took her a moment to identify what was disagreeable about it too. He had merely clutched the edges of her hand, curving his to prevent their palms touching.

"…chicken in wine sauce. I hope you don't mind," Bernie was saying as he guided them to the table. She hadn't been paying attention.

"That sounds just fine. Delicious, in fact." She hobbled to the table and slid onto the cushioned bench.

The smaller of the two tables in the salon was fixed next to a semicircular bench, upholstered in some kind of canvas, while chairs stood on the outer side. An overhead panel of six lights could illuminate the area at night, but at the moment, late-afternoon sunlight poured in from the salon window next to it. The tabletop, inlaid in green marble, was set for three.

"I think you'll find Abdullah's cooking much better than hospital food," Bernie said. "It took us awhile, but we finally found a cook who could make the kind of meals we're used to. Wine?" He held up a freshly opened bottle of chardonnay.

Joanna raised her good hand. "Thank you. Not for a couple of days. I'm still taking an antibiotic."

"Ah, yes. Of course." He smiled agreement and filled his own and Kaia's glasses. Kaia smiled as well, though stiffly, and her eyes darted back and forth nervously between her husband and Joanna.

"I want you to know how grateful I am that you're taking care of me this way. I can't imagine how I'd manage in the hostel, with no access to food. You're so kind…"

"Don't even think about it," Bernie said with paternal gruffness. "We're all just working to get you back to what you were doing before the accident. And while we're on the subject, what *was* that exactly? Something to do with the underwater art project, isn't it? We've seen a few pieces being lowered into the water."

The change of subject was deft, but Joanna brightened at a chance to talk about her work and nodded while she finished chewing her first bite of chicken. "Yes, I'm one of the artists contributing. What you probably saw were parts of the 'Great Balance' of my friend Marion." She sipped her iced tea.

"I'd love for you to tell us about the project in general. I've noticed a few articles in the paper, but I confess, I haven't been paying much attention." Kaia seemed relaxed now and took a swallow of wine.

Joanna wiped her mouth. "Well, it's essentially a two-purpose undertaking, a coral-regeneration project and an art exhibit. The larger structures, the walls and arches and so forth, were brought down months ago. The whole point is to create a coral city, you see, so most of the surfaces are made of porous marine concrete and seeded with algae, porifera, hydrocorals, hard and soft corals. The official name of the project is some pompous title that ends with 'Ecological Art,' so you can see its purpose. Most of us just call it *al medina*."

"The city." Kaia translated, revealing at least a tourist's knowledge of Arabic. "So where do you enter the picture?"

"Well, professionally I'm a marine biologist, and I specialize in coral. People who don't know the ocean think that coral is a plant or, at most, a single animal, but it's not. It's not even a single species. It consists of colonies of species, all occupying the same niche. The huge variety you see in a healthy coral reef is a mix of cultures, if you will, competing just enough to keep each other in check but no one dominating. It's quite fragile, actually."

"Uh-huh." The confusion on Kaia's face told Joanna she had wandered a little off topic.

"What I mean to say is that I was chosen to contribute a work to the underwater city precisely because I was a marine biologist, like some of the other artists. Our sculptures will add to the coral reef that Egypt wants to build but also make the city more like an art exhibit, presumably to attract tourists."

"And you? What will your piece be?" Bernard asked.

"I'm doing a fountain and several figures."

Kaia threw her head back. "Ha, what a fantastic joke. An underwater water-fountain."

"It's an even better joke than that." Joanna laughed. "We've made an air fountain, with a reservoir of air underneath. Divers can blow into it or pump air in from their regulators, and the air will bubble out very slowly from the top. Depending on how much air they pump in, the fountain could emit bubbles for up to an hour. But I'm also adding a group of statues."

"Of course, you need people. Will they be like the god statues we saw?" Kaia asked.

Joanna shook her head. "Marion actually chiseled her statues the old-fashioned way in basalt and some other materials. The one of Osiris is made of some blue mineral. Mine and those of a few others will be different."

"How different?" Bernie asked, scraping off the last food on his plate, though his monotone suggested he asked out of courtesy rather than interest. No matter. Joanna answered for Kaia's sake.

"It's a process developed by a British artist Jason Taylor for his underwater museum in Cancun, Mexico. He made casts of actual people, hundreds of them, of all sizes, ages, races, types, etc., then poured special marine concrete into the molds. The finished statues were exact models of the people with facial expression and everything. But because they were porous and in some cases seeded, within a year, they were covered with coral."

Kaia winced. "That doesn't sound so appealing, having faces disappear under vegetation. Statues sprouting wiggly growths seems, I don't know, a little creepy."

"Sounds like a waste of time to me. I mean why not just put down blocks and grow more coral?" Bernie poured himself another glass of wine and topped up his wife's glass.

"I suppose the idea was to blend people into the environment, you know, a sort of dust-unto-dust theme." Joanna redirected her attention to Kaia. "But I agree with you. When I saw the evolving photos, I also didn't like watching a human face turn into a bush of coral. But I do like the idea of putting portrait statues under water."

"So what are you doing with your statues? They'll just be people standing around? I'd love to see them." Kaia's interest seemed genuine.

Joanna sighed. "They don't exist yet. I have the designs, but the accident brought everything to a halt. I want to have three women of different generations and a male figure, standing separately. That one will probably be Charlie, my partner. He's got a very sculpture-worthy face. But for the women, I'll be looking around El Gouna for the kind of faces I have in mind. Once I find them, the sculpture part goes pretty quickly. About two days for each statue."

"Why go through all that trouble looking when the faces will disappear in a year anyhow?" Bernard's tone was dismissive.

"Well, my idea is to use the marine concrete only for the body. For the heads, I'll use something smoother, more resistant to growth. That way, the coral will grow up as a sort of blanket around the figures while their faces remain distinct. Not forever, of course. Nature eventually wins."

"Hardly seems worth it." Bernie helped himself to a second portion.

"All things pass. In a year, or a decade, or a century. You, me, this boat, everything. But that shouldn't stop us from creating something lovely in the interim and cherishing it, should it?"

Kaia glanced over at her husband and Joanna instantly regretted the remark. These people were caring for her, and she had no business challenging their opinions, however subtly. "Anyhow, it's fun while it lasts, and who would turn down two weeks diving in the Red Sea?" she added cheerfully.

"Mmm, whatever floats your boat," Bernie replied, and emptied the wine bottle into his glass. "Me, I dive for the fish."

"Oh, you're a diver too. I should have guessed. With this fantastic boat, you can dive anywhere you want."

"Yep, and I have too. Got all my own gear and even a compressor to fill my own air cylinders. Don't have to depend on the shoddy crap they give you at the dive centers."

Shoddy crap seemed an exaggeration, but Joanna veered away from the subject. "So you love the fish too. I'm always astonished by how gorgeous they are. Like living flowers."

"No, I dive for fishing. I'm a spear-hunter from way back. I've also hunted big game on land, but who's got time to go on safari every year, right? Spearfishing is almost as good and you get to sleep on a yacht instead of in a tent."

Joanna hesitated a beat at the unexpected shift from beauty to blood sport, then replied pleasantly. "What sort of fish do you hunt?"

Bernard busied himself opening a second bottle of wine. "Whatever's out there, but I've had particular luck with rock grouper. I've harpooned a few sharks too, just for the challenge. You know, one alpha hunter against another. And I always win. Too bad I wasn't there when your shark attacked."

Joanna wondered at the comparison between a beast hunting for food and a man hunting for pleasure, but declined to remark on it. "Yes, too bad," she said.

Kaia spoke up gently. "Unfortunately, we found out that spear-fishing is illegal in Egypt. A shore-patrol boat came by last week just as Bernard was coming aboard with a catch. They confiscated the fish and we had to pay a large fine. We can still fish from the surface, if we go far enough out, but it sort of put a damper on things."

Bernard refilled their glasses. "Yeah, but it takes more than a little fine to stop me. That incident was near Ras Mohammed where the eco-fanatics are on the lookout. But south of Hurghada you can still spear a few and not get caught, and the risk is part of the fun."

Joanna could think of nothing to reply to the boast of criminality but noted that Kaia was also silent. "Do you dive too?" Joanna asked her.

"No. I keep asking Bernard to teach me, but he hasn't got the patience. I suppose one of these days I'll take a formal course. It does look like fun."

"I just don't like the idea of you being on the scene while spear-hunters are shooting off their darts," Bernard said. "And even when no one's spearing, there are too many ways to get injured down there. We want to protect that pretty face, don't we?"

Joanna's hand went involuntarily to the side of her cheek, and an awkward moment of silence followed.

Kaia filled it. "Oh, by the way, Charlie called this afternoon while you were sleeping. He asked if he could come visit you tomorrow and I told him yes. Is that all right?"

"Of course. That's fine. Charlie's been so good, and we need to talk about how to proceed from here. I couldn't do without him."

Bernie looked at his watch. "Ah, nine o'clock. I promised to meet someone in El Gouna this evening for a drink." He wiped his mouth with a linen napkin and stood up from the table. "If you'll excuse me," he said, and walked through the salon. He stopped on the other side of the glass doors and drew a cigar from his shirt pocket. He bit off the tip, lit it with a Zippo lighter, and descended the stairs to the stern deck.

Joanna watched him, puzzled at his brusqueness, then shrugged inwardly. "Can I help you with the dishes?"

"Dishes? Oh, no. That's what we pay Abdullah for. Come on. If you're not too tired, we can go and sit on the stern deck for a while." Kaia stood up and helped Joanna to her feet, picking up her cane from the floor. "Is that what they gave you at the hospital?" she asked, holding out the aluminum stick with the blue plastic handle.

"Yes. Ugly, isn't it? I'll be glad to get rid of it."

Kaia was silent for a moment, as if considering something. "You know, I have a carved walking stick from my father. I've had it for years, thinking I'd use it sometime on a hike. But you know, I just don't ever hike. Why don't you use it for a while, until you're back on two feet? It's probably not as efficient as this one, but it's much more attractive. Or has that remark just revealed how shallow I am?"

Joanna smiled at the self-deprecation. "Of course not. One wants to limp stylishly. I'd be honored, but are you sure? I mean, it's a family heirloom."

"It's only a walking stick, and yes, I'm sure. Just wait a minute while I look for it. I'm pretty sure it's in the storage locker under the bow."

In a few minutes Kaia was back, holding a curious object, not at all what Joanna had expected. The main stock was twisted wood stained and varnished. Its handle, fastened diagonally at the top of the stock with a metal band, was a bright-red bird with black wing tips and a long, curved salmon-colored beak.

"It's lovely. What kind of bird is it?"

"A bird native to Hawaii called the 'i'iwi. They live on nectar, like a hummingbird, and they have a song that sounds like a creaking door, or ii-wii. They were hunted for centuries for their bright scarlet feathers, but they managed to survive extinction. A flock of them lived near the house where I grew up on Molokai. Anyhow, my father had this carved as a walking stick, but he only got to use it for a short while before he died. I've kept it ever since."

Joanna ran her finger along the smooth red- and black-tipped wing. "I don't know if I dare. What if I fall on it? I could never face you."

"Don't worry about that. I'm sure my father would like the idea of a pretty young woman using it. Try it out. See if it suits your height."

Joanna exchanged her aluminum cane for the *'i'iwi* stick and practiced steadying herself on it. It was a bit higher than the hospital cane, but she'd adjust to it. "I love it, and I promise to take care of it."

"Good. Now let's go outside for a bit of fresh air. Do you think you can manage the steps?"

"I'm willing to try."

Kaia led the way slowly through the glass doors to the stern, and Joanna kept pace, though with an awkward lurch, even negotiating the narrow staircase to the stern deck.

The swiveling fisherman's chair presented some difficulty until Kaia held it in place while Joanna lifted herself onto it. She relaxed against the chair back, laying the artful new cane across her knees. "Such a magnificent boat," she said as Kaia took the other seat. "It must be wonderful living this way, being rocked to sleep each night."

Kaia gazed out over the dark water on the other side of the dock.

"It's fun in the beginning, but the charm wears off. And then, of course, I have to go back to work to pay for it all."

"What made you decide on Egypt? I mean, you're both Americans. Wouldn't the Caribbean be closer to home?"

"It would. But I was here a few years ago filming *Queen of Thebes* and fell in love with the Red Sea so we began coming here for vacations. I have a big birthday soon, and since I'm not working this month, I got Bernie to agree to three whole weeks. It wasn't exactly a big sacrifice for him. The fishing's good, even when you do it legally."

A big birthday. That could only mean her fiftieth, Joanna speculated, but knew not to ask. A frightening number for an actress, she supposed, but it explained Kaia's complex sensuality. She was suddenly jealous of Bernard Allen's claim to it.

"I love the evening quiet." Kaia's soothing voice drew Joanna's attention to the soft night sounds—the lapping of water, the faint murmur of men talking a few boats away. "The evening view is nice enough, but it's much better at dawn in the other direction. If you can manage to be up that early, you can see how spectacular it looks from the bow."

"Well, that view is spectacular enough," Joanna said, tilting her head upward toward the clear night sky. "I learned to identify a few constellations when I was in school, and it's always nice to spot them."

She pointed directly overhead. "That one is Ursa Major. I think the Americans call it the Big Dipper complex. And that one over there is Orion, the hunter. You can always tell by the three stars on the belt. He's supposed to be chasing the Pleiades, the seven sisters, but I can't locate them now."

"Killing animals, chasing girls. A bit of a thug, isn't he?" Kaia remarked.

Joanna laughed softly. "Yeah, but in the end, the scorpion brings him down. Scorpio is also a constellation, but I can't find that one either."

Kaia glanced over at her. "I guess there's no point on sailing to America with you navigating, then, is there? You'd get us lost for sure."

Joanna chuckled. "If you're aiming to get to America from the Red Sea by star reckoning, you'd be better off with Peter Pan. You know, 'Second star to the right and straight on till morning.'"

"You actually *remember* lines from *Peter Pan*? I thought I was the only adult on earth who still did that. My favorite was always, 'When the first baby laughed for the first time, its laugh broke into a thousand pieces, and they all went skipping about, and that was the beginning of fairies.'"

"Oh, I've got a better one than that." Warming to the game, Joanna thought for a moment, getting the words in the right order. "'Stars are beautiful, but they may not take an active part in anything, they must just look on forever. It is a punishment put on them for something they did so long ago that no star now knows what it was.'"

"Peter Pan astronomy is so much more fun than the real thing. How come you know the book so well?"

"My father played in a London performance of it. I heard it being rehearsed. A lot."

"Oh, I'm so impressed. I've always loved that story, and now I know someone who's related to someone who's been to Neverland. It's like you've brought a little magic onto my boat."

Though the darkness concealed it, Joanna felt the heat of her blush.

❖

The tapping on her door woke Joanna from dream-filled sleep. Flashes of it came back to her. Something about Orion lumbering after a group of young women, then being stung by a scorpion and turning into Peter Pan.

She shook herself awake. "I'm just getting up," she called, struggling to get out of bed with a stiff and unyielding leg.

"No hurry, Joanna. Take your time." Kaia's voice came through the door. "Charlie's here. Call us when you're ready and we'll send him down."

Throwing back the covers, Joanna examined her leg. It had ached during the night and she could see why. It was still swollen, and the area around the stitches was bright pink.

"Great!" Joanna massaged her leg for a moment and then lurched toward the shower.

A little practice revealed that she could operate the shower handle with one hand while she supported herself against the wall. She poured shampoo onto her scalp and massaged it with her free hand, then rinsed it with lukewarm water as not to scald her facial scar.

After drying herself, she hobbled back to the bed where she wrestled her clothes on. Putting on her cargo pants was the hardest, since the weak leg refused to bend at the knee and she had to lean far over to slide the pants leg over her foot. But she finally had everything in place, and, after running a comb through her disheveled hair, she put on a shirt and limped with her cane to the doorway.

"Please tell Charlie he can come down," she called up the stairs.

"Ah, her ladyship is receiving, is she?" Charlie laughed, said something to his hosts, and descended the staircase. "Hey, beautiful. How're you doing?" He embraced her quickly and pretend-punched her shoulder. "How's the arm and leg?"

"Tolerable. Come on in and talk to me." She sat on the edge of the bed and patted the mattress next to her.

Charlie perused the cabin. "Hey, nice digs. No wonder you don't want to come back to the workshop."

"But I *do* want to. This pampering is fine for a few days, but it's killing me not to be able to work. What's the news from the committee?"

"Good news. I spoke to the chairman and there's no problem with the postponement. I explained about the drop-off behind Site 13, and they said they'd assign you a new location once the entire layout was decided. I also told them about what we found down below."

Joanna frowned. "What did we find down below?"

Charlie studied her for a moment. "You really don't remember anything before the shark attack, do you?"

"No, why? Is there something important I should know?"

"Yes, something very important. On the other side of the drop-off, at thirty-eight meters."

"Well, what? Don't be so mysterious."

"I'm not sure." Charlie dropped his voice, as if someone might be listening. "Metal objects and clay tablets were scattered all around, so I would guess they were signs of a shipwreck. We brought a few things back. A cup—gold, I'm pretty sure—and two of the clay tablets. You're sure you don't remember?"

"I'm sure. Why didn't you tell me sooner? Did you notify the committee?"

"Of course I did. And I handed over everything. I was sure they'd want to translate the tablets and send divers down to look for more, but so far they've been silent."

"You *know* how the Egyptians are. Everything takes longer. It's bureaucracy times ten. Too bad our guys at the London Museum couldn't take a look at them."

"Funny you should mention that." He gave an exaggerated smirk. "I suspected the tablets would disappear into the Department of Antiquities once I handed them over, so I took a bunch of close-up photos and sent them back to the museum for transliteration. To Nigel Castor, in Ancient Middle Eastern Art. Then, a couple of days ago, I dove down for a second time and brought back another one, along with a plate. I decided to get a different perspective, so I sent the second set of photos to Judy Zytowski in Semitic Collections."

"Good idea. They can investigate while we get on with our work," Joanna said. She rather liked the idea of the discovery in general, but with no recollection of the objects themselves, she couldn't share Charlie's excitement. "Speaking of the museum, we're going to have to ask for an extension of leave."

Charlie patted her good hand. "Already taken care of. First of all, they'd already heard about the shark attack. It made the London papers, you know. So when I called the chairman and explained that you were all right but we had a scoop on a possible shipwreck discovery, he was happy to give us another two weeks' leave."

"Well, that's London taken care of. What about the Egyptian committee?"

"Sharks are always bad publicity, especially when you're setting up a tourist site, so they're treating the attack as insignificant, and they're bending over backward to accommodate you. They want the unpleasantness to all go away."

"In practical terms, what does that mean?"

"It means we have it until mid-June. Everything has to be under water two days before the opening. In the meantime, I've calculated approximately how much material we'll need for casting the statues and have ordered it under your name. It'll all be waiting for you the minute you come back to work." He stood up. "So just relax and enjoy hanging out with a big-shot movie star."

Joanna released a long exhalation. "Maybe now I can. But you're wrong about the big-shot part. Kaia's been very down to earth. It's easy to forget she's a movie star."

"But not so easy to forget she's beautiful, right?" Charlie leered amiably.

"No, but as you've noticed, she's well and truly married, and her husband is my benefactor. I never forget that either."

"Benefactor maybe, but I don't like him. He seems like a bully, and he stinks of cigars. There's something phony about him too. I wouldn't be surprised if this was the boat where the shark bait came from." He glanced overhead as if the culprit were still there.

"Charlie, stop being so cynical. You're jumping to conclusions. I seem to recall several boats around us when we entered the water. The bait could have come from any of them. Anyhow, he's been very generous, so I think you should just let it be."

"All right, for your sake, I will. So enjoy your convalescence, no questions asked." He grasped her good shoulder, giving it a squeeze, and stood up to leave. "I'll stop by in a couple of days to see how you're doing."

"Thanks, Charlie." She watched him mount the stairs and heard him exchange pleasantries with her two hosts in departing. Then she relaxed against her pillows and gently massaged her damaged leg, brooding. What if someone from the *Hina had* caused…No. She wiped the thought from her mind. Everything was going well and she was being coddled; what was the point in throwing it all away on a mere suspicion?

Another knock at the door broke her train of thought.

"Kaia? Is that you? Come in."

The door moved slightly and a somber face appeared in the opening. Directly below the face was a tray of food. "Ah, you must be the invisible Abdullah. Come in."

A tall, lanky man crept all the way in. He seemed about forty, with thick lips and a heavily weathered face. Muttonchops curved down both cheeks, drawing attention away from his long hooked nose, and he looked more like one of Ali Baba's thieves than a cook. He smiled gently as he approached, stopping a polite distance from her bed, even though she sat fully clothed on its edge.

"Thank you, miss. Missus Allen said you cannot to climb the stairs, so I have bring you breakfast." His willowy form curved over her briefly, but once he had placed the tray on her lap, he retreated to the doorway. "An English breakfast, you can see."

She glanced down at what might have passed as a cartoon of an English breakfast. "That was extremely kind."

Tucking the cloth napkin into her collar, she cut into one of the three-inch long tubes of fried meat and chewed it thoughtfully. It was pleasing, but unfamiliar, with far more flavor than the English bangers she was used to.

"This is obviously not pork, is it? And I don't taste any bread filling in it."

"No, miss. It is lamb. With spices. But no bread." His eyelids fluttered slightly, as if to waft away the whiff of insult.

"It's quite good—delicious, actually. And these green slices are grilled tomatoes?"

"No, miss. Fried okra. With spices."

"Ah, yes. I should have recognized that. These are baked beans though, right?"

"No, miss. They are *fuul*. White beans with parsley, onion, garlic, and lemon."

She tried small samples of each item and found them all very tasty, but alien, so that each one required a conscious decision. Only the mug of tea tasted absolutely familiar.

"Earl Gray tea. Perfect. Just the way I like it, with milk and sugar."

"The same as Missus Allen."

She took another series of bites, tasting each item carefully, and concluded that it was far superior to an English breakfast. "Thank you, Abdullah. It's the best breakfast I've eaten in years."

"Then I am happy." He nodded in the hint of a bow and let himself out of the cabin.

Joanna finished the meal with relish and set the tray on the end table. Sated, but faintly bored, she relaxed against the headboard, holding the tea mug on her stomach. Strange the places where fate could bring you, she mused. Six months earlier, she could never have imagined she'd be lying on a yacht nursing shark bites after being chosen to place an exhibit in an underwater museum in, of all places, Egypt.

Six months ago she had been plodding along monitoring the collection in the Biodiversity Department of the British Museum of Natural History. She had been single for over two years after Ingrid had left her for a voluptuous German mezzo-soprano, and nothing was going on in her life but work.

Curiously, she hadn't missed the sex as much as she did the operatic world Ingrid had brought with her. Joanna had tried to keep music around her, going to concerts and playing her old CDs. But the house seemed quiet and dreary since Ingrid's larger-than-life friends no longer animated it.

For two years Joanna had watched the women come and go from the museum—colleagues, visitors, anyone who crossed her path. But no one sparked any interest.

A renewed interest in sculpture, a long-lasting form of art, had filled the emotional void. A university course years before, in which she'd banged out a few busts and horse figures, made clear both that she had moderate talent and that sculpting was a great deal of fun. And a trip ten years later to the underwater sculpture of Jason Taylor in Cancun had shown her that marine biology and art could go together. Apparently Charlie Hernie, a colleague from her own department, had made the same discovery.

But now there was Egypt, and…She felt the pause separating that thought and the next. And now there was Kaia. But what did it mean, "Now there was Kaia"?

For the first time in a year and a half she sensed a long-dormant emotion. But no, it was sheer folly to imagine that Kaia was offering anything other than simple kindness, and Joanna dared not abuse it. She would have to be on guard every moment against a misstep, an improper touch, remark, or look. If ever she had encountered forbidden fruit, it was this.

Chapter Seven

A nd on the third day she rose," Joanna murmured to herself, amused at her own wit. She'd spent three restful nights on the *Hina*, and strength was returning. She still needed her cane and had to plan each venture up the circular staircase carefully, but the weak leg would support her now between steps. Her forearm sported an angry bruise down its length but was almost back to normal strength and the scar running down the side of her cheek mostly itched.

"Hey, good morning!" Kaia met her at the top of the stairs, radiant in the bright morning sunlight that shone through the port windows of the salon, though it could have been the white calf-length pants and linen shirt that seemed to catch the light.

Behind her, Bernard entered the salon from the galley, his navy-blue golf shirt introducing a sudden spot of darkness. "Just in time for breakfast," he said, guiding her to the smaller table in the salon. "Abdullah's made eggs Benedict this morning. I told you he was good." He seated her, and before she could agree to the heavy breakfast, he called back to the galley. "Another one, Abdullah!"

"Yes, thank you. That'll be lovely," she said, defeated. She glanced toward Kaia at the other side of the table, squinting in the sunlight on one side of her face. She seemed unusually cheerful, considering the continuous disagreements they'd been having, though the muffled sounds Joanna kept hearing from the forward cabin or from overhead were never clear enough to make out words. Thank God the quarrels seemed to be over.

"Would you care for orange juice?" Kaia asked suddenly, holding a plastic pitcher over Joanna's glass. "Abdullah squeezes it fresh but only on special occasions."

"Yes, thank you. Are we celebrating something?" That might explain the general cheer.

"You could say so. Bernie is flying today to New York to hash out the final terms of a major contract. For a film called *Tribulations*."

Joanna searched her memory for a moment. "Isn't that the series of novels about the end of the world where only the chosen are saved while the rest of the world suffers war and chaos?"

"Yep, that's the one," Bernard said, shoveling a quarter of an English muffin and egg into his mouth. While he chewed, Kaia explained.

"They want me to play Katherine, the adulterous wife left behind when angels gather up her husband and children." Kaia slid the coffee pot toward Joanna, who poured herself a cup. Steam rose into the beam of sunlight that crossed the table.

"Hmm, that does sound like the sort of role you usually play."

"Yeah, it's another bad-girl role, like Delilah. Except this time, the good guys aren't the Hebrews but the Christians. My career doesn't really need a Christian movie, but they're offering a huge fee, and money we can always use."

Bernard had finished chewing. "It's a perfect role for you, Kaia. I've even made them expand it for you, write a bunch of new scenes. You can act your ass off, get yourself another Academy Award. Besides, two million bucks, after taxes, will soothe the embarrassment, I'm sure."

Nervously curling the end of her napkin, Kaia seemed a bit more uncertain. "Yes, you're probably right." She looked at her watch. "In any case, you'd better get going if you want to catch your flight. You know how busy it gets at the Hurghada airport this time of year."

"If I didn't know you better, I'd think you were trying to get rid of me," Bernie said, wiping his mouth. "But, yeah, I should be getting a move on. Egypt is great for vacationing, but unfortunately no one's taught them how to run an airport."

He stood up from the table and bent over the railing of the staircase. "Jibril, hurry up with my suitcase, will you?" When he emerged dragging the cumbersome bag, Bernard groused, "What were you doing that took you so long?"

Without waiting for an answer, he patted his pockets, mumbling, "Wallet, passport, cigars..." Then he gave Kaia a perfunctory kiss. "Don't worry, I'll be back in time for the big day," he said, and strode through the glass door. He stopped and lit a cigar, then headed down the steps and out of sight. Jibril followed him struggling with the suitcase.

Kaia visibly relaxed and poured herself another cup of coffee.

"What did he mean by 'big day'?" Joanna asked.

"He was talking about my birthday, June 15." She stirred in sugar. "We're not planning a party or anything. There's no one to party with, and that's sort of the point—being away from the noise and fakery of the industry, I mean. I just didn't want to turn fifty under spotlights, with a thousand people who hate me sending me congratulations on growing old."

"I understand. But June 15 is the opening of the exhibit. Perhaps you can celebrate a bit with us."

"That would be nice. Anyhow, you and I are on our own today. What would you like to do?"

"Do? You mean other than loll around on a luxury yacht enjoying the sunshine? What are the alternatives?"

"I was thinking of going into the water. Are you able to swim yet? I mean, do you still have any open wounds? Or are you nervous about sharks?"

"I don't remember the sharks, so I'm not worried about them. They don't come around much unless there's food, anyhow. As for my wounds..." Joanna touched the delicate skin on the side of her face. "This is closed, and so are the bites on my leg. I could use a nice swim. I hope you don't mean here by the dock, though. The water's pretty nasty."

"Oh, not here, of course. We can swim around some shallow reefs farther out. Don't forget that we still have your fins from the day of the accident."

"Oh, that's right. But I lost my mask that day. I've got to pick up a new one from the dive center."

"Don't worry. We have lots of masks and snorkels lying around."

"Sounds like fun. I don't have a bathing suit, but I suppose I can just swim in shorts and an undershirt."

"All right!" Kaia slid from the cushioned bench toward the pilot's cabin and opened the door. "Hamad, we're all fueled up, aren't we? Good, as soon as Jibril gets back, unhook us from the dock and take us out to Shaab Abu Galawa, would you?"

❖

As they drew close to the reef called Abu Galawa, Joanna could already see the plateau that formed its highest point. The bare tips of a few coral formations jutted out of the water, but all around just below the surface she could see the reds, greens, and browns of a living coral garden.

Supporting herself on one side with her bird cane, she groped her way awkwardly down the stairs to the stern deck less than a meter above the water line. The midday sun was pleasantly warm, but she was self-conscious of the discoloration on her lower leg. She'd seen it often enough in the shower, but it must have come as a shock to Kaia.

Kaia looked anxiously down at the damage. "Are you sure you're up to swimming? I don't want to push you. We can just as easily sit here and enjoy the sight."

Joanna surveyed the plateau. "Oh, no. I definitely want to swim. Obviously we need to stay away from the reef, but it should be fine around the edge. How strong is the current, I wonder?"

"Don't worry. Even if we do get pulled along, Hamad can swing the boat around and pick us up farther downstream. We've also got a dinghy he can hop into at a moment's notice."

"You really trust these guys, don't you?"

"Of course Why not? They know their business." Kaia unbuttoned her shirt and dropped her pedal pushers, and Joanna tried not to stare at the lithe golden-brown form in a two-piece emerald bathing suit. Only a slight thickness above the hips suggested the passing of youth to maturity.

"I'm sure you'll want these." Kaia bent over the locker and pulled out Joanna's battered yellow fins. I've been looking forward to the day when I could give them back to you."

"Me too." Joanna wiggled her feet into them and examined the borrowed mask and attached snorkel. She spat onto the inside of both lenses and then washed them off with a quick spray from the deck hose. "It feels good to be back in uniform," she said, ignoring the sting of the mask skirt on the fresh scar. "Ready when you are."

Kaia duplicated the routine and donned her own mask. "Off we go then." They flapped in three penguin steps to the edge of the stern deck, nodded to each other, and leapt in unison overboard.

Joanna was slightly chilled without a wetsuit but knew it wouldn't matter for the short time they'd be snorkeling. She located Kaia next to her and let herself float leisurely with her face in the water, keeping the wall of the reef on their right side. Immediately a row of bright-yellow angelfish passed directly under them. A bit farther on a single black one with a garish yellow tail hovered, pursing its little fish mouth in a continuous and soundless *oh...oh...oh.*

Gaining courage, Joanna began to take shallow thirty-second dives, experiencing the familiar joy of being under water. It was also pleasing to know that Kaia hovered close by, keeping an eye on her.

She dove again, corkscrewing in the water, and Kaia followed. Like two sea creatures they circled each other, though Kaia, frog kicking gracefully with her hair streaming back, seemed the more mermaid of the two. *What a shame she's masked,* Joanna thought. *Those wonderful full lips distended by the snorkel.*

Kaia swam under her suddenly and Joanna dove after her. Kaia was on the sea floor some three meters below, peering over the edge of the shelf into a crevice. Joanna swam closer, tracing the line of the crevice clearly visible in the crystalline waters. It spread downward to a deep drop-off and then to a sort of channel. With a jolt, Joanna recalled another crevice, and memories crashed in on her. She backed away and allowed herself to drift to the surface.

Kaia emerged a few feet away from her and spat out the snorkel. "Is everything all right?"

"It's...the crevice. I remember now, what happened just before the sharks." She turned onto her back, closed her eyes against the afternoon sun, and tried to relax, letting the water support her. But the details began to crowd in with no particular order, and the deep water seemed more menacing.

"Can we go back? I'm sorry. I just need to rest a little and sort things out. Is that all right?"

"Of course. I never meant for us to stay in very long, and I'm getting cold anyhow."

They hadn't drifted far, and after a short swim they arrived at the boat. The fishbone ladder accommodated Kaia's fins, and she climbed up first. But after a single useless lurch, Joanna realized she wasn't yet up to ladders. She struggled halfway up with her hands and one good leg, until Kaia and Abdullah lifted her under her arms and hauled her aboard. She stood there for a moment, her shorts dripping, and Abdullah handed her one of the several thick towels he'd brought.

"If you can make it up to the sun deck, we can lie on the cushions and dry out. It's a great place to take a nap." Kaia was already pulling on a shirt.

"Sun deck, yes. That would be good." Ridding herself of fins and mask, and retrieving her cane and shirt, she labored up the staircase to the salon and then to the upper deck.

Kaia had dragged foam mattresses into the shade of the canopy, and Joanna dropped down gratefully onto one of them. The sun-soaked pad was warm to the touch, and for a blissful moment her cold back absorbed the delicious heat. "Ah, so good," she breathed.

"Yes, but sunlight isn't," Kaia commented next to her and she pulled a white plastic tube from some pocket. "You'll be needing this, even in the shade." She squirted a glob of cream onto her palm and smeared it gently on Joanna's cheek.

Joanna closed her eyes as Kaia's fingers slid across her nose to the other cheek, then along her chin. The gentle touch both paralyzed her and sent a sudden burst of hot moisture between her legs. But the hand stopped and returned to the tube. "You should also put some on your legs. Otherwise you'll roast," Kaia said, and offered her the tube.

Joanna was embarrassed by the triteness of her arousal. The applying-suntan-lotion scenario was just as clichéd and trashy as the "oh, let me give you a massage" fantasy, and she hoped her blush wasn't obvious. Averting her eyes, she slathered the cream on her forearms and legs and lay back on the mattress, pretending indifference.

Next to her, Kaia finished oiling her own skin but remained upright. After tucking away the tube of cream, she produced a massive loose-leaf book and began to read.

Joanna rolled onto her side and supported her head on her palm. "That looks ponderous. What are you reading, *The History of Everything?*"

Kaia chuckled. "If only it were. Unfortunately, it's the script for *Tribulations*, the movie Bernie is hanging on me. If I'm going to agree to this crap, I might as well start learning it. I'm looking at the scenes that he made them add. Katherine arguing with the angels about world suffering."

"Does she win the argument?"

"Of course she doesn't. Her argument is shut down the way it always is, by the God-has-a-plan answer."

"Yeah, I recognize that one. Suffering is to teach us a lesson, and in the end, everything will prove to have a meaning because God's plan is good. The simplest sort of tautology."

Kaia peered over the top of her sunglasses. "I'm not sure what a tautology is, but I'd call it a cop-out."

"A tautology is an argument that simply repeats the premise, so it turns on itself. Like God is good and everything He creates is good so anything that looks bad can't be from God because God is good. In other words, you're right. It's a logical cop-out."

"Oh, yes. Now I remember. It's the logic of 'I hate spinach and I'm glad I hate it because if I didn't hate spinach, I'd eat it, and I hate it!'" She laughed at her own joke. "Besides, the angels they've written in here give me the creeps. They have such soothing speeches about love and redemption, while they're condemning billions of people to suffering."

"How does it end? I mean, is Katherine redeemed in the end?"

"Ah, no. Her sports car crashes and burns. Presumably after she dies, she's in for more of the same, for all eternity."

"Sounds like a revenge-on-Hollywood film." Joanna tried to rub away the itch on her nose, though the coating of sunscreen prevented a satisfying scratch.

"I suppose it is. If it weren't for the money, I swear, I'd dump this thing for the trash that it is." She sighed with exasperation. "I'm sorry. I don't want to plague you with my little problems. I'll stop whining now and let you enjoy the day." She turned a page.

Joanna's elbow ached from lying on her side, and she suddenly sat up. Was it her imagination, or was Jibril glaring at them from the other end of the deck? He turned away abruptly and disappeared down the stairs.

"How long has Jibril worked for you?" she asked.

Kaia glanced up from her typescript. "Just this summer. Why do you ask?"

"He was staring at us. I also heard him saying his afternoon prayer in one of the cabins. I wonder how he feels about working for Western women who lie around in bathing suits and shorts."

"I'm sure he considers it shameful. The whole country considers it shameful. But that was his choice when he signed on. If he does or says anything improper, you should let me know. Otherwise, we have to put up with his disapproval the way he puts up with our shamelessness."

"I guess you're right." Disquieted, she glanced back toward the top of the stairs where he had been standing, then decided it wasn't worth worrying about. She had other things to think about, such as the shark attack. She closed her eyes again, letting memory seep back up from her unconscious.

The first image was the sudden drop-off and the crevice. She could see it now, Charlie just beneath her. She had glanced at her wrist computer—nearly forty meters down, farther than they had planned for. A stupid idea and a dangerous one. But she could see her own hand, no, it was Charlie's hand, lifting something metallic, then some things square and dark, covered with sand. Charlie rubbed off the sand as they gradually surfaced. She remembered waiting at the decompression stop and examining the objects in Charlie's net bag. A cup. A block, covered with marks. No, with cuneiform. A tablet. Now she understood why Charlie was so excited. The pieces had to be old. Breathtakingly old. And she had been so stupidly wrapped up in her own misery she'd brushed him off. She owed him an apology and a lot of questions.

She felt suddenly overwhelmed, and under the shaded Egyptian light, she surrendered to sleep.

❖

A hand on her shoulder shook her gently. "You've slept for two hours. That's probably enough, don't you think?"

Joanna sat up, stupefied. "Umpf. Yeah, I guess so. Was I snoring? Or drooling? Why didn't you wake me?"

"Neither one, dear. And you looked so peaceful, I knew you needed to rest. Don't worry. I covered you with the towel so you wouldn't burn." Kaia was dressed now in a white shirt and old blue jeans, her feet and hands bronzed against the washed-out fabrics. She'd combed her hair and put on earrings. Even a little makeup.

Joanna glanced away and asked casually, "What time is it?" It had to be late. The blue sky in the east was already graying with evening. In the west, the sun was nearing the horizon in a gaudy field of pinks.

"Six thirty, more or less. We're on our way back to El Gouna, where we'll eat in about half an hour. Here, I brought you a heavier shirt and some wine. You're off the antibiotics now, aren't you?"

Joanna drew on the shirt, that still held Kaia's fragrance, and shifted around to prop herself against the bulkhead. "Yeah, there's no problem with medication. But wine on an empty stomach? I don't know. I wax philosophical when I'm tipsy. At parties, I can empty the room in two minutes."

"Drink up, then. The sun will be setting shortly and we're out on the Red Sea. A perfect time for philosophy, I'd say." Kaia filled two glasses and handed one of them over.

Joanna tapped her glass against Kaia's. "To the Red Sea. Over it and under it." Then she took a long drink. It was a good wine, even she could tell, but how soon would it go to her head?

"I love it too. Best place to escape Hollywood."

"Really? Millions of people would kill to be *in* Hollywood."

"They don't know about the constant pressure to make nice with narcissistic actors, the kowtowing to egotistical producers and directors, the invasive fans. I realize it's the price you pay for fame, but it's a high one." She took another drink and smiled toward Joanna. "I'm guessing you love the 'under' part more."

"Yes, of course. It's both work and vacation. I'm grateful to be part of this ingenious, deeply poetic project. Imagine, creating a city of art, an international one, and then surrendering it to nature. I can't imagine a better way to spend my energy."

"I know what you mean. I feel that way about the theater."

"I thought you just said you wanted to get away from that."

"No, I was talking about Hollywood films. The live theater is something else. I've only done three or four plays, before my film career took off. But it felt so much more honest. You don't film five minutes of action, then take a break to adjust makeup and lighting and change angles. Even the steamy love scenes consist of ten different takes, and all the while your leading man is sweating and getting a hard-on. No, I'll take the stage anytime. Even something as difficult as Shakespeare. I'd give a lot to do Lady Macbeth or Hamlet's mother."

"Gertrude." Joanna supplied her name. "I know what you mean. Live theater is classy. It goes back to the Greeks and requires an engaged audience, while movies are for the popcorn-eating masses. If there was narcissism, I don't remember it, just the theatrical personalities. My father was an actor."

"Yes, you mentioned that. You said he acted in Peter Pan. I was very impressed."

"He played Captain Hook and Mr. Darling, the father, too. It's a mixed good-guy/bad-guy role. Actually, that sort of describes my father too. A unique experience being the child of an actor."

"The apple has really fallen far from the tree, hasn't it?" Kaia laughed. "Is he still acting?"

Joanna shook her head. "Oh, no. That was a long time ago. He died in a boating accident when I was young. He was celebrating the end of a long run of the play by partying with friends in Westcliff-on-Sea. Apparently they all went out on a boat, everyone a little drunk, maybe a lot drunk, and my father went missing. They never found him, so they assumed he fell overboard and was swept out to sea."

"Oh, how terrible for you." Kaia laid a comforting hand on Joanna's wrist.

Joanna smiled. "Thank you for your concern, but it was, um… twenty-five years ago, so I'm sort of over it. Anyhow, I still have relatives in theater. An uncle in administration and a cousin who is an actor, but I never see them. It's a different world from mine."

"I'm sure it is, but not different in the phony plastic-and-glitter way that the film world is. Well, maybe one day…" Kaia shrugged. "So what got you interested in sculpture? I mean, you're a marine biologist, aren't you? They don't usually go together."

"No, they don't. Anyhow, I'm primarily a scientist, and I'll never make a name for myself as a sculptor. Basically I can only record what's already there. In fact, I started in photography, doing close-ups of mammals and fish, comparing their individual faces."

"Faces on a fish? Oh, c'mon. All fish faces are alike." Kaia's tone was faintly mocking.

"Ha. A lot you know." Joanna mocked back. "Fish recognize each other, don't they? And they probably think we all look alike. But seriously, the biological world is all about replication, generation after generation of the same thing, while individuals—with faces—emerge and nudge the pattern into variation. It's the delicious dichotomy of evolution, and it's been operating since the dawn of life."

Kaia chuckled softly. "I see what you mean about wine making you philosophical. Here, have some more. I like you this way." Kaia filled their glasses again and raised her own toward the burning white ball approaching the horizon. "Here's to the Red Sea at sunset. Both art and nature, wouldn't you say?"

Joanna held up her drink to the blazing red sky. "Nature, art, religion too. Isn't there a Hawaiian god of the sunset?"

"A goddess actually, called Hina. I've had a little plaster statue of her since forever, and of course the boat's named after her. I love the Hawaiian gods. One of the worst things to happen to the islands was the arrival of the missionaries."

"So I've heard. Do you miss Hawaii? Do you still have family there?"

A few cousins, my ex-husband. Sometimes my daughters go back to visit him. But mostly it's a memory of leisure and innocence. A lot of days like this one."

The word daughters brought Joanna up short. "You have children? I didn't know that. Somehow I just never imagined—"

"Yes, two daughters. Kiele and Mei. Grown up now. I married in Hawaii when I was very young and had babies the first two years. Then I discovered acting and moved to the mainland. Bernie downplays that information to the public because he thinks it hurts my image."

"And Bernard adopted them?"

"No, they were nine and ten when we married, and they never really hit it off with Bernie. He was expanding his agency and working to promote my career, and they always preferred their Hawaiian father. There was a lot of tension. Misunderstandings." She looked out over the water for a moment. "And now they're on their own and doing just fine."

Grown daughters, young women whom Kaia loved. Joanna felt a twinge of jealousy. "They live in Hawaii?"

"No, in Los Angeles. One of them teaches elementary school, and the other is starting graduate school at Stanford. I don't see them as much as I'd like, but we telephone every couple of weeks.

"Why did you leave Hawaii?" Joanna sensed she already knew the answer.

"I traded it for a career. There's no film industry in the islands. I left the kids for a while with their father and went to acting school in New York. That led to a few off-Broadway plays. After a couple of years of that, Bernard discovered me. He was just reinventing himself as an agent after years of making short commercial bits and some shadier films. But once we got the connections and the screen tests, there was no turning back. We got married and the girls came to live with us."

"That must have been the early '80s. I remember you in *Bravados*."

Kaia laughed. "Yes, Bernard's first coup, to get me cast in a Western along with Clint Eastwood. As an Apache, of all things."

"Yes, and then you were a gypsy in *Carmen of the Factories*, a gangster in *Vendetta*, Delilah in *Samson in Delilah*, and after that a pharaoh in *Queen of Thebes*. Always the bad girl, never the ingénue."

"I'm flattered that you remember. That was Bernard's doing. He wanted to mold the image and decided that playing bad girls suited my exotic persona, as he called it."

"And now you're playing another one in a Christian movie."

Kaia's expression clouded. "Yeah. The Temple Institute is financing it and they're willing to pay a huge salary. Frankly, with this yacht and the houses and Bernard's standard of living, we need it. I've never questioned his judgment before, but this is about as far as I'll go."

Joanna was beginning to feel the effects of the wine and she rubbed her face, trying to keep her thoughts clear. "The Temple Institute. Aren't they the ones who are running the campaigns against abortion and gay rights? They've also brought a lawsuit against some high school, I can't remember where, to force creationism to be taught in science classes. They're pretty high profile."

"Are they? That's too bad. I hate the thought of being part of that sort of thing." She shrugged. "But an actor's got to work. And it's not like we have a say in the message of the films we play in. Half the time we don't even *know* the message of the film. We recite our lines, sometimes take our clothes off, and emote. Then we collect our paycheck. At the end of the day, we're high-priced whores." Kaia's words were slurring a bit too.

"I don't know if I'd go that far. Actors also love to perform, don't they?"

"Yes, we do. Stage actors and maybe the Independents still have that sort of honesty. But once you get into the big leagues, with the million-dollar contracts and the Academy-Award nominations, you're 'on' all the time. You never dare go outside without makeup because of the paparazzi, half your friends are doing cocaine to keep their weight down, and you're terrified that you'll go a year without working." She scowled out at the setting sun for a moment.

"If you want a Hollywood income, you have to live the Hollywood life. You take dubious roles, just to be seen, give TV interviews where you gush over people you despise, go to the cocktail parties where the directors can feel you up, have sex with producers and agents, and get your first facelift at fifty and another one every three years after that."

Joanna frowned. "I can't believe you've done any of that. And if you have, I don't want to know."

"Well, I haven't done the facelift part yet." Kaia chuckled. She set down her glass. "But let's not talk about age and mortality, any of that. Fate has given us this stunning sky, and it would be boorish not to enjoy it."

"And we certainly don't want to be boorish, do we?"

"Shush, now. Just look. Talk later."

Obediently, Joanna gazed up at the spectacle of orange and fuchsia streaks that spread across the sky as the last particle of the sun sparkled on the horizon.

Kaia. She formed the word silently in her mouth, uttering no sound, holding the name inside of her like a captured bird.

CHAPTER EIGHT

Charlie took a seat at his favorite table in the El Gouna Sun Bar and signaled for a beer. The waiter, a strikingly handsome boy with huge eyes and a narrow chin who could have stood model for Tutankhamun's mask, nodded acknowledgement.

Charlie wiped his hands on his thighs, feeling the powdered grit that remained from drilling into the stone stele, and was extremely pleased with himself. Not only had he finished the lines of poetry on schedule but had done so even after a last-minute change of text. The new verse was so much more appropriate than the Shakespearean sonnet he'd originally proposed, and he knew Joanna would love it too. Then, to make sure she didn't see it until it was installed, he'd covered the stele with a tarpaulin and arranged to have it moved the next day to the holding lot. With a little luck, it would be under water before she was back in the workshop.

Then, with an hour to spare, he'd also done an experimental mix of the alginate that Joanna would need. The first mixture went well so he was fairly confident that everything would be ready for the casting once Joanna was up and running again. *Well, maybe not exactly running.* He smiled at his own thought. He'd settle for her standing in one place and slapping liquid alginate on her first subject. Until they heard from London about the tablets, she had an art project to finish.

"*Ach,* zere you are," someone said, and he glanced over his shoulder. Marion patted him on the back, then slipped into the cushioned booth next to him. "How is going it?" she asked, as she did every day, and he answered "Coming along" as he usually did. He saw no point in correcting her grammar.

"*Und* Joanna?" she asked, and before Charlie could reply, Gil appeared and slid into the booth from the other side. "Yeah, is she on her feet yet?" he asked.

"She's walking with a cane and can get up stairs, but only just. I went down to the dock today and the boat was out at sea. So I guess she's having a good time."

The waiter set down Charlie's beer and took the other orders.

"Is she going to make her schedule?"

"I hope so. They gave us two additional weeks. The blocks and basin for the fountain are ready to be dropped into the water as soon as the committee assigns a spot. Then it's just the statues. Once Joanna's back in the workshop, it'll go pretty fast. It just depends on how soon she finds the faces she's looking for."

"So why not use you and me? Or Gil? We have nice faces. I look around the bar, everywhere, great faces." Marion waved her hand vaguely at a woman leaning with her elbows behind her on the bar. "Her especially." The woman, who looked European, stared in their direction.

Marion took a long drink of her beer. "I love this place. Very... umm, *Weimar Republik, nicht*? All kinds of people. Old men, boys and girls together, boys together." She pointed with her chin toward a couple of young men hunched shoulder to shoulder over their drinks.

"That's the good part, but there's also the guys watching us from outside. Those I could do without." Gil tossed his head toward two men who stood in the doorway. Their Islamic three-day beards sharply contrasted to the smooth, mostly European, faces in the bar.

Charlie let the matter drop and turned toward the placid Gil. "How far along are you on the train?"

"Almost done. The cars and the caboose are already under water and the locomotive's being delivered to the holding lot tomorrow. But I checked inside the little train station they set up. It's fine on the outside, but inside, the concrete reinforcing rods are exposed and some of them simply jut into the interior space. They're going to rust right away."

"That shouldn't make any difference. People will only see the outside, won't they? The inside is fish habitat."

"Eventually yes, but you know divers are going to want to go inside of everything. Someone could get caught on those rods. I'm wondering how many other buildings in the exhibit have the same hazards inside them. I've filed a request for them to be covered in some way."

"Don't hold your breath, so to speak," Charlie quipped. "I mean, you know those guys take their own sweet time to get things done, especially when it concerns changes to something they've already agreed on."

"Yeah, you're right. But they could at least post signs. By the way, we were laying the tracks under water today, and I took a look at Joanna's site. There's nothing to it. It drops right off. Did you report it to the committee?"

"Really? You were at Site 13?" Charlie's inner alarm went off. What if Gil had gone down the crevice and seen the artifacts? Neither Gil nor Marion was the pillaging type; he was sure they'd behave ethically and report the find the same way he did. But he felt a certain proprietary right to the discovery. Besides, Joanna's part in it was the best possible gift to offset her suffering, and he didn't want her to have to share it. "Yeah, I told them it was useless. We've already requested another site. It's no big deal."

Marion held up an empty beer glass. "*Scheisse*. Dying of thirst here and no waiter. I'll get it myself." She slid out of the booth but got only as far as the woman who leaned against the bar.

A few couples had come into the center of the bar to dance to the generic soft-rock music. Well-toned young people, they presumably had come to El Gouna to holiday and snorkel, some to dive. He'd passed some of them on his way into the bar, speaking French, English, German. One of the women, in shorts and a halter top, caught his attention. Pretty daring for Egypt, but she was obviously a foreigner and didn't care.

He glanced toward the door. The bearded men in the doorway were gone, and a quick check of the crowd showed they hadn't come inside. No surprise. The Sun Bar was far too free for the religious. Gil's elbow jabbed him gently.

"Looks like Marion's having a good time."

On the periphery of the dance floor, Marion and the woman from the bar were dancing, though not quite together. About a meter apart and not looking at each other, they seemed to be dancing solo, each to her own interpretation of the music. *So*, Charlie thought to himself, *that's how it begins. Clever.*

He glanced down just as Khadija Saïd appeared, slipping into Marion's place at the table. "Don't you guys ever do any work?" she asked.

"Hey, there." Charlie clapped her amiably on the shoulder. "What are you doing here slumming with the infidels? I thought you didn't drink."

"I don't. Disgusting habit that kills brain cells. But I can treat myself to a soft drink after finishing a project, can't I?" She waved toward the waiter. "Cola, please."

"You're done too, eh? Great news," Gil said.

"Yep. Last of the figures delivered to the lot this afternoon. Everything goes down to *al medina* tomorrow. How's Joanna?"

"She's coming along," Charlie reported. "We've got an extension on her deadline, but I'm sure she'll want to go down before that to see the other installations. Yours is the ring of children, right?"

"Women and children, standing around two armed Israeli soldiers." The cola arrived with a fresh round of beers.

"Political statement, eh?" Charlie helped himself to a fresh glass.

"Is anything a Palestinian does *not* political? We're being crushed by occupation, after all."

"Yeah, sorry to be insensitive. I'm looking forward to seeing it under water. Marion's work is done too, as well as mine, and last I heard Yousef's horses were down. Japhet's "Brothers" statues too. International and multicultural. All we need down there is a miniature copy of the Sun Bar. That would be the finishing touch on our City on the Plain. A shame no one's thought of it."

❖

"They make me sick, these people." In a café close by, Najjid the barber bent over his coffee and stirred in more sugar. "They come here with their money and their offensive behavior. And the Egyptians around here grovel in front of them, just to earn a few pounds."

His cousin Mazhar nodded agreement. "Or dollars. The pigs aren't even loyal to their own currency. It's a complete betrayal of our culture." He scratched his neck under his chin, where his beard was still sparse.

"Did you see the women? Dancing and exposing their bodies like whores. They don't care who looks at them. If my sister dressed like that, I'd kill her."

"You'll never have to worry about that," Mazhar assured him. "Your sister is pious and pure. Anyone can see that. She's only twelve, but she'll be ready to marry in a year or two. So maybe now is a good time for me to ask if you think I would be a good match. I mean, I respect and honor your whole family, and if your father was alive, I would be discussing it with him."

Najjid reached across the table and squeezed his cousin's shoulder. "Mazhar, you are like a brother to me, and I would love to give my sister to you, but right now, you can't afford a wife and children. I know your intentions are honorable, but I have to look out for Djamila's welfare. Let's talk about it later, when you have a job, all right?"

"Fine, but I can assure you, when I do have a job, it will be a good one. I'm studying computers and I'll be a specialist one day. But I refuse to work for one of those European companies that have invaded the country. Colonialist dogs. It has to be an Egyptian company that's respectful of God's laws and allows time for prayer. If a man gives up his prayers for money, he's thrown his life away. Believe me, I am sincere."

"I believe you are, my brother. I too would like to be rid of European and American businesses, or at least force them to follow Sharia. What a disappointment it's been that the Brotherhood has shown so little muscle against them. Even *Al-Gama'a al-Islamiyya* seems to have forgotten the meaning of jihad."

"They are certainly useless when the tourist hotels keep growing and the bars keep filling up with foreigners and immoral women," Mazhar grumbled. Sometimes I even see Muslim women drink with the foreigners. A dishonor to their families."

"Not only the women. Did you see those two boys at the bar? They were almost kissing. It is a regular Sodom in there. *'They are a transgressing people. They commit such immorality as no one who has preceded them in all the worlds.'*"

"Ah, I see you know your Quran," Mazhar said. "My father used to quote that to me when I was young."

"Yes, I know the Holy Book very well. I was blind before but now I see all the offenses and I am an angry man." Najjid braced himself on his elbows. "In the old days, our grandfathers would have grabbed them by their necks and dragged them outside and killed them. But not now. I bite my fist at what has become of Egypt."

"It's the foreigners. They brought their filth with them. What's to be done?"

Najjid stirred what was left of his coffee. "I have prayed a long time about this and have read the Quran every night looking for wisdom. More and more I find encouragement to act. Just last night I opened the Holy Book at random and guess what I found." He did not wait for a reply but continued with upraised index finger. *"O believers, fight them until there is no more mischief and the way of Allah is established."*

Mazhar looked perplexed. "But how are we supposed to fight them? If we draw attention to ourselves, even to do what is right, we'll be arrested."

Najjid held up two fingers now, for greater emphasis. "The Quran also says, *'If there are twenty among you, patient and persevering, they will vanquish two hundred; if there are a hundred then they will slaughter a thousand unbelievers, for the infidels are a people devoid of understanding.'"*

"But we are not twenty. We're only two. I have complete faith in Allah and am willing to die if need be. I know that martyrs live jubilant in Paradise and so we should have no fear and no cause to grieve. But it's just you and me."

"What if I knew someone who knew someone who knew how?"

Mazhar dropped his voice to a murmur. "What do you mean? Someone who could actually strike a blow?"

"Yes, one that would draw blood so that the infidels would remember it." He paused, as if to add strength to his remark. "I know someone who has great skill with explosives."

Mazhar's voice became a whisper. "You want to make a bomb?" He let his gaze sweep around the cafe. "I…I…guess that *would* strike a blow."

"You sound afraid. Remember that the Quran says, *'We shall put you to the test until We know the valiant and the resolute among you, and test all that is said about you.'* Allah could wipe them out in the blink of an eye, but he calls on us to fight them, in order to test us. Do you have the courage?"

"Don't worry about me." Mazhar's jaw thrust forward. "I will stand the test, you'll see. If Allah wishes to punish them by my hands, I will do it, for Allah is all-knowing. I will do even better. My mother's brother Jibril works for the rich Americans on their yacht. Some Hollywood agent. Jibril goes every day to wait on them like a servant and he complains often about the man who insults him. I'm sure I can convince him to join us."

Najjid nodded triumphantly. "You see? Already Allah is giving us the tools. Your uncle will be very useful to us. I have a good feeling about this, my brother. I believe we can do great things."

"Inshallah," Mazhar mumbled uncertainly.

"Yes, if God is willing," Najjid repeated. "More and more it looks like you are the right man for my sister."

CHAPTER NINE

Joanna reached the top step of the circular staircase that, after four days of laborious climbing, she knew intimately. But this time, when Kaia emerged from the galley, Joanna met her with both hands free.

"Look!" she said, her feet spread apart to steady her. "No cane. I made it up on my own legs. And I can almost walk without lurching." She demonstrated by carefully pacing the length of the salon and returning. "The limp's pretty bad, but I'll get better."

"Oh, that's wonderful. You're really on your way." Kaia took hold of Joanna's left arm and slid her sleeve up. "It's looking better. Just the faintest sign of a bruise and the little scars from the teeth. What about your leg?" She glanced down at Joanna's jeans.

"Still a little blue-greenish, but it holds my weight now. Unfortunately, that's all it holds. It won't yet support me carrying the air cylinder, the equipment, and the diving weights."

"But it's so warm now. Can't you dive without the wetsuit? At least then you wouldn't have to carry so much lead."

"Only in shallow water. Below ten meters it's still cold, and after half an hour down there it gets pretty numbing. I'd love to do a shallow dive to get back in shape. But I can't go under alone. Too dangerous."

"Can't I go with you? I was meaning to ask if you would teach me anyhow. I can use Bernard's vest and regulator. We've got air tanks, and Jibril can fill them with the compressor."

Joanna frowned. "A beginner and a recovering invalid. Not a good combination. Besides, you're supposed to start in shallow water, not by jumping from a boat."

"I know that. But why can't we do it from the beach? I bet Charlie would be happy to come and help carry your tank. If I do something dumb under water, we can just stand up and walk back to shore. It will be good for you too. One step closer to returning to work."

Joanna still hesitated. "I'm not really qualified to teach, you know. That's more Charlie's domain."

"Well, let's give him a call and see what he thinks. Is he still working on his project?"

"I should think that by now he's probably done. But it still doesn't seem wise."

Kaia half closed her eyes, in the temptress look Joanna recalled from several of her films. "Come on. You *know* you want to get back in the saddle. I saw how much fun you had the other day snorkeling. And frankly, after all you've told me, I want to see your city and your underwater fountain. I can't do that unless someone teaches me to dive."

Joanna let out a long breath, defeated. "All right, maybe we can do a little 'baptism.' But only in the shallow water. And only if Charlie agrees to come babysit both of us."

"Fair enough. So go and call him while I get Abdullah to make us a quick breakfast." Her deep-brown eyes grew large and she clasped her hands. "Oh, this is going to be so much fun."

❖

"Excuse me, Missus Allen. You want me to do what?" Jibril's scowl was almost comical when Kaia explained the need for two tanks of compressed air. "I am sure Mr. Allen will not like that."

Kaia was already hauling the compressor motor onto the stern deck and checking the gasoline reservoir. It was nearly full. "But Mr. Allen is not here, and he has given no order for you to refuse to fill the tanks. Besides, you work for me too, don't you? Come on, Jibril, don't make me do this alone. I might make a mistake."

Jibril looked defeated. "All right, missus. I do it for you, so you don't hurt yourself. Here, this place is for to connect output hose to tank." He stood the steel air cylinder in its cradle and screwed in the valve of the compressor hose. "This is most important thing," he said, taking hold of the long pipe jutting upright from the top of the compressor.

"This is where air comes in for to be compressed. You must to keep it far away from the compressor motor. Very bad if exhaust gas goes in. You must also to use compressor in open space where is a good wind."

"Yes, I understand." Kaia hauled over the second empty tank and laid it on its side. "That's the reason the pipe stands so high. Okay, let's start this thing."

With a final sigh to underscore his reluctance to abet the whole endeavor, Jibril started the motor and the compressor pistons began their rhythmic cadence.

❖

Joanna shaded her eyes as she swept her gaze along the shoreline while Hamad brought the yacht within some three hundred meters of land. They came to a halt and Hamad dropped anchor. The beach that lay in front of them was flat and empty, far from the big hotels. Perfect for kindergarten diving.

"Look, there's Charlie. He's just driving up to the beach now. You gave him good directions." Joanna kneeled down to fill a large net bag with masks, snorkels, weight belts, and fins.

"It wasn't all that difficult, just at the end of Bikar road. Come on then, let's get going." Kaia gathered up the two buoyancy-control vests and regulators and went down the stairs to the stern deck where Jibril stood with the newly filled air tanks. With a final grumble of disapproval, he slid them into the dinghy.

When they were seated, Kaia started the outboard motor, and as they moved away from the yacht, Joanna attached the vests and regulators to the tanks. Soon they were within a few meters of the beach where Charlie already waited with his own equipment in a heap next to him. He waded out to meet them and help tow the dinghy toward shore. Kaia and Joanna slid over the side and splashed through the shallows along with him.

"It's good to see you in the water again," Charlie said over his shoulder.

"It's good to *be* in the water again. Kaia talked me into this, but now I'm glad," Joanna said as they hauled the dinghy up onto the sand. "I've attached the tanks and regulators, so all we have to do is inflate the vests and float them out to where we can hoist them on our backs."

She dropped down onto the sand to put on fins and weight belt and to spit-clean her mask. Kaia followed suit.

Charlie lifted the tanks and vests out of the dinghy and laid them at the water's edge, then inflated the vests until the soft incoming waves lifted both kits. Taking hold of her own kit and checking that Kaia had hers, Joanna led the way out into the water. When they were at chest depth, it was easy, even in her weakened state, to slide on her own gear and tank while Charlie assisted Kaia.

"Did Joanna show you the basic hand signs?" he asked.

"I already knew them." Kaia held up index finger and thumb forming an *O*. "Fine." Then she spread all the fingers of one hand and made a rocking motion. "Problem." She crossed her forearms, "End of dive," and then made a thumbs-up fist. "Back to surface."

"Very good," Charlie said. "What about air supply? Can you read the gauge?"

"No problem. And the signs are palm over the fingertips for *half full*, fist plus one finger for *reserve plus one bar*, and fist on the head for *I'm on reserve. Get me the hell out of here*." She thought for a moment. "Wait, there's one more." She tapped the edge of her flat hand against her throat. "*Out of air*. I guess that's the most important one of all, isn't it?"

"Charlie, Kaia knows all the rules, and she even knows how to empty the mask underwater. She's really ready. I think we should just sit down together under water for a minute, make sure everything's in place. Then you and I can stay on either side of her while we swim out in a circle and end up back here."

"Sounds good. Okay, everybody: masks on, mouthpieces in, and under we go."

They dropped down together in place to sit in a circle. Joanna watched to see if Kaia showed any sign of distress, but she immediately gave the *fine* sign. To demonstrate her prowess at emptying her mask, she let it fill with water, then tilted her head back and blew gently through her nose, refilling the mask with air. Charlie gave a silent underwater applause.

With Charlie and Joanna flanking the neophyte, they began paddling in a diagonal out from the shore. Kaia swam with her hands and arms as well as with her fins, like most beginners, but she seemed in her element. Though the fauna were sparse so close to shore, a few cardinal fish passed alongside of them and Kaia pointed, then gestured *Fine!* like a child learning to talk.

But Joanna saw nothing childlike about Kaia's adult body swimming with such natural grace next to her, as she had when they snorkeled. Even the cumbersome air cylinder stayed balanced on her back. A childhood on the beaches of Molokai had obviously taught her to be at home under water.

For Joanna's part, her legs and arms began to ache from so many days of inactivity, but it was the pleasant ache that told her she was using her muscles again.

When they completed their circle and returned to shallow water, Charlie signaled *surface* and Joanna checked her watch. They had been under water for less than seven minutes.

Kaia raised her mask to her forehead. "That was fun. When do we go down to the shipwrecks?"

"Um…let's wait until tomorrow for that," Joanna said. To Charlie she remarked, "I think she's ready for air sharing now, don't you agree?"

"If you stay in shallow water, yes. Try it first kneeling on the bottom, then—"

"Fine, let's go," Kaia said, popping the regulator back into her mouth. She dropped under the water and made the hand slice to the throat, though she still breathed from her own tank. Laughing inwardly, Joanna reached over and tugged the mouthpiece out of Kaia's mouth. Even through the mask, Joanna could see the surprise, but Kaia remained calm and had the presence of mind to signal again.

Going by the book, Joanna linked her left arm into Kaia's right one and pulled her close, at the same time transferring her mouthpiece to Kaia. She took two long pulls of air, then passed it back to Joanna, who inhaled conspicuously only once but deeply. Soon they exchanged the mouthpiece back and forth comfortably with Charlie nodding approval.

Without breaking the rhythm, Kaia pointed out to deeper water and signaled, "Let's go." Pleased, Joanna rose off the bottom still gripping Kaia's upper arm, and they set off in the same circle they had made before, with Charlie shepherding them.

Though Joanna had shared air a dozen times before, it had never felt so intimate. She swam pressed against Kaia on one side, and the plug of hard rubber went from mouth to mouth, one breath for each, until it became almost natural. Each time she sucked in a lungful of air, she sensed the trust of the woman who held onto her, waiting for breath, and they were like twin creatures, nourished from the same vital source.

But the paddling was awkward, and Joanna's muscles began to remind her she was still recovering. Worse, it was her weak leg that was pressed against Kaia's thigh, and it ached the most.

Finally they were back in shallow water, and Charlie signaled with crossed forearms that the exercise was over. She let go of Kaia and felt the cool water on her newly exposed arm.

Kaia stood up out of the water and raised her mask. "That was brilliant!" she exclaimed, slightly breathless. "I want to do more of that."

Charlie turned to Joanna. "How do you feel?"

"Better than I thought I would. I guess I'll be ready for work soon." She omitted mentioning a specific day.

"Good. Everything's waiting for you. But look." Charlie glanced down at his watch. "Gil's finishing something up this evening and I promised to help him. So if you two are all played out, I'd like to call it a day."

"Thanks, Charlie." Kaia undid her vest. "It's been a lot of fun, and I hope we can do it again. Even better, I hope to be able to dive down to see the pieces you're working on."

"My pleasure, ma'am. We'd love to have you see them." Charlie helped them deposit their gear into the dinghy and shove it from the beach back into shallow water. "All right, ladies, I'll leave you to your own amusement and get on with what I was doing." With that he turned and hiked back up the beach to the rented car.

Joanna watched him return to work and felt the first twinges of guilt. They were soon overshadowed, however, by the real twinges of pain in her leg and shoulder. She lay back against the inflated gunwale of the dinghy and closed her eyes against the Egyptian sunlight while Kaia motored them back to the *Hina*.

They were back on the deck within minutes, and the yacht returned to the dock long before sunset. Joanna withdrew to her cabin to change into dry clothes and made her way up to the salon, pleased at how well she could handle the stairs in spite of her fatigue.

Kaia was on the far corner of the long sofa bench, her shampooed hair still damp and in ringlets, her knees drawn up. "Come here and have a glass of sherry," she said. "It'll be another hour before Abdullah makes dinner." She held out a small goblet of golden liquid.

Joanna took it and curled up next to her. "To the sea," she said as they clinked glasses. She took the first swallow and the sherry went down, warming her like the amber glow of the evening sunlight that still filled the salon. She took a second sip of the luminous liquid and wiped a fleck of sugary residue from the corners of her mouth.

"It was a lot of fun today," she said. "But I've got to get back to the workshop."

Kaia nodded wistfully. "It couldn't go on forever, could it?" She bent toward Joanna and ran a fingertip gently down the welt on the side of her head. "The scar, it's healing quite well, isn't it? It doesn't tan, like the rest of you, but it's definitely shrinking. I'm so relieved."

"Me too." Joanna inhaled the scent of rose hand lotion and wished the lovely hand would stay on her face. "You can hardly see the slashes on my arm now too." She held out her left arm and Kaia ran a finger along the curve of pink welts. Joanna shivered with pleasure. "You've been so kind, you know. Taking care of me all this time. You're not only beautiful, you're a saint."

"Oh, someone's had a bit too much sherry." Kaia suppressed a smile. "You're rather beautiful yourself, you know. And you don't work for sleazy people." Kaia's hand was still on Joanna's wrist and Joanna held very still, willing it to remain.

"You don't have to, you know. Under that gorgeous face is also a good heart and a conscience. Maybe you could buy a smaller yacht."

Kaia's hand was warm and did not leave its resting place. They had breathed together that day and been locked arm in arm. Joanna wanted to breathe with her again. She studied the huge brown elliptical eyes, the wide Hawaiian cheekbones on flawless tan skin. She let her face drift closer and Kaia didn't move away. She smelled of sunbaked skin and her lovely full lips opened.

With a swish, the glass doors slid apart and Bernard strode in from the aft deck.

❖

Joanna leapt to her feet as if bitten and stood nonplussed for a moment. "Welcome home," she said awkwardly, forcing cheer into her voice.

But Bernard seemed focused on the glasses they held. "Hard liquor in the afternoon?"

Kaia stood up as well and edged toward the galley. "It's just sherry. Can I get you a glass?"

He set down his attaché case where Kaia had been sitting. "You know I don't like that stuff. But you can fetch me a glass of beer." He took off his linen jacket, revealing a rumpled white shirt. His slightly red face indicated the exertion of the trip and the hike along the dock in the still-hot sunlight.

"I have the contract here, all negotiated and with the higher salary. They screamed like pigs but finally agreed. You just have to sign it and it's done."

Kaia all but fled to the galley and Joanna backed away, wanting more than anything to be in her cabin, on the dock, any place but in front of Kaia's husband and his sleazy contract. But Bernard blocked her way. "It looks like you're finally up and about. That's good. But stick around. We'll celebrate."

In a moment Kaia returned with a glass of beer and handed it to him. "Bernie, we have to talk."

"Not now, Kaia. We're celebrating. We're making a new movie and we're going to be rich. Well, richer." He held up his glass. "To G-rated movies, our bread and butter," he said, and downed half the glass.

"Bernie, I don't want to do it."

He wiped his mouth with the back of his hand. "What!? What the hell are you talking about? Don't be a twit." He set down the glass and opened the attaché case. "We talked about it. It's a done deal, for chrissake."

"It's financed by the Temple Foundation. They're fundamentalists trying to force religion into politics and schools. I don't want to be part of that."

"How do you know what they're trying to do? Suddenly you're an expert on politics?"

"You know yourself it's religious propaganda, and Joanna told me the Temple Foundation is lobbying against women and gays. They're creationists."

He turned toward Joanna. "What the hell are you doing giving my wife advice? This is our private business. You aren't *allowed* to have an opinion about her acting contracts and what she should or shouldn't do. You understand that?"

"I'm sorry. I wasn't trying to intrude on your business. We were just talking about the Temple Foundation and I told Kaia what I knew. And those are facts. They *are* creationists and that movie looks like one of their vehicles."

Bernard's well-tanned face grew pinkish with anger. "You ungrateful twit." It seemed to be one of his favorite words. "I pay your medical expenses and invite you into my home to recover, for chrissake, and while I'm away, you poison my wife's mind."

Kaia's voice remained soft. "She didn't poison my mind, Bernie. She just made me realize I had some principles."

"It's way too late for principles. We passed *principles* two million dollars ago. As for you..." He turned toward Joanna. "You've worn out your welcome by a long shot. It's time you left my boat."

Joanna had already retreated to the dining area, and she set down her glass. "I'll do that, right away. I'm sorry for the trouble I've caused." She turned and hurried down the circular staircase, anger and frustration suppressing the pain in her leg. While she threw her few possessions into her rucksack, she heard Kaia and Bernard upstairs quarreling. The word twit occurred again.

Fortunately, she traveled light so it took only moments to pack. She zipped up the rucksack and checked the charge on her cell phone to make sure she could call Charlie from the dock. Her face grew hot at the embarrassment. Bernard was right; she had been out of line. She had forgotten she was a visitor in a world she knew nothing about. And now Kaia would be left to deal alone with the wreckage.

"Excuse me, miss." A crewman stood in the doorway.

"Huh? Oh, it's you, Jibril. Listen, thank you so much for all your help this last week. I feel terrible that it's ending this way. They've been so kind and now I've sort of thrown a wrench into things."

Jibril stepped into the room and closed the door behind him. "They are not so kind as you think, miss." He dropped his voice. "It was Mr. Allen who caused the sharks to come. He threw a rotten fish into the water and that brought them. We told him that was not allowed and divers were around us, but he didn't care. Then they decided to take care of you for to make you not cause trouble. It was not kindness, it was…" He searched for another word.

Joanna stared at him, appalled. "Calculation."

"Yes, miss. It was that." Lowering his eyes, Jibril let himself out of the cabin and went below to the engine room.

Joanna dropped back onto the bed. She was breathing heavily and her heart pounded, but uncertainty paralyzed her. How could she get through the salon to the dock with a modicum of dignity? How could she face the two people who had pretended to be her benefactors when the whole time they had been exploiting her?

She heard another knock at the door, but before she spoke, Kaia came in and closed the door behind her. Joanna stood up from the bed. "I apologize for Bernard's rudeness," Kaia said. "He explained the importance of the contract and how I can't get out of it." She shrugged faintly and seemed to droop in helplessness and defeat. "So it's really my fault that it came to this ugly scene."

Joanna could think of nothing to respond, and so a moment of tense silence fell between them.

Kaia forced a weak smile. "But we had fun this week, didn't we? And you've gotten better, which was the whole point, wasn't it?" she added limply. "Maybe I can come and see you at your workshop sometime?"

The bile rose in Joanna's throat. So that's how far things had advanced in those five minutes. The Hollywood couple had reconciled, doubts had been extinguished, and all that remained was for them to get rid of the gullible guest and thorn in their side.

"I don't think so." Joanna wanted the remark to sound solemn, but it came out a croak.

"What? Why not? What have I done?" Kaia backed away a step.

"Jibril told me about Bernard throwing the rotten fish into the sea. And that you both conspired to bring me here to prevent litigation. So very American of you."

Kaia recoiled visibly then glanced around, as if searching for an explanation somewhere in the cabin. Her hands came up in supplication. "I swear to you. It's not what you think. Maybe at first I wanted to do what Bernard suggested, but soon I really liked having you aboard. I *wanted* you to stay. I loved every minute of it."

It all looked and sounded too theatrical, and Joanna would not be made a fool of again. "Of course you're going to say that. No one wants to admit taking advantage of an injured person, a person *you* caused to be injured." She took a breath. "I trusted you, I *groveled*, thanking you every day for your kindness. But it was all play-acting. All the while I thought you liked me, cared about me." She heard the whine creep into her voice but couldn't stop it and was on the edge of tears. "That's so… humiliating."

Kaia's hands went up again, more helplessly this time. "Listen, you have to believe me. Right away, I was sorry. Right away, I started having fun with you. And it's been six wonderful days. What can I say to convince you that I *do* care about you? That I care *for* you?"

"Nothing. There's nothing you can say that won't sound like acting. It's your trade, after all." Joanna took hold of her rucksack and was about to step toward the door when she spotted the Hawaiian cane with the carved scarlet *'i'iwi* bird propped against the wall. She snatched it up and held it out to Kaia.

"I thought that you were giving me a tiny bit of Hawaii, and this bird seemed a little like you, exotic and vulnerable. I was wrong. You're as common as a shark, you and your creepy husband. Thanks for everything," she said bitterly, and dropped the cane onto the bed.

She stepped toward the cabin door and tried to pivot past Kaia, but the hand on her arm spun her back around.

"Maybe you'll believe this." Kaia grasped her by the shoulders suddenly and pulled her close, covering her mouth with her own. Astonished, Joanna froze for a moment. Then she felt the moist inside of Kaia's lips, the pressure of her teeth, and tasted the sherry they had both just drunk.

Was the kiss a trap too? The thought shot through her mind. But she had yearned too long for Kaia's touch and so she kissed back, cautiously, then with ardor, pressing against the sherry-sweet mouth. They had shared air a few hours before and now their two breaths streamed across each other's faces. She encircled Kaia with her arms, feeling the expansion of her ribs in rhythm with the hot exhalation on her own cheek.

"Jesus Fucking Christ, what are you doing with my wife?"

Kaia broke away and looked toward the doorway where Bernard stood filling the space.

Joanna searched for words but found none. It was a frightening moment, yet excruciatingly banal. Husband finds wife cheating. She had no words. Only Bernard said the obvious.

"Get the hell off my boat, you pervert."

With a last dazed look at Kaia, who was ashen, Joanna snatched up her rucksack and brushed past him in a fury.

Chapter Ten

Taciturn and sullen, Joanna limped up the steps to her room at the artists' hostel. Directly behind her, Charlie carried her bag, less out of necessity than as a gesture of comfort. Even without reporting the details of the confrontation, Joanna knew that he sensed something unpleasant had happened, for he was suddenly very solicitous.

Hanan, the widowed manager of the hostel, met her at the top of the stairs. As always, she wore a galabaya of some indiscriminate dark color and a black headscarf, in spite of the heat. To Joanna's surprise, Hanan set aside her broom and embraced her lightly.

"Praise God!" She threw up her hands in rejoicing. "Welcome back, Dr. Boleyn. I was so sorry when Charlie tell me about accident, but God has bring you back. We prepare your room for you. Very nice now."

"Thank you," Joanna said, touched. "I'm afraid I left it in rather a mess the morning I went to dive. I know this isn't a hotel with room services, and you've gone way beyond the call. I'm very grateful to know you've cleaned it up for me."

"Fahimah, my oldest, made the clean. And don't to worry. She was very careful everything. She wants to be diver, but I tell her not to touch of your dive things."

Joanna glanced down the walkway and saw a young woman with a broom. She had the same dark skin and narrow Arab face as her mother, though she wore no headscarf. Egypt's generation gap. "Is that Fahimah? Please thank her for me."

"No, that is Fayruz, the young one. They both help me with the work. You are needing anything? A bottle of water is already putted in the room."

"You're very kind, but I'm fine. I just need to get a good night's sleep."

"That is good," Hanan declared. "If you need me, I am there." She pointed toward the painted concrete house across the parking lot where the family resided. "If you want to send message, you know computer connection and fax machine are in office. We close at six, but for you we will open special."

"Thank you again. Fortunately, Charlie has been taking care of that for me. We don't need to send anything this evening."

After another embrace, Joanna continued to her room and unlocked the door. It was, in fact, pristine. Her clothes were hung up, and all her books and spare equipment were neatly arranged on the floor. An unopened bottle of water stood on the night table.

Charlie loitered for a while in the doorway while she unpacked. "Are you sure you don't want a bite to eat? We can go to Falafel Ali's, which you really liked before."

"Thanks, Charlie, but I'm not hungry and not much up for conversation either. Please understand. I'll see you in the workshop tomorrow. At eight, say?"

"Yeah, sure," he said neutrally. "Eight o'clock is fine."

When he was gone, Joanna let herself drop limply onto the perfectly made bed. She trusted her own abilities, physically and mentally, to go back to work the next day, but for the moment, she was paralyzed. Fury, humiliation, and a sense of betrayal churned in her stomach. She imagined a dozen revenge scenarios, beginning with a lawsuit and ending with a hand-grenade attack on the *Hina*. She snickered at the latter image, imagining herself blithely buying a grenade in the El Gouna souk.

As for the lawsuit, she wouldn't have considered it, but Bernard Allen had all but precluded it anyhow. By paying her hospital bill and providing a place to recover, he had eliminated any claim to damages she could make. And of course a week on a luxury yacht with one of the perpetrators, who happened to be a world-famous actress, rendered ridiculous any assertion of emotional distress.

So there it was. Bernard had laid his trap well and Joanna could almost have congratulated him on his guile. No wonder he was a millionaire businessman; he knew how to make the law—and people— work for him.

But the emotional trap was far worse. Every time she brushed her fingers across her lips, she remembered Kaia setting her on fire, then backing away and returning to her man. It was the cruelest kind of taunt, and she resolved to never fall for it again.

Finally she roused herself from her bleak brooding enough to undress and take a shower. With the warm water flowing over her, she scrubbed herself roughly with the bar of soap, as if to wash the whole episode away. *To hell with them*, she thought. *To hell with them both.*

❖

"Playtime's over," she muttered to herself as she unlocked the door to the workshop the next morning. "Time for the grown-ups to get back to work." Ignoring the dull ache that persisted in her leg, she strode across the concrete floor to the drafting table and unrolled her drawings. She had a schedule now, and she would keep to it.

The design she'd made was still distressingly vague. The fountain part was clear, and the fountain itself was ready for installation under water. But the figures that were to accompany it had no character. Two would be sitting and two standing, to create a pleasant little scene. But she had no narrative. Who would they be? What would be the message? It seemed frivolous to make them anonymous.

She grimaced, hating her lack of inspiration. Time was running out and she had to start doing the casting, narrative or not. Well, she could start with one standing female figure. Nothing more archetypal at a fountain than a woman. And since Marion was done with her own sculptures, maybe she could be convinced to stand as model.

She rolled up the drawings again and had just turned away from the workbench when Charlie appeared in the doorway. He stopped melodramatically, waving several sheets of paper over his head, then came inside.

"Have I got something for you!" he exclaimed, all but dancing to her side.

"Mmm? What?" His cheerfulness annoyed her.

"Remember I told you I e-mailed photos of our tablets to Nigel Castor, in Ancient Middle Eastern Collections? Well, he's just sent back the first transliteration."

"So? Out with it. What does it say? Please don't tell me it's a grocery list." She pulled over one of the workshop benches and sat down.

Charlie straddled the bench next to her and unfolded the typewritten printout. "Nope, not groceries. It's cuneiform, all right, and the language is Akkadian. And you're not going to believe this. It's the story of Lot."

"Lot? You mean the one who escaped from Sodom?"

"Yep, except in this case it's Gomorrah. In fact, this whole account is different from what we all learned as kids. Even weirder, one of his daughters tells it. Here, have a look."

Joanna took the three-page fax from his hand and began to read.

This is the testament of Aina, born of Gomorrah, the second daughter of Lot of the tribe of Abraham. I bear witness hereby to Sodom, which God smote for its iniquity, and to Gomorrah, which the Lord destroyed for reasons I know not.

The city of Sodom was within sight on the horizon, half a day's ride away from our own. Men who traveled there said it was very like Gomorrah. And yet, our father Lot and his father's brother Abraham spoke oft of its corruption. And lo, one evening, upon an outcry, we climbed atop our house to see a terrible light glowing over Sodom in the distance. The city had gone ablaze just before dusk, and from our roof it seemed we could hear the screams carried on the wind across the plain.

On the morrow, as the conflagration sank to ashes, the men of Gomorrah betook them to the ruins, and when they returned, they trembled, telling of the carnage. The people had burned in their houses or fallen in their blood in the streets. Women lay charred with their infants in their arms, the goats and lambs were slaughtered in their pens, the crops in the fields were scorched. Yet our father forbade us mourning the Sodomites, for the fire was God's retribution for their sins and their worship of false idols.

We took this judgment in faith, ne'er imagining the same might befall Gomorrah, for our city was fair in our sight and pious. Its fountain offered welcome to all who wandered in, and this seemed a godly virtue. We gathered at the fountain upon the sunrise, that the women might fill their jugs and the foreign tradesmen might water their beasts. The goddess Anat stood protective o'er the spring, and never was a hard word spoken between ourselves and the strangers.

But the righteous Lot was scornful of the many idols of Gomorrah and the elders of the city for their sufferance of them. Even more did he abhor that the people took those of their own sex as their beloved companions.

He spoke menacingly of the Angels of God, for it was they whom God had sent to destroy Sodom and reveal His almighty power. Hearing this, I prayed each day for God to spare our city and watched each night in dread of his blazing hosts descending from the sky.

Yet when the angels came to Gomorrah it was by foot. They stood before the city gate and cried out, "You are a transgressing people. You commit such immorality as no one who has preceded you in all the worlds."

The people were sore afraid, all but our father, who brought them in to sup with us. And in our house, they were as other men, with feet that need be washed. Their names were Yassib, Mesoch, and Gebreel, and though they had no blazing wings, the fire of God was in their eyes. Only Gebreel, who scarcely had a beard, spoke gently with our mother.

And so it was not long before the elders of the city appeared before our house. They arrived with their wives or their favorite boys, and curious folk attended them, and all clamored for the strangers to come out and explain themselves.

Lot barred his door to their entreaties, nor did the angels want to be thus confronted. But the crowd would not relent, so our father thrust us, his daughters, into their midst. To shame them, he called out that they should satisfy their lust upon us, who were maids that never knew a man.

But the shame was upon us who were given unto them, though in truth, we came to no harm, for the crowd was all our neighbors and the women of the fountain. Two of the men grew angry at the insult and pounded on the door. And lo, when the door opened, Mesoch threw hot coals into their faces, scorching them, and proclaiming that Gomorrah would burn as well, as Sodom did for all its wickedness. Only the righteous Lot and his women would be spared.

But the people did mock them, even as they withdrew, and it was their undoing.

"Flee," the angels said, and though it was night, we took the donkeys our father had packed with provender and fled into the hills. From there, we could see the fires breaking out, spots of light here and there, then ever more of them, until the entire city was aflame.

We wept, embracing our mother, for Gomorrah was all the home we had known, and life had been good. Only our father drove us onward, into the hills as the angels had instructed him. But at the ridge that overlooked the burning city, our mother fell upon her knees and would not rise again. Lot pressed on, leaving her, and brought us to a cave where we found shelter.

Lamenting, we made a fire against the chill and waited for Lot to fetch our mother back. After much time had passed, he returned, bringing dreadful report. God's wrath was upon her for her disobedience, and He smote her. We cried out bitterly, for she was the best of mothers, but we dared not question. We were meek before God and before our father, who knew His will, and so lay down in the darkness and gave up our anguish in prayer and weeping.

That night, I heard fearful moans in the dark but knew not what it was. I prayed to God for protection and no harm befell me that night. But on the second night, my father came unto to me with force, pressing his hand upon my mouth. "Do not cry out, my daughter," he whispered, and the smell of the fermented grape was on him. "It is God's will that my line continue and your mother bore me no sons. Be still now and let God's commandment be fulfilled that the kin of Abraham and Lot shall multiply."

I felt a sharp pain inside me, for I was a maid, and the touch of my father was repugnant. But though I wept the while I bore it, I was ever obedient.

On the morrow, while my father slept, Astari drew me by the hand outside the cave. "If what our father has done to us is by God's command, then God's will is done. But I will not stay one day more under his authority, for his touch is loathsome to me."

"What can we do?" I asked, for I feared the wilderness more than my father's force. I could not bear another trial after so much had happened. But then God showed His hand again, for Gebreel, the fairest of our angels, appeared and bade us leave our father. He pointed toward a break between the distant hills and said, "Go thither to Zoar, for there are men of your tribe. Ask for the family of Bessem, and they will take you in."

*He helped us pack the donkeys with provender for the journey and
gave his blessings. Smoke still rose from the ashes of Gomorrah as we
set off eastward toward Zoar under this new guidance.*

*The house of Bessem did take us unto them as the angel prophesied,
and within the month we were betrothed. We dared not speak of our
condition, for we were certain no one would believe us, and when our
sons Moab and Ammon were early born, our husbands beat us and
threatened to abandon us. But Lot himself came to Zoar, honored as the
one righteous man of Sodom and Gomorrah. He told his half-true tale,
and though he cast it as our assault upon him, he declared it to be God's
will and purpose, and so we were forgiven.*

*But surely this is not justice, for if the planting of the father's
seed upon his daughters was by God's design, then there is no shame
in telling the truth of it. And if there is shame, then wherefore is it from
God? Let him who reads this solve the puzzle and proclaim the truth of
it for all the world to know.*

Joanna dropped the fax to her lap and glanced up at Charlie,
stunned. "This is authentic?"

"Assuming the tablets are authentic. But why wouldn't they be
real? It's not the sort of thing that people want to fake."

Perplexed, she perused the transliteration once again. "Do you
realize what we've got? This is equivalent to the Dead Sea Scrolls. No,
they're even more important because the Dead Sea Scrolls simply give
earlier versions of most of the Old Testament books, plus a few new
texts. None of them actually *contradict* the stories the way this one
does." She held up the pages.

Charlie shrugged. "Maybe it's a parody or something."

"This doesn't sound like a parody, and people who wrote cuneiform
tablets did not usually engage in comedy. That didn't arise until fifth-
century Greeks, with Aristophanes and his ilk. Plus, this is written in
first person. I don't know of any instances in archaic literature of people
inventing tales about themselves. It sounds to me more like a cry for
justice. Do we have anything more to go on?"

"Nigel faxed me several pages of background explanation." He
pulled them out of another pocket. "You can read them here. Or would
you like me to summarize them?"

"Please summarize. I'll read the details later tonight. For now, I just want to know how he can be sure he's got it right. The date, for example. Where does it fall, and how does he know?"

"Well, for starters he can figure it out from the choices and variety of cuneiform characters. According to Nigel, the language emerged in Sumer around 3,000 BC as pictographs. These became simplified and increased to about four hundred in the Late Bronze Age, when it was adapted for many languages: Akkadian, Elamite, Hittite, and a bunch of others."

"So how does he figure out which one he's dealing with?" Ancient languages were well outside Joanna's expertise.

"Well, he said it was Akkadian, and who am I to question it? It was the dominant literary language of the Fertile Crescent, and Akkadian cuneiform had a unique combination of phonetic symbols and syllabic signs. Anyhow, it disappeared as writing around the second century CE."

Joanna squinted as she did the quick calculation. "So our tablet is at least two thousand years old."

"Judging by the content, I'd say easily twice that age."

She shook her head. "That leaves me speechless."

"Nothing leaves you speechless, my dear. But it *is* exciting."

Joanna stared into the distance, calling up other questions. "If it's Akkadian, where does he propose it comes from? How big a territory are we talking about?"

Charlie shrugged. "He doesn't say, and I don't think he can make any better guess than we can. Assuming a shipwreck, the tablets had to be brought on board somewhere on the other side of the Red Sea. I'd say from anywhere between the Dead Sea to the eastern shores of the Red Sea. I'd be more concerned with making sure it's not a fake."

"If it's a fake, it's not a modern one. No one's going to learn Akkadian just to create a counterfeit and then drop it into the sea hoping someone will find it. And an ancient fraud, well, why would anyone bother? I'm not an antiquities scholar, but I've never heard of myth parody, least of all one told in the first person. If this account is authentic, we have to not only rethink the story of Sodom and Gomorrah but to acknowledge that it was real. Nasty and real."

Charlie chortled. "It's going to piss off a *lot* of rabbis."

"It won't be just rabbis. Christians and Muslims refer to Sodom and Gomorrah too. It's the biblical basis for condemning homosexuals. Lot's a kinsman of Abraham, and he *is* called righteous, so no one's going to like finding out he was a rapist. Especially of his own daughters."

"Disgusting, isn't it?" Charlie grew somber. "I've got a daughter. She's grown up now, but just the thought of any man doing that to his child makes me want to puke. If I was in the same room as someone like that, I swear, I'd break his teeth."

Joanna appreciated his vehemence. "I bet you were a good father, Charlie. I can just see you waiting up at night till your daughter got home from a date. Poor girl."

"Well, I tried to be subtle in cases like that, but hell, what good is a man if he can't do right by his children."

"The problem with fathers is that they're men, and parenting gets all mixed up with pride and honor. You know, it's all about the son's toughness and the daughter's chastity. It seems to me the best kinds of fathers are the ones who act like mothers, who love you no matter what. Given that, my father gets high marks. He had a drinking problem too, but it just made him amusing, until he drowned in a drunken accident, like I've already told you. No pride or honor there."

"Well, it sounds like your father was doing his best, so you can't compare him with Lot, who was simply a creepy bastard."

"I'm curious now to see what the other transliterations say, not to mention all the tablets that are still down there," Joanna said. "Maybe there are more creepy bastards."

Charlie stood up from the bench, folded his fax, and slapped the ubiquitous concrete powder from his jeans. "If they're from the same period, we could have some serious biblical revisions." His face suddenly brightened. "This discovery could make us famous."

Joanna ran her fingertip along the still-sensitive scar on the side of her head. "Let's hope it's 'good' famous, and not the kind they burn at the stake."

CHAPTER ELEVEN

W hat the hell did you two get up to while I was gone?" Bernard came from the galley with his second beer.

Kaia looked through the salon windows toward the darkening sea. "We didn't 'get up' to anything. I just took care of her, like you ordered me to do. We became friends. I found her much more interesting than I expected. And attractive."

"So it seemed. Listen, you can't go doing things like that. It's one thing to have the queer boys admiring you, but lip-locking with dykes, no matter how attractive they are, that's out of the question. The tabloids would eat it up, and the only roles I could get for you would be prison wardens and gym teachers. I don't want to see her around this boat again, you hear?"

Kaia didn't reply, just leaned against the salon doors, her mind in turmoil. Bernard stepped into the silence. "Look, you've got to trust me on this. You're the talent, but I know the business. I picked us both up off the street and got us into the big time, and I can't have you second-guessing me. I've made your career. Christ, I've made you fucking *rich*."

"Yes, you have. I appreciate that your connections in New York and Hollywood got my career off the ground, and I've always gone along with the roles you found for me. I think I can do better than play vampy stereotypes, but you're right. They paid for all this." She glanced up at the ceiling of the salon. "But this religious propaganda is a bridge too far."

"I don't get what you're so up in arms about. What's wrong with a religious movie? You don't believe in God?"

"What I believe is beside the point. It's going to be an awful movie. People will associate me with fundamentalist propaganda. I just don't like the message."

"Okay, so it's a little bit over the top and it's not Shakespeare. But what's wrong with that? It's going to bring in large audiences. And what bothers you about the message anyhow? It's just about obedience. It wouldn't hurt you to learn a little of that."

"Ugh. What is it about men that makes them want women to be submissive?"

"Because we're stronger, period. There's a reason we've always run things—corporations, armies, countries. If you want to know why men are in charge, just try arm-wrestling with one." He unbuttoned and pulled off his soiled shirt and rolled it into a ball. "Has Jibril done the laundry recently?"

"I don't know. I haven't been paying attention. You can ask him."

Bernard dropped the ball of shirt onto the floor and scratched the patch of hair at the center of his bare chest. His pectorals were getting flabby, she noted.

"Anyhow, next time, make sure he gets all my shirts," he said, his tone softening. His expression, too, became gentler and he approached her. "Look, this thing with Joanna. I don't know how she managed to get her hands on you, but it's over now. Things are back the way they're supposed to be. Starting next month, the big checks will start coming in again, and you'll see that this flirtation happened because you were bored."

He slid his arm around her waist. "You know, seeing you two together was a shock but also a turn-on. I've got a nice hard one right now, so let's go celebrate your new movie with a little male dominance. I'm so horny I could do it twice." He pressed against her from behind, his erection obvious. Arguments, especially the ones he won, always aroused him. They also made him stink, and she pivoted away from him. "I don't think so."

His eyes narrowed. "I could force you."

"You've already forced me, by tying my cooperation in bed to my career. It's as if I've been on the casting couch for twenty years. I've always given you what you wanted, even when it was rough or strange. Come to think of it, it's been strange from the beginning, and I'm fed up with it. You can jack off tonight, as rough as you want. I'm sleeping in the guest cabin."

She took the first step down the spiral staircase and looked back over her shoulder. "And I'm not signing the contract."

CHAPTER TWELVE

Joanna assembled her tools, made lists, cleaned her worktable—anything to block out thoughts of Kaia and Bernard.

"Hello?" Someone called from the open doorway of the workshop. An Egyptian in a suit. Nice looking with a full head of graying hair and, like so many Egyptian men of his age, a well-trimmed mustache. Omar Sharif plus thirty or so pounds. The man stepped inside and held out his hand, first to Charlie, then to her. "Rashid Gamal. Pleased to meet you. I'm from the project committee."

Joanna brightened. "Are you here to assign us another site in place of the one that disappeared?"

"Unfortunately not. The committee is still working that out. You see, the Ministry of the Interior issued a specific area of the reef for our use, and now that a portion of it has collapsed, we have to request additional space."

"What!?" Charlie expressed the anger they both felt. "You mean we still have no place to exhibit just because one of your engineers was clumsy enough to destroy a part of the reef?"

Gamal raised both hands in a conciliatory gesture. "There is no need to be upset, Mr. Hernie. Your own piece is already installed, as you know. As for relocating Miss Boleyn's fountain, you must be patient. The committee extended your deadline, so I suggest you simply complete the work, and by then the matter will have been settled."

Joanna was not reassured. "Is that what you came here to tell us?"

"Uh, no. In fact, it is my job to, shall we say, monitor the displays to ensure their, um, political and religious neutrality."

Joanna frowned. "But the designs were reviewed months ago. Everything was approved."

"Yes, I know. That was on the basis of their suitability for the exhibit. But we must still determine whether they give the right message."

"Message? Excuse me, but what does that mean? The message of the fountain is 'Fountain.'"

"I'm pleased to hear that. But please understand. One of the purposes of this exhibit is to help bring Egypt into a cosmopolitan worldview without destroying its Arabness. There is Western influence all over Egypt—modern hospitals, universities, businesses, and hotels. But the countercurrents of conservatism are powerful, and we must be sensitive to them."

Joanna set one fist on her hip. "You really think that your bearded Islamists are going to put on wetsuits and dive down to scrutinize the political correctness of each piece?"

Gamal chuckled patiently. "No, but they will see pictures of them in the newspapers, and they will hear about them in the mosques. We just do not want to step on any toes."

"The Brotherhood's toes, you mean."

"If you must put so fine a point on it, yes. But Egypt has several conservative religious groups, and they all fundamentally demand the same thing, that Islam be respected."

"Well, the committee has already seen my designs, but I'll show them to you again." She fetched the rolled up drawings from under the worktable and laid them out. "Two basins, with a pipe in the center leading to a reservoir beneath. There will be a valve here," she pointed to a spot slightly below the emerging pipe, "that will prevent a backflow of water into the reservoir. An intake pipe will emerge just here," she pointed to a spot on the lower basin, "that will allow divers to blow air into the reservoir. When the pressure is sufficient, bubbles will emerge from the fountain."

Gamal tapped a finger on the drawing. "Clever idea. What about the statues?"

She drew out two more sketches and laid them side by side. "These are the female figures that will be dressed in generic drapery. As you can see, two of them will be sitting at the fountain, and the third and fourth will be standing nearby. A male figure will be involved, but I haven't finished positioning him."

"Gamal nodded approval. "Women around a fountain. Very nice. Biblical almost."

"Yes, I suppose so. Would that be a problem?"

"I shouldn't imagine. Obviously we can't have gods and saviors and crucifixes and madonnas. And of course there must be no representation of God or Mohammed. That would certainly stir up trouble."

"What about the Egyptian gods?" Charlie interjected. "One of our colleagues has a sculpture of the weighing of the heart in the underworld, with three or four gods."

Gamal chuckled again. "There are plenty of those all over the country, aren't there? I'm sure a few radical imams would like them to go away, but this is Egypt. It's who we are. No one's going to object to Miss Zimmerman's statues."

Joanna was pensive for a moment as she rolled up her drawings. "Would there be a problem if a scene were obviously and intentionally biblical?"

"To the extent that the scene is a general message of morality, one that is common to both our traditions, that would certainly be acceptable. Who would ever object to that?"

"Exactly," Joanna said. "Who would ever object?"

"Well, I am glad we have that settled," Gamal said, and brushed imaginary dust off his hands. He straightened his jacket and gave a brief nod, suggesting a bow. "It's been a pleasure. Please let me know if I can be of any further assistance." Smiling, he let himself out of the workshop, passing Marion in the doorway.

"Interesting," Joanna murmured as the one departed and the other arrived.

"What's interesting?" Marion asked.

"Assuming that Bible stories are always moral."

Marion looked nonplussed. "They're not?"

"Never mind that." Joanna's thoughts were elsewhere. "Charlie, have we got a drill bit for the sander?"

"Of course we do. I did nothing but drill all the while you were recovering. What do you need it for?"

"You'll find out. But now let's start on the first figure. Are you ready to be cast, Marion?"

"Sure. As one of your girls?"

"A goddess, actually."

"Fantastic!" Marion beamed. "Finally, someone who appreciates me."

❖

"Everything taken care of?" Joanna asked.

Marion counted off on her fingers. "Let's see. Pee pee, *ja*. Hair in plastic, *ja*. Vaseline on skin, *ja*. Tubes hanging out of nose, *ja*. Everything is good."

"All right, then. So sit down here and be prepared to be imprisoned for half an hour inside a mask of goo. But listen. The dental alginate mixture will dry very quickly. We've got a window of opportunity of about ten minutes to apply it, but it will start to dry even while I'm working. Once we start, you can't move at all."

"Fine. So less talking and more spreading." Marion closed her eyes.

Joanna dipped a spatula into the creamy concoction and laid the first smear over her forehead, then another over her eyes.

"*Scheisse*. It's cold."

"Hush. You can't move your face muscles. You can only moan or grunt, okay? Moan for something bad, grunt if you agree." She slathered another strip over Marion's mouth, troweling it up with the palm of her hand toward her ear.

"Uhn," she grunted, apparently in agreement.

Once the first thin layer was applied and there were no evident holes or bubbles, Joanna laid a netting of sisal over both cheeks to support the next layer.

"How's the breathing? You still alive in there?"

"Uhn."

"I'll take that as a yes," Joanna said. "So let me explain. Charlie made up the cement mixture we're going to use for the actual casting. It's the usual type-two marine cement, but he's added a little sand, micro-silica, and fiberglass. Then we're going to polish it smooth," she added, laying on the creamy compound until Marion's entire head was encased.

"Sit still now. It'll take about twenty minutes to set all the way through."

She'd turned to gather up the mixing tools when someone called from the open doorway, and she looked up, annoyed, as George Guillaume sauntered in.

"Looks like you're back to work again," he said. "Don't let me interrupt you."

"To what do we owe the pleasure?" Joanna picked up the scratch knife and wiped it clean with a rag.

"I just wanted to stop by and take a look at the competition." George wandered around the shop, examining tools, poking at packages of materials.

"Competition? We're not competing, George. We're all in the exhibit now. We've all won."

"Some people seem to have won more than others." He held up a concrete sander. "Nice tool. Did you bring it or buy it here?"

"Charlie bought it while I was recovering."

"How much did you pay for it?"

"Not much. About 240 Egyptian pounds."

"You were robbed. You should have asked me. I know how to deal with these people. You have to be tough with them or they'll screw you. Don't buy anything else until you've checked with me."

Joanna tapped gently on the drying cast on Marion's head. Another few minutes and it would be ready. "Thanks, George, but I don't need any help buying from Egyptians. Charlie and I do just fine."

"All right, then. Go ahead, keep on paying double. I don't care. You seem to have enough friends here to help you, so maybe it's worth it."

Joanna ignored him, focusing on inscribing a line with the knife along Marion's neck past her ear and over her head to the other side. Marion twitched slightly when the rod passed her ear.

"Don't worry, I won't nick you. I just need to make a cut where the mold will separate."

"Uhn."

George persisted. "No matter what you do, someone bails you out. I wish I had your connections."

Joanna turned around to face him directly. "George, what are you here for?"

He scowled for a moment. "I wanted to ask you something."

"Ask me what? As you can see, I'm pretty busy."

George leaned his hip against the worktable, examining the sander. "Well, Gil said you asked the committee for a postponement and for a new site, and they gave it to you."

"Only the postponement. We still don't have a site. Why are you asking?"

"But you do know someone on the committee, right? Someone who decided on your case. A friend of yours, maybe?"

"I don't know who Charlie talked to about my *case,* but I can assure you I don't have any friends on the committee. What do you want from them?"

He shoved his hands deep in his pants pockets. "My exhibit is a plane crash. I've got some scrap airplane parts, fuselage, wings, torn-up seats, some luggage, and I have to drop them down in a nice pattern."

"So what's the problem?"

"It needs a wide area. Planes don't crash in little patches."

"Didn't they know that when you submitted the drawings? They're supposed to coordinate the works with the space."

"Apparently not. They're idiots. A bunch of Arabs on the take. I specifically requested the center of the town square, and they said maybe but then took it back and gave me a shitty narrow strip on a slope. And guess who they gave the prime space to? One of their own, of course."

"One of their own? What do you mean?" Joanna was losing whatever faint interest she'd had in the conversation.

"Khadija, that Palestinian woman with her little propaganda scene of women and children and Israeli soldiers. Pure anti-Semitic politics. It just makes me sick."

Joanna declined to comment, recalling that George had gotten an invitation to the underwater city because his father had been on the USAID committee that had provided some of the financing. Yes, it was all politics, but there were different kinds of politics.

George was still talking. "Anyhow, since someone on the committee already gave you a break, I thought you could ask him to help me out. It always helps to be female."

"No one gave me a break. I was mauled by sharks, didn't you hear? And I still don't have *my* space either."

"Yeah, well, you got a postponement, so obviously you have some good will on the committee. I'd like to have a little myself. Or is that only for Arabs and women?"

"George, you aren't even making sense, and you're getting on my nerves. I can't see that you've got a problem anyhow, and coming here and insulting me certainly won't fix it. So please, leave me to my work. As soon as I'm done with this head casting, I've got to do the body, so I really don't have time to talk."

"If you're going to be such a bitch about it, I'll confront them myself. But make a note that I'm not someone who lets people walk all over him." He dropped the sander onto the table less gently than Joanna would have liked and stormed out of the workshop.

Joanna shook her head to dispel the thought of him and tapped Marion's plaster-encased head. "Good news. It's time to take this off now."

"Umm!"

She ran the scratch knife again along the separation line between the front and the rear parts of the casting and began separating them. After half a dozen tugs from each side, the two parts pulled away.

"Wuhh!" Marion said, taking a deep breath of air. "Damned hot in there. Dark and hot. So, is it good?" She peered into the negative space inside the casting at her own face.

"Looks great. If all the castings go this well, we'll be right on schedule."

"Hey, girls!" It was Charlie, arriving with a sack of concrete over his shoulder. "Did I miss anything?"

"No, we just finished the head." She helped him unload the sack and slid it under the worktable. "And you're here just in time. As soon as you and Marion are ready, we can start with the body."

"I'm ready, if I don't have to cover my head again. That was half an hour of my life I never want to relive." She ran her fingers through sweat-damp hair and rubbed her neck.

"Don't worry, this one is just standing in place for half an hour, but your head will be free. Maybe you should make another trip to the toilet, and while you're there, strip to your underwear and put these on." She held out two pieces of soft canvas.

"The smaller one ties around the waist and the larger one drapes over the shoulder, comes around the back, and tucks into the waist. I'll arrange it when you come out."

"Why is it so oily?" Marion examined one of the pieces with an expression of distaste.

"To keep it from absorbing the plaster. Trust me. I learned that through a lot of trial and error. Oh, here, don't forget the sandals."

"*Ja, ja.* Sandals." Marion trudged off toward the bathroom scratching tiny pebbles of alginate out of her ear.

Joanna turned back to the worktable and set up the mixing vat. "Your mixture worked fine for the head, but I'm going to use a coarser and tougher plaster for the body mold." She measured out water in a bucket and handed him a standard wooden spoon. "Here's where I can use your muscle."

"Ah, so good when a man feels needed." Charlie began to stir the powder-and-water mixture until it had the consistency of creamy oatmeal. At his side, Joanna unwrapped a bundle of gauze cloths and dropped half a dozen of them into the mash.

By then, Marion had returned in her generic desert-dweller clothing. Joanna adjusted the canvas drapery to her satisfaction. "Looks fine. Come stand over here in a position you can hold for about forty-five minutes. Weight on both feet. Okay? Now, hold both hands out in a sort of beatitude."

Marion complied, rotating her shoulders first to relax them, and struck a generic saint pose. "This good?"

"That's fine. Think 'earth mother' and you'll be fine."

"How do you want to do this?" Charlie asked, taking hold of one of the gauze squares by two of its corners.

Joanna took it from his hands. "We need to get a rhythm going. While I'm draping one batch of gauzes on her, you soak the next half dozen in the plaster so I have a steady supply." She turned to Marion and draped the dripping patch over her chest and one shoulder.

"Oh, that's cold. Your statue is going to have hard nipples."

"Don't worry, I'll sand them off."

"*Ach, Gott.*" Marion winced. "Can we talk about something else?"

"Sure. Why don't you tell us about *your* sculpture? I hear it was one of the biggest. What is it called again?"

"The 'Great Balance.' Sometimes called 'Weighing the Heart in the Underworld.' Egyptian final judgment but not so much of good or evil." Marion shivered again as the first wet patch was laid on her back. "More like to see if you have, um…lightness in the heart."

"The assumption being that the heart was the seat of conscience?" Joanna asked.

"Exactly. One dish of the balance has the dead person's heart and the other dish has the feather of Maat."

Joanna bent over and tucked another sheet of creamy gauze under Marion's ample breasts. "She ruled over harmony, justice, order, and morality, right?"

"*Ja.* If the dead person's heart is light and just, it balances the feather and he can enter the underworld. But if it is heavy with injustice, his dish crashes to the floor and the feather of Maat flies off the other dish."

"What happens to him?"

"A monster eats him."

"Ah, always someone eating your soul," Joanna grumbled, moving down Marion's back and laying the dripping cloths on her hips and buttocks.

"I've seen the sculpture," Charlie said. It's a real balance, with dishes hanging on chains from two arms that pivot on a central fulcrum. Looks great."

"What about you, Charlie? Your project is done now too, *nicht*?

"Yep, it went down days ago, inside the long gallery. Gil's finishing up his locomotive too. Actually almost everyone's done or close to. Even Sanjit. You know, the Indian guy? He wanted to do the Hindu gods."

"Can't see Rashid Gamal approving that." Joanna pressed a series of metal rods around Marion's whole form and covered them with the next layer of plaster-soaked cloths.

"In fact, he did smuggle them in." Charlie handed over the next cloth, leaving a trail of dripping plaster between them. "He just made an elephant that happens to be Ganesh, a lion that Indians will recognize is Vishnu, a monkey who is Hanuman, and some kind of mixed animal with horns. Sly devil, that Sanjit." He stirred several more patches into his plaster batter.

Joanna knelt now, wrapping plaster cloths around Marion's legs. "Didn't the Japanese woman also make a dragon?"

"That's Yoshi," Charlie said. "'Ryūjin,' she called it. Dragon god."

Joanna chuckled. "Well, with all that, and Marion's gods of the underworld, they've got themselves a wild pagan city, haven't they?"

She stood up and surveyed her handiwork. "I think we're done plastering you, Marion. Can you hold that position for about forty minutes?"

"I think so. But I'm thirsty. Got any beer?"

"Are you sure you want to drink something?" Joanna asked. "What are you going to do fifteen minutes later, when it passes through you?"

"*Ach, ja.* Good point."

Charlie patted her lightly on the cheek. "You can hold out, old girl. And when we break you out of that thing, we can go to the Sun Bar and you can drink all you want, on our tab."

"Ah, a good reward. You see, Joanna? That's the way to comfort a German."

George needed a drink. Several of them, in fact. But the last place he wanted to go was the Sun Bar, where he'd run into the other project sculptors and have to be polite. He was fed up with the whole thing. The exhibit was obviously bogus, rigged by the Egyptians to make themselves look cultured.

He wandered toward an open-air beer kiosk near the dock and sat down at the bar. While he waited, he mentally inventoried the ethnic groups represented in the exhibit. There were the Egyptians who constructed the walls and buildings, so that was about five right there. Then there were Saïd, Faisal, Mansouri—all Middle Eastern. And a Japanese, a Congolese, and an Indian. Damn. That left only four who were white. He was in the minority. No wonder they were treating him like shit.

The beer arrived, and while he nursed it, he stared down at the long dock and watched the foot traffic coming and going along the row of boats. Divers, boat owners, Egyptian workers, they all had something to do. Only he was stuck waiting on the whims of a bunch of ignorant Arabs who were trying to ape Western culture.

He regretted ever entering the competition. What was he trying to prove, after all, coming to a primitive country to let himself be made a fool of? He had his own yacht, or at least his family did, on the Chesapeake Bay, bigger than most of the boats at the dock in front of him. He should have stayed with his own people and not screwed around with Third World art exhibits.

While he brooded, a man came along the dock toward him, his clean white shirt and tailored pants marking him as one of the boat owners. The stranger approached the kiosk indifferently, then sat at the bar, a seat away from George.

George glanced over at him desultorily, careful not to make eye contact. The stranger drank half his beer, twirled the glass for a moment in the ring of water on the bar counter, and seemed in a bad mood. George could certainly relate to that.

The Asian couple sitting at a table behind him finished their drinks and went off, leaving him and other man as the only customers at the bar. After a few moments, ignoring each other became more awkward than acknowledging each other. When the boat owner finished his beer and held it up to order another one, he glanced sideways. George smiled quickly and remarked, "Not such great beer, is it?"

"About what you'd expect in a Muslim country," the man answered, then added, "You're one of the guys on the art project, aren't you? I heard you talking with someone on the dock."

"That's right, I am. Who might you be?"

"Bernard Allen. I'm here on holiday. The big boat toward the middle of the dock." He poked a thumb over his shoulder in the general direction of the row of yachts.

"Uh-hunh," George said. "A Princess 85, isn't it? We looked at something like that, but decided on a Princess 76. A little smaller, but faster. My father likes that."

"Oh, I've had 'er up to a pretty good speed, but whatever floats your boat, eh?" Bernard chuckled at his own witticism. "What brings you here? Oh, right, the project thing." He sipped his second beer, making apparent that his interest was slight.

"Yep, I'm one of the artists," George said again. He liked the ring of it. "I'm held up a little at the moment, but things will settle out. I'm the only American though."

"Yeah, I noticed that too. I don't hear much English. That's why I spotted you."

"Well, there's two people from London and an Irishman, but the rest are foreign." It struck him as he said it that foreign was probably not the right word. But another American would understand what he meant.

"The ones from London. One of them's named Joanna, right?"

"Yeah, how do you know her?"

Bernard snorted. "I saved her ass. Pulled her out of the water after a shark attack. Not that she showed any gratitude."

George raised his eyebrows at the whiff of scandal. "Oh, *you're* the one. That's right. She was staying on one of the yachts with some actress-and-agent couple. Well, you could have saved yourself the trouble. She's just as arrogant as the rest of them."

Bernard finished his beer and held up two fingers toward the barman. "I'm inclined to agree with you. We wined her and dined her for a week on our yacht, first-class treatment, at our expense. I go away for a few days, and what do I find when I come back? She's making a pass at my wife. Of course, I asked her to leave."

George laughed out loud for the first time in weeks. "Really? She's a lezzie? Well, that explains a lot. My condolences to your wife."

The beers arrived and Bernard slid one of them toward George, who held it up in salute. "Thanks. As for women, you can't trust any of them these days."

"Right you are, my friend. This women's lib business. The lesbians are behind it, of course, but the normal women fall for it. I don't know where it's going to end."

George hunched forward conspiratorially. "Listen, at this point I've had it to here with women in general." He tapped his throat with the edge of his hand. "When they want something from you, they're all tits and ass, and when they've got it, they're suddenly liberated and flip you off. You'd think the Arabs of all people wouldn't fall for that crap, but they do."

"Arabs. To hell with them all. So you were cheated on by an Egyptian?"

"Na. Nothing like that. It was a professional screwing, not a personal one. I mean, I was supposed to set up my exhibit in the center of what they call the city, but someone got paid off and suddenly they gave my site to a woman. Some Palestinian. Smug little bitch got the prime spot. And I've seen her stuff. Pure propaganda." He sucked air through his teeth and muttered, "Now they're letting terrorists have art exhibits."

"That's a real crime." Bernard swirled the remaining beer in his glass, creating a little vortex. "Women. You can't live with 'em, and you can't live without 'em."

"Well, it can't be so bad in your case. I mean you got a beautiful actress in the deal."

Bernard snorted again. "She *was* beautiful, twenty years ago. Tits like a Barbie doll. But all things pass, my friend. When they're young, they make you do things you shouldn't, and when they're old, they kick you in the balls. No, my friend. They're daughters of Eve, all of 'em. Nothing but deceit. They look appetizing, but there's poison in each bite." He wiped his mouth with the back of his hand. "Here, let me buy you another beer."

CHAPTER THIRTEEN

Jibril removed his shoes and sat down before the fountain outside the mosque to perform his ablutions. He murmured the opening verse of the first sura, washed his right hand up to the wrist three times, then did the same with his left. Following the protocol, he rinsed his mouth and spat out the water three times and rubbed his teeth with his finger. He sniffed a bit of water from the palm of his hand into each of his nostrils and exhaled it. Three times again, he washed his face from hairline to chin and ear to ear. Then it was his arms, up to the elbow, three times on the right then on the left.

To purify his head, he passed wet hands once over his hair, around his ears and the back of his neck.

Last of all, he cleansed his feet according to the formula, starting with the right foot, from between his toes up to his ankles, three times, all the while mumbling, "There is no god but God, and Mohammed is the messenger of God."

Then he was ready to enter the holy place, right foot first, through the main entrance with the men. He walked midway into the mosque and sat down at the end of a line of worshippers who were in quiet prayer or reading softly from the Quran. Closing his eyes, he made his own prayers, a combination of ritual utterances and personal supplications to God to be kept pure. When the call to prayer came, the words were as familiar to him as his heartbeat. *God is great. I bear witness that there is no god but Allah, that Mohammed is his messenger. Come to prayer, come to success, God is great, there is no god but Allah.*

The imam ascended the pulpit and began the sermon, this time on the subject of *jihad*. He began neutrally enough, talking about the obligation of each man to strive to perfect himself before God. But when he quoted the Quran, his message became more pointed.

The Jews say, "Ezra is a son of God" and the Christians say, "The Messiah is a son of God." They resemble the saying of the infidels of old! God's curse be upon them! How are they misguided? They take their teachers, and their monks, and the son of Mary to be equal to God, though bidden to worship one God only. There is no God but He! They would put out God's light with their mouths. God hath sent His Messenger with the religion of the truth, that He may make it victorious over every other religion, even those who assign partners to God.

The verse had always confused Jibril, for he knew who the Christian Messiah was, but he had not heard of Ezra being one of the Jewish gods. Still, if it was written in the Quran, it had to be true. Perhaps the imam would explain.

But the imam offered no interpretation and simply continued in a vein of thoughtful condemnation. He did not specify violence or hint in any way at aggressive action, but Jibril knew the ninth sura and had long ago memorized it.

Make war upon those to whom the Scriptures have been given but believe not in God, or in the Last Day, and who forbid not that which God and His Apostle have forbidden, and who profess not the truth, until they pay tribute and be humbled.

What did that mean? Were they supposed to drive out the Americans and the Europeans? That's what some believers wanted, but he needed for the imam to draw the parallel before he would be convinced.

The Brotherhood was always on his mind. Illegal though it was, it pervaded the political discourse, as well as the day-to-day talk of the men in the coffee shops. The message was a noble one: that the Quran and the Sunnah constituted a perfect way of life and revealed the social and political organization that God had set out for man. He agreed that governments should be based on this system, for only this system would achieve social justice, eradication of poverty and corruption, and freedom under Sharia law. Above all, he was in sympathy with the

Brotherhood's hatred of colonialism, even the cultural variety that had seeped into every corner of Egyptian life.

He listened carefully, reflecting on the way in which his own life and livelihood flew in the face of the demands of his faith. He'd always been a good Muslim and tried to live every day in such a way as to please God. But he felt utterly unable to do so. Bad enough that he found bodily purity so difficult to maintain, but he'd also fallen into the trap of wanting more money than the life of a shopkeeper could provide.

He'd relinquished the inheritance of his father's pathetic little shop in the souk to his brother and taken jobs with the foreigners because they paid so much better. That was the beginning of his torment. His previous employers at the hotel had been decent men, but they were infidels and had led him off the path. His gravest mistake was allowing them to cajole him into going to the El Gouna cinema and seeing *Queen of Thebes*, and that had forever changed his view of women.

He wanted to marry, desperately. At twenty-eight, he was long ready and weary of restraining his desires, and in a year or so he would have enough money. But now, every pious woman he looked at seemed drab and boring when he compared her to the image on the screen, the image of Kaia Kapulani, which had swept him off his feet. When he had learned that the actress and her husband not only had a yacht in the harbor, but were looking for an all-purpose crewman, he had applied, and to his surprise—and his father's horror—he had been hired.

And now he worked for rich Americans, waiting on them, carrying their bags, delivering their laundry. It paid well, and it brought him in contact with the actress, but all that did was confuse him, since it was obvious she represented all that his faith condemned.

What was happening to him? To Egypt? The Red Sea beaches were now all but completely owned by Westerners and their tourist businesses and bars. Infidels with money and power, and women in bikinis. It was tearing him apart.

The sermon ended and then came the second call to prayer. He stood up with the other men, shoulder to shoulder, lightly touching elbows, in a straight line facing the niche that pointed to Mecca. Together they began the ritual prayer. The cry of God is Great, the recitation of the first sura of the Quran, a bow, a second recitation, a prostration, a rising, a second prostration, a final rising. When the prayer was completed, he exchanged the required salutation with his two neighbors, offering a light embrace to affirm brotherhood.

Calmed by the service and the sense of community with other good Muslim men, he donned his shoes and began the walk home. But he had gone scarcely a hundred meters when the two of them caught up with him.

Mazhar clapped him gently on the back. "Hey, Uncle. Why did you hurry away from the mosque? We could have walked back with you."

"I have to get to work. You know my job is important."

Najjid snorted. "I know that your boss is a beautiful whore who makes movies. Is that why you're in such a hurry?"

"You should control your mouth, Najjid. I am as good a Muslim as you, and I do not lust after women I should not."

"Then why do you work for those people? If you got an honorable job, you wouldn't be around nearly naked women all the time. And you wouldn't have that pig of a boss pushing you around."

"It's none of your business why I work for them. Did you catch up with me simply to berate me for my employment?"

Mazhar raised his hands. "I'm sorry, Uncle, honestly. We are family, after all, and you are as a father to me. I hate those rich Americans as much as you do, not just for what they do to you but for how they have dishonored Egypt. You know that's the whole point of our group, to stand up to them. Why don't you join?"

Jibril kept on walking, but slowly now, and the two others kept pace with him. "What would joining entail, exactly?"

"Not a lot. Just meeting with our group now and then. Discussing how to deal with the problems. Maybe helping us out when we hold a demonstration."

"Let me think about it," Jibril answered, and turned away onto the path leading to the dock.

❖

"Have you got a good grip?" Joanna looked down at Charlie's hands. "Okay, now slowly, you pull from the back while I take it from the front. Marion, try to stay in place while we take it off you."

Tugging gently, centimeter by centimeter, they pulled apart the two sides of the cast along the lateral cut, the bottom layer of gauze splitting with a soft ripping sound. A moment later, they stood with the two negative halves of the figure while Marion stepped away from them, rubbing sensation back into her arms.

"Is it good?" she asked, rolling her shoulders with obvious relief.

Joanna inspected the inside front, nodding. "Looks fine. Picked up a lot of detail too. More than I'd hoped."

"Thank God that's over." Marion dropped down onto the bench and vigorously scratched her legs. "That itch has been tormenting me for half an hour."

"How long before you can pour the concrete?" Charlie asked. "I want to see our first figure."

Joanna laid the two pieces horizontally on the worktable. "Tomorrow, first thing. That way we'll be sure that the entire mold will be dry. Can you come tomorrow morning at eight?"

"Sure. The earlier the better. I've promised to help Gil put his locomotive in place in the afternoon. It'd be great if you could be there too. Are you up to diving again?"

"Should be. I've got to stop by the diving center tonight and buy a new mask and wetsuit. The last one got cut to pieces in the hospital, remember? Then tomorrow, while we're on the dock, I have to get my fins back from the *Hina*," she added with forced neutrality.

Marion stood up. "Okay, I go now to my room to take a shower, but *somebody* has promised me a beer."

"Beer it is," Charlie said. We'll meet you at the Sun Bar in half an hour. I could use a shower myself. Joanna, can you take care of the cleanup? I'll do it tomorrow."

"Go wash your smelly bodies. I'll be fine here." Joanna waved them away and turned to study her first casting. It was good, really good, and now she could stop worrying about it. She dried her hands on a towel.

With the satisfying success of the first casting, she tried to plan the remaining figures. But her thoughts wandered obsessively toward an actress whose kiss tasted of sherry.

"I think we're done here," Joanna announced early the next afternoon. She hit the switch, cutting the power to the miniature concrete mixer that had been grinding away on the workbench. The special marine concrete with its additives of silicone, fiberglass, and powdered coral had slowly filled the mold of the female figure. She and Charlie had poured extremely carefully, but if any bubbles rose to the surface, she'd catch them at the sculpting stage.

"Now let's make sure we don't get any leaks or splits," she said, wrapping strips of duct tape around the mold at intervals and wedging it upright between two stools.

Charlie checked his watch. "Hey, it's only one o'clock. We've got plenty of time to get to the dock for some of the drop-downs."

"What was the schedule today?" Joanna asked. "Weren't they bringing down Khadija's work, too?"

"Her group went in this morning. Gil's is scheduled for two o'clock."

Joanna washed powdered concrete off her hands and forearms then reached for the towel. "The whole city is filling up. Poor George. Looks like he's stuck with his narrow slope."

"Oh, that reminds me. I forgot to tell you. George is out."

"What?" She held up the damp towel, noting that it needed laundering. "Out of what?"

"Apparently he barged into a committee meeting yesterday and started shouting at them about discrimination, racism, what have you, and when they tried to get him out, he popped one of them in the face."

"Ohmygod!" Joanna exclaimed. "He's lucky they didn't put him in jail. What happened then?"

"I don't know the details. I suppose they simply hauled him out of the building. But he's definitely out of the exhibit now."

"Too bad." Joanna wiped off the worktable with the soiled towel. "All he had to do was compromise a little. Now he's got all that airplane junk to get rid of."

Charlie shrugged. "Guys like George don't know how to compromise. For them it's win or lose."

"Yeah, I know another man like that," Joanna muttered as she slid her diving sack and new wetsuit out from under the workbench. "Which reminds me. I need to stop by the *Hina* and get my fins before we dive." For the second time, merely naming Kaia's boat gave her a faint shiver of pain.

❖

The dock was hot under the midday sun, but Joanna scarcely noticed. On the drive over, she had worried that the *Hina* might be out on the water for a day of fishing, but already she could already see that it was docked, with its stern facing in.

Would she be able to talk to Kaia? Did she even want to? What would she say? But upon approaching the yacht, she realized the questions were moot, for Bernard Allen was on the stern deck. In baggy shorts and khaki shirt, he stood with his back toward the dock. Jibril worked next to him, coiling some plastic rope.

"Good afternoon," she said as cordially as she could manage.

Bernard spun around. "What do you want? I told you to stay away from my boat."

"Your boat doesn't interest me. I just want my diving fins. I forgot them when...when I left."

He raised his hand, waving her away. "I haven't seen them. You must have lost them someplace else."

Joanna stood her ground. "No, I'm sure they're here. The last time I used them was from your boat." It galled her to say 'your' boat. "Could you look around a bit?"

"No, I couldn't." He did an about-face, terminating the discussion. Not bothering to look back at his crewman, Bernard climbed the steps to the main level and entered the salon, the doors hissing closed behind him.

"I found them, miss," Jibril said, alone now on the stern deck. "I put them in the locker." He knelt and rummaged through the equipment locker, and in a moment he had both bright-yellow fins in his hand.

Joanna stepped tentatively onto the boat as he held them out. "Thank you, Jibril." She took them from him and tucked them under her arm. "How's Kaia?"

"She's not here now," he answered noncommittally. "She went to the village."

Joanna nodded. "Ah. When she comes back, please tell her that I was here and that I...just tell her I was here."

"Yes, miss." He replied in a monotone and returned to coiling his rope.

❖

Joanna quickened her step, to get away from the *Hina* as fast as possible. Charlie waited for her at the end of the dock and was loading their tanks and flotation vests into one of the inflatables. She braced herself on the dock post as she struggled to force her weak leg into the tight new wetsuit, but when that was accomplished, the rest slid on more easily.

Charlie zipped her up from the back and she stepped into the inflatable. It did feel good to prepare for a real dive again, and once she was in the water, the stiff wetsuit would loosen a little too.

They motored the few hundred meters toward the barge that held the final piece of Gil's exhibit, and as they pulled up alongside it, they slid on vests and tanks. Glancing up at the barge, Joanna could see that the locomotive was encased in half a dozen large, heavy-duty balloons. Gil stood in front of it already in full diving gear and waved a greeting.

"Balloons?" Joanna called out.

Gil patted the closest one. "The only way to control the descent," he called back. "Once we get it over the track, we'll release them." He laughed. "So watch your toes."

Charlie tied the inflatable to one of the barge ladders and he and Joanna dropped into the water. Joanna floated, checking Charlie's location and her own buoyancy. Gil jumped in from the barge, and the three of them watched as the crane operator lifted the locomotive from the deck and swung it out over the water.

Joanna followed the motion, amazed at the precision with which the operator seemed to be able to direct the heavy machine, cranking it down centimeter by centimeter. Though the heavy load swayed and turned in the air, it stopped moving when it touched the surface. At that moment, she deflated her vest, dropped to a depth of ten meters, and watched the massive object descend toward her.

In fact, the balloons were a good solution, for they inhibited the rate of descent of the locomotive just enough for the crane and the two technicians to direct it. Two other divers already waited in front of the station, and she joined them while Charlie and Gil helped to guide the huge machine sideways onto its track.

When its wheels were at eye level, she and the other six divers took hold of them to steady them. It edged downward a centimeter at a time until finally the steel wheels barely touched, the rails. At a signal from Gil, two of the balloons were released and the locomotive dropped.

The coral sand flew up in a cloud for a moment at the impact, and when it settled, Joanna could see that the wheels were solidly in place. She turned to the diver next to her, whoever it was, and shook hands. Gil paddled around the locomotive, releasing the remaining balloons one by one, and though his mouthpiece prevented him from smiling, Joanna could tell he was relieved and happy. She hoped his luck would spread.

With half a tank of air left, she allowed herself the pleasure of exploring the train. The steel locomotive and cars were too small for a diver to enter, but he had put a series of dummies inside them near the open windows. The effect was a bit disarming, for, unlike the standing statues at the station, the seated passengers gave the impression of being trapped and drowning.

She paddled away and made a quick round of the developing exhibit, enjoying the pleasure of a real dive again, then returned to the train station. Gil was still photographing his technicians at different locations on the locomotive. When she was finally low on air, she signaled to Charlie that they should surface, and they motored back to the dock.

The whole operation had taken over an hour, and as she tugged off her wetsuit and put on shorts and tee shirt over her bathing suit, she felt the pleasant kind of tiredness of having completed a good dive. Only after she hefted the steel air cylinder onto her back for the trudge back to the car did she sense real exhaustion setting in.

They hiked together along the dock, and as they came within sight of the *Hina*, she forced herself to look away. She refused to let Bernard insult her again. But movement on the lower stern deck caught her eye.

Kaia, waiting for her.

Joanna stopped in front of the yacht, her heart pounding, while Charlie gave a quick wave and diplomatically continued on.

Kaia smiled with sorrowful warmth. "How are you?"

"I'm all right. Back working." She hated the banality of their conversation. "You?"

"Struggling. I miss you."

"Really? Why don't you visit the workshop?" The question seemed obvious in retrospect. "You can come any time."

Kaia shrugged ambiguously. Was she afraid of Bernard or of Joanna's expectations? Both thoughts made Joanna slightly nauseous.

"Too much going on. I'm sorry."

I'm sorry. Joanna hated that expression. *I'm sorry* is what women said when they dumped you. "I understand," she answered, the sickness in her stomach spreading to her chest, making it hard to breathe.

"I told you not to come around my boat," a male voice called out. Bernard Allen stood on the upper deck, his mere elevation lending him authority.

Kaia cringed visibly, and Joanna unconsciously took a step back. She thought of a dozen things she could shout back at him, but none of them would change the anger or the longing that roiled inside of her. "Well, good-bye, then. Take care," she said impotently, and continued along the dock to the shore. The weight of the steel cylinder on her back forced her to hunch forward, in the posture of defeat.

She had been through so much in the last two weeks, but at that moment, for the first time, she felt like breaking into tears.

CHAPTER FOURTEEN

As Charlie turned the car into the parking lot of the hostel, Joanna tried to shake off her depression. She was a scientist and a sculptor, she told herself, chosen from among hundreds to contribute a piece of art to a major exhibit. Moping around like a lovesick teenager was ridiculous, and she deserved a good slap in the face for it. Charlie, ever the diplomat, said nothing, but his gentle silence only added to the embarrassment.

They unloaded their diving equipment from the trunk, set aside their tanks for return to the dive center, and hung their dripping wetsuits on the outdoor rack along with the others. As they passed the hostel office, Charlie waved her on. "I'm going to check for mail."

"Yeah, sure," Joanna mumbled, and climbed the stairs to her room. Maybe showering and shampooing the salt out of her hair would help her pull herself together. She let herself into her room and kicked off her sandals. Her shirt was soaked through and she hung it up on a hanger, then changed out of her bathing suit.

Someone knocked. "Joanna, it's me. Let me in."

"Just a minute." Throwing on jeans and a dry shirt, she opened the door. "What is it, Charlie?" She couldn't keep the irritation out of her voice.

Charlie stepped in, unfazed. "A fax came in from the museum. Hanan was holding it for us especially. You want to read it or shall I?"

She dropped down onto her bed, energized by the news. "You read it. It's your baby, really."

Charlie pulled up the only chair in the room and unfolded the fax.

"Nigel made some remarks at the beginning, about problems with a few of the words, etc. But let me jump to the translation itself."

This is the testimony of Astari, first daughter of Lot, who is kin to Abraham and the father of my child Moab. I swear before the One God it is the true account of the destruction of Gomorrah and our flight from it as God's chosen family.

Gomorrah was a cheerful city of mixed peoples and their gods, though none but the family of Lot worshiped the One God. Lot was not a son of Gomorrah but wandered to the city on the plain from elsewhere, while my mother was native to the town and a follower of Anat. When she was given unto Lot as wife, she renounced that cult and took into her heart the One God.

For all that my father preached, the people remained indifferent to our God, yet Lot took great offense at theirs. His righteous anger waxed with his years and yet none would hear him. And so it came to pass that he spoke of a Reckoning, of the One God's wrath toward the idolaters, and of His avenging angels. When we looked upon their work in the ashes of Sodom, we knew he spoke true.

And verily, after the ruin of Sodom, within the cycle of the moon, God's angels came to Gomorrah. Lot met them at the gate and bade them come into his house. They entered in and spoke their names: Mesoch, Yassib, and Gebreel.

We knew for a certainty they were our special angels, for they spoke of Abraham, the head of our clan, and of his supplication to God to save us, the only righteous ones. My mother fell to trembling, and Gebreel, the fairest of the angels, cast a gentle eye upon her in her distress. It was as if God's love was in his face and God's wrath in the faces of the others.

While we prepared the evening bread, the men tarried in the other room whispering among themselves. I yearned to listen, for surely the matter touched us deeply, but alas, though our mother wept, our duty was to serve the men their supper.

When we sat at table breaking bread, the people of Gomorrah came unto us with great vexation. Men and women of the city and the elders with their wives and boys. They feared the angels, who had prophesied doom already at the gate, and demanded to confront them. But Lot's heart was hardened, and he mocked the people from the doorway.

"This is a house of true believers, where none but the righteous shall come in. Here, satisfy your appetites on maids who have known no men, for it is better you violate their innocence than that you molest an angel of God." Thus saying, he thrust my sister and me into their midst.

"Violate? Molest?" One of the elders laid a gentle hand on my shoulder. "Wherefore do you speak of molestation? We have no interest in your daughters, but only in those who call themselves angels and who entreat heaven for our ruin. Let them come before us and explain themselves." He spoke clamorously for Lot had closed the door.

"Why do you withhold them? We want only to speak with them," another shouted, pounding on the door. And lo, the door did open, but a shower of burning coals was cast from within and did blind him.

The people departed then to attend the injury, and our mother drew us back inside. But there was no peace, for the angels commanded that we flee. Not from the crowd, which had dispersed, but from the conflagration that was to come. By some foreknowledge, perhaps in prayer, Lot had already bidden the servants load the donkeys. And though it was eventide, the angels were adamant and drove us before them into the hills. Hardly had we reached the heights when the darkness below became lit. We looked back and saw the fires here and there, small at first, then increasing, until the city, our home, was all ablaze. Our mother cried out and fell upon her knees, pounding the ground with her fists.

While we mourned with her, our father did but raise his hands to heaven. "This is the wrath of the One God," he called out. "Praise be unto him." Beside me, my mother only whispered through her tears, "My Tiamat."

"Enough lament." Lot reproached her. "Your sorrow is not meet, wife, for God has other plans for us. Just ahead is a cave where we can dwell until the punishment is past."

Our mother would not turn away but stared yearning toward Gomorrah. I beseeched her to come but she would not hear of it. "No, I will tarry here, for my heart is broken. Go with your father, dearest child. If more calamity falls, you must look after your sister."

Those were my mother's last words to me. For verily, God's testing of us was not done, and there were yet more tribulations. That very night God struck down my mother for her disobedience, and out of fear of Him, I submitted to my father's will. But I could not endure to abide by him, and so by first light, I crept down the hill to seek my mother's spirit. Where she had knelt and looked back upon Gomorrah, I found her grave, marked by a pillar of salt, and I prayed it was a sign that God had forgiven her in death. I returned to the cave holding to this consolation, but on the second night, my father did force himself upon my sister, taking her innocence as he had done mine, and I was once again in despair.

Again, at first light I rose, and drew my sister with me outside. I thought to take her to our mother's grave, but lo, an angel of the Lord appeared. Gebreel it was, gentle and fair, and he comforted us and sent us to Zoar, where God had opened the hearts of the men to welcome us.

At Zoar, we were betrothed within a month and hastened to marry. When the time was come, we both bore the sons of our father. Shortly thereupon, Lot came to Zoar, and, though they were amazed, the people accepted his claim of fathering our children against his will but at God's command, for such a righteous man could ne'er be doubted.

My sister and I have ever been servants of God but cannot fathom how this deed serves His majesty. And what of our mother? What was her sin but mourning? Surely it has all been part of God's mysterious plan, though I wonder. If plan there be, deceit cannot be a part of it. If Lot is righteous, he need not have lied.

Thus, it is in piety that we endeavor to set the tale right, and the blessing of wisdom be upon him who reads this testament and sees God's justice in it.

Joanna shook her head. "What a bastard. I never did trust that tale of the one righteous man."

Charlie folded the fax in half again. "I don't put much stock in Bible stories, especially one about virgin daughters seducing their father. How often does that happen, anyhow, compared to the times fathers rape their daughters? I can't wait until we publish this."

Joanna stood up and paced the few feet that made up the length of the room. "Oh yes. We'll publish it for sure. But you know? This has come at just the right moment. It's given me an idea."

"What's that?"

"I'm going to change the installation, at least its meaning. The women seated at the fountain will be Aina and Astari."

"You think they'll let you make changes in the design?"

"No, no. The design stays the same. But the figures didn't have names before and now they do. Aina and Astari." She savored the sound. "You know what's so outrageous? I mean beyond the incestuous rape by that scumbag of a father. The girls are so incidental to Lot and his male offspring, who *are* named, that they're simply called 'Lot's daughters.' They're raped, lied about, and become the founders of two lineages, and they *still* remain anonymous. It's enough to make you sick. Well, my fountain will be a monument to them. And the best part is, it's already been approved."

Invigorated, she threw open the door of her room and stepped out onto the walkway. Just below, Hanan was sweeping in the parking lot. Joanna leaned over the railing and called down to her. "Hanan, do you think Fahimah and Fayruz would like to pose for statues for me?"

"Oh, yes," Hanan called back. "This would be a great honor, I am sure."

Charlie was beside her now. "All very nice, but no one's going to recognize the scene but you and me. How will you identify it as Gomorrah?"

"You'll see," she replied cryptically, play-punching him on the shoulder and re-entering her room. "I have it all worked out. And you know what else?" She spun around to face him again. "I want to go down and get more tablets."

"Oh, I like that." Charlie's avuncular face lit up for a second, then darkened again. "But it'll be hard to do discreetly. They're putting in the installations every day now. There'll always be other divers in the city, and they'll see us bringing things up."

"Not at night," Joanna said, holding up a pedagogical finger. She gave him the narrow-eyed smile of the conspirator. "Tomorrow night. Will you take care of getting us fresh tanks?"

"I love it when we do skulky stuff. Okay, tanks and lamps. You got it. Now, go rest up for the big caper." He walked off, waving behind him.

Joanna watched him disappear down the stairs, smirking at the notion of engaging in a "caper." *Yeah, I can do skulky,* she thought. *I even have a nice new black neoprene outfit for it.* Snickering softly, she pulled off her clothes again, ready for a shower and restful sleep.

CHAPTER FIFTEEN

At eleven o'clock at night, the half-dozen cars and vans in the parking area near the dock were dark and silent, their owners, or renters in most cases, settled in for the night on their yachts.

Without commentary, Joanna and Charlie put on their wetsuits and hoisted vests and air tanks onto their backs. Fins and torches in hand, they started down the long dock toward the inflatable boats tied up at the far end. "You're not worried about people seeing us?" Joanna asked. "Aren't we supposed to be doing this in secret?"

"Stop worrying. These boats are full of tourists and fishermen who know divers are working on the project. No one's going to blink an eye if they see us. Relax and wave."

Relaxed was the last thing Joanna felt, especially as they were once again passing the *Hina*, still docked in the same place. Bernard seemed to have lost his enthusiasm for Red Sea fishing or spear-hunting for that matter. Why else would they stay docked all the time? As they passed, Joanna peered toward the upper deck of the yacht, though she could hear no voices nor see any activity. The only sign of life was the warm golden light that shone cruelly from the salon, reminding her that Kaia was inside and she herself was not.

She quickened her pace, and in a few moments they were at the row of inflatables reserved for the project divers. "You're sure we can find the exhibit in the dark?" she asked, untying the first of them in line.

"Yeah. I went out there once at night with Gil while you were still sick. The only hard part is spotting the buoys, but once we're under water, it'll be easy. Gil's railroad station on the west side, Marion's temple to the north, the long gallery on the south. Khadija's women and children in the middle, Yukio's dragon southeast. It's like a village for crazy people now."

"Except for no streetlights."

"Good point." Charlie laughed. "Maybe next year."

They were in the boat now and were silent until they spotted the first buoy. "This one should be directly over the train station. I'll tie up here."

Joanna had made night dives before, a few dozen of them. It was an adventure in the beginning, a plunge into a mysterious, dangerous realm, where one was threatened with the absence of both light and air. But the added frisson of risk was offset by the elaborate precautions, and soon the inconvenience outweighed the pleasure. Even now, they went through a list.

Flashlight? Check. Backup lamp? Check. Blink light on vest? Check. Air turned on? Check. Vest inflated? Check. "You've got the net?"

"Hanging on my vest. Ready? Go."

And then they were in the dark sea, waiting for their bodies to warm up the layer of water that seeped into their wetsuits.

"Everything okay?" Charlie asked.

"Everything okay." Joanna deflated her vest and sank into the darkness.

Except it was not dark. As they dropped ever closer to the railroad station, she could see a dull green glow beneath them, coming from somewhere in the center of the city. They descended farther, skimming just over the top of the locomotive as they swam toward the light. At that moment it jerked into movement.

By then she had made out the figure of another diver just ahead of them. She shone her own light in that direction, but the diver was beyond the reach of her beam. Then the light faded as the diver disappeared around the corner of the block of archways. All she could see for a moment was a dull shimmer and the outer edge of the wall in silhouette. Then that, too, went black.

Charlie had obviously seen the same thing, for he shot forward toward the spot where the diver had been. Joanna followed until he halted suddenly right over one of the IDF soldiers.

His flashlight beam swept along the line of women and children, stopping at the last figure—decapitated. Its head lay on the ground, next to the hammer that had smashed it. What madman would do such a thing? She was pretty sure she knew, but they couldn't make accusations without evidence.

Charlie took off in pursuit of the light, making a sharp right turn past the dragon and around the corner of the arcade. Joanna followed close behind so as not to lose him. The arcade building ran parallel to the railroad tracks, but while the front had a series of arches, the rear was a solid, unbroken wall, with no place to hide. She could clearly see another diver ahead of them silhouetted against the sphere of dull light from his own flashlight.

They pursued him almost leisurely along the rear wall, confident that he couldn't navigate among the objects without light, and even if he halted and cut his beam light, theirs would illuminate his bubbles. Then he turned again around the far corner of the building and disappeared.

As they came around the corner themselves, Joanna was sure she spotted him vertical in front of the train station, but when she neared, she saw it was merely one of the statues that had been lowered the day before. She swung her beam in an arc, revealing them all—anonymous concrete passengers about to board the train that would forever stand at the station.

No bubble columns. The diver had swum out of flashlight range or surfaced. Charlie opened his hands in an exaggerated shrug, indicating that they abandon pursuit. They had their own job to do and now limited air to do it.

They paddled along the inner side of the arcade and, shining her flashlight beam across the square, she could see the Egyptian temple where Marion's underworld gods stood with their balance. No time to examine them though. They returned to the dragon on the southeast side of the square and swam past it toward the hole that was supposed to have been Site 13. The white limestone gravel opened like a grave beckoning them into oblivion.

After first checking that Charlie was by her side, Joanna dropped feet first into the crevice. She descended until her wrist computer indicated thirty-five meters. Still the crevice dropped away. But to her relief, it bottomed out at thirty-eight. She forgot the fugitive diver as she spotted the pale limestone gravel and wondered what other stories they would find. Were more blasphemies there waiting to be uncovered?

But they found nothing. They swept their light beams back and forth across the entire swath of limestone sand but saw no sign of other tablets. Had they come to the wrong spot? But no, Charlie ran his fingers through the sand and brought up a fragment of what appeared to be fired clay. It was the original site, where they had discovered the tablets, but in the meantime, someone had come and collected all the others. It could only have been the Antiquities Department.

Damn, she thought, glancing at her wrist computer. They had reached their time limit for forty meters and had to begin the ascent if they were going to have time for the decompression stop. They already had less air than they'd planned for.

They ascended slowly and, upon emerging again at the city, they swung northward toward Marion's balance. As good a place as any to linger, letting some of the nitrogen in their blood dissipate. Still half distracted by the puzzle of the missing tablets, Joanna studied the Egyptian animal gods: the comical ibis head of the Scribe God Thoth and the sharp jackal snout of Anubis. The balance itself loomed large over her head, its two dishes swaying slightly on their chains. She tugged on one dish, the one with the heart, and the other dish rose. Very clever. She'd have to tell Marion how impressive the display was.

She glanced down at her computer, letting another minute go by. Idly, she swept her flashlight around the square of the city. Something odd was happening on the other side of the locomotive. She cut her beam for a moment and signaled Charlie to turn off his. In the darkness that engulfed them, she could see another light in the distance, flashing off and on. The signal for distress.

Reacting at the same time, they both switched their lamps on again and paddled toward the light. Soon she could see that bubbles rose from the upper corner of the doorway to the train station. They had to be from the fugitive diver. He must have hidden there in the first place, his bubbles temporarily collecting over his head, which would account for why they had missed him before. Joanna dropped down to the entrance of the train station and shone her light beam inside.

George Guillaume stared back at her, his eyes wide in terror. She thought at first it was fear at being captured, until he made a sharp chopping gesture with the edge of his hand toward his own throat. The sign every diver dreaded ever having to use.

Out of air.

She shot toward him and, with well-trained reflexes, yanked her secondary "octopus" mouthpiece from its clip on her shoulder and offered it to him. He spat out his own mouthpiece and sucked in long breaths from her tank while she checked his pressure gauge.

He was right. He was at the bottom of his reserve tank, breathing the last of his air. He must have seen that he had only minutes left and in his terror had used up his air even faster.

Charlie came behind her and shone his own torch over her head onto the ceiling of the miniature station, and she saw the problem. The reinforcing rods of the concrete blocks were exposed, and the valve of his oxygen tank had become wedged between them. He must have tried to kick his way out, because his long fin was caught up awkwardly behind him, in such a way that he couldn't pull his foot from it. And there he'd waited in terror while his air ran out.

She saw no point in trying to dislodge his tank, which was empty anyhow. So they set about freeing him from his vest. He flinched with obvious pain as they twisted his foot out of the fin between the steel rods and pulled him from the station.

Joanna checked her own pressure gauge and saw to her horror that she was also deep into her reserve. George, in his terror, was sucking it up at an enormous rate, and they wouldn't have enough to surface together.

She signaled the problem to Charlie but knew there was no good solution. George might be able to surface now on a breath if he had the common sense to exhale while rising, though it would be a stretch from fifteen meters, and he was already in a panic. But she and Charlie had been down to nearly forty meters and needed to decompress before surfacing or risk decompression sickness. Whether Charlie had enough air for both of them was an open question, but it was certain he couldn't support three.

George was out now, kneeling on the ground next to them and taking long, deep breaths from Joanna's air reserve. She made an instant decision and unhooked her vest and tank, threading George's arms through it. It was awkward holding a flashlight, so she laid hers down and worked in the sphere of Charlie's light. Dropping her own mouthpiece, she shoved George upward, allowing him to use the remaining bit of her air. It might take him to the surface. If not, he could probably manage the rest. Then she turned to Charlie, who already grasped the plan. He handed her his auxiliary octopus and she took her first breath, trying to remain calm. She shone her light on his gauge; it was also on low reserve, only slightly higher than hers had been but almost enough for two people.

Almost.

George disappeared above them as they both rose, measuring their rate by their wrist computers. At six meters they stopped. She dared not look at Charlie's gauge; she knew when the moment came, they wouldn't have enough air to inflate his vest for both of them and would have to drop their weight belts. A cheap sacrifice.

Her wrist computer showed zero. Decompression stop over. She held it up in front of Charlie and shone her flashlight on it. Then she dropped her weight belt and kicked upward, exhaling her last breath slowly, trying to even the pressure. Six meters was doable, but in the dark, they seemed endless.

With the air in her lungs expanding as she rose, her exhalation lasted far longer than it would have done at the surface. But when it ran out, she was still under water. She kicked upward, but the water wouldn't end and her brain screamed for her to inhale. Had she miscalculated? Had her wrist computer failed? How much longer? Her ears began to ring and her stomach lurched and still she kicked. If only she didn't black out.

She broke the surface gasping and Charlie's head popped up next to her, his hair a dull spot of white on the black water. They both sucked in air.

"You okay?" Joanna asked, panting.

"Tip-top. You?"

"Yeah," she said, unable to form a longer sentence. "Gotta rest…a min." Without the weight of the tank, her wet suit kept her at the surface, so she lay back spread-eagled in the water and floated, catching her breath. For a moment, she wondered if George had made it. Or would someone find him floating in the sea in the morning? She didn't much care.

They floated without speaking and Joanna stared dizzily up at the stars, her chest still heaving. Ironically, for all her misery, she could still make out the three stars that identified the constellation of Orion. The hunter, looking down on them. Or was it Peter Pan's stars to Neverland? She was too spent to laugh at her own meanderings.

After four or five minutes of immobility, she felt the pounding in her chest subside and her strength return. "You ready to swim, Charlie?"

"You bet. And look, the inflatable's tied up just behind you."

"Okay. Then, let's get the hell out of here."

With the last bit of air in Joanna's tank, George managed to fill her vest and surface. Floating for a moment, he glanced around, getting his bearings. He saw no sign of the inflatable he'd motored out on, but he'd dived into the city from the other side so it was probably still tied up to one of the other buoys. New panic struck him briefly when it seemed he'd never find his way back, but then he saw the lights of the docked boats in the distance. There was no appreciable current in the harbor, so he paddled awkwardly toward it with his remaining fin. He'd swum only a hundred feet or so when he heard voices behind him and knew the others had surfaced too. Rescue or not, he had no interest in facing them again, so he quickened his stroke. Then the voices went quiet, which at least meant they weren't chasing him. Not yet, anyhow. With renewed vigor, he splashed toward the ladder and hauled himself up onto the dock.

"Shit," he kept thinking, furious at how everything had gone wrong. He dropped Joanna's vest and empty tank on the boards next to him and pulled off his fin. What the hell was he supposed to do now? No way would he allow himself to be confronted about the smashed statue. He'd been out-maneuvered, beaten, and was now deep in shit. Christ. His father was going to have a fit.

Abandoning the useless single fin, he staggered up the dock barefoot and in his drenched wetsuit. Fuck. This had to be just about the worst night of his life. The whole idea of being in the exhibit was a mistake. What was he thinking? "Fuck the exhibit," he said out loud. "Fuck Egypt." He was getting out of this place on the first flight in the morning.

"Is everything all right?" a male voice called out to him. He glanced up to see a man with a cigar lounging in a fishing chair on the stern deck of his boat. The fragrance of the smoke told him the cigar was an expensive one.

"Oh, it's you, the Hollywood guy. Yeah, I'm okay. Been better though."

"A night dive, eh? Where's the rest of your gear?"

"Oh, long story." George ran his hand over his dripping hair.

"You look like you could use a drink."

George glanced over his shoulder but saw no sign of pursuit. Christ, he was exhausted and trembling. The last thing he felt like doing was running the length of the dock. "Are you offering?"

"If you drink Johnny Walker, I am."

"Sure, but I should get out of this wetsuit. Maybe we could go inside?" He stepped onto the stern deck, and with the speed fueled by fear, he peeled off the dripping neoprene and let it fall to his ankles. As he slid his feet out of the crumpled suit, he finally heard the ignition of an outboard motor in the distance. Shit, that had to be them. But Bernard was already standing by the sliding-glass doors, and George bounded up after him.

"Just a minute. I'll get you a towel. Don't want any footprints, you know."

George waited patiently, shivering slightly in his bathing trunks, until Bernard returned and handed him a beach towel. He draped it around his shoulders and it warmed him immediately. Glancing nervously over his shoulder, he rubbed himself until he was passably dry, then slipped into the salon where Bernard was already pouring him a double.

Once inside and out of sight of anyone passing on the dock, he was able to relax. He draped the towel over one shoulder like a toga and perused the interior of the yacht. Impressive. No doubt about it.

"My wife's sleeping, so we should keep our voices down. We don't want her to come up and think we're partying." He set down the bottle and George could see it was Johnny Walker, Blue Label. Jesus. The guy drank only the best. Even George's father saved the Blue Label for Christmas and funerals. He pulled out one of the chairs and sat down.

"Here, warm up with this. I think you'll find it a slow, intense, multilayered experience. At least that's what their ads say." Bernard handed over the glass and, pulling the towel tighter around him, George took the first mouthful.

Wow. An explosion of flavor rose to his palate, a mix of aromas both sweet and smoky. He swallowed, feeling the heat run down his throat to his chest, then detected the satisfying aftertaste of smoke and pepper and a final touch of spice.

He set the glass on his knee and nodded. "That's the best whiskey I've ever tasted. I'm guessing you didn't buy it here."

"Naw, of course not. I picked up a few bottles in Sharm el-Sheikh. Wouldn't miss it. Goes great with a fine cigar too." He took a sip from his own glass and sucked it through his teeth. "What the hell are you doing diving in the dark? I did a little night diving in my time, but it wasn't worth the trouble. You can't spear fish in the dark. Or are you such an art lover you decided to check out the exhibit by flashlight?"

George took another drink and half closed his eyes as he followed the developing tastes. He liked this man. Bernard Allen was his kind of people, men who knew what was good and what was crap. Someone who would understand what it was like to deal with imbeciles. Still, he didn't intend to admit what had happened and sound like a fool.

He sized up the yacht again. Wow. The guy must have a bundle. A pity he was on his way out of the country. Bernard Allen was someone to cultivate. But maybe he could make a connection after all. A sort of trade-off. The one thing he had at that moment was information, knowledge that could pay off big. And maybe he could still enjoy the profit in a roundabout way. It never hurt to have a Hollywood big shot owe you something.

"I was just checking things out, up close and personal, and I'm telling you, the exhibit is shit. Just a phony 'politically correct' collection of a bunch of self-indulgent artistes." He said the last word with derision. "But there's something else down there you might want to know about. Something I couldn't get to, but you could."

"You don't say." Bernard reached for the Johnny Walker bottle.

George held out his glass for a top-up and granted himself another sip before continuing. "Not very many people know it, but I think our friends, Joanna and Charlie, discovered something down there. It has to have been in the drop-off where Site 13 was supposed to be. At least that's where Charlie came up from. I took a look at the spot later but didn't have a chance to go down to the bottom, and I'm sorry now I didn't. I think there's sunken treasure down there."

"Sunken treasure, eh?" Bernard sounded skeptical. "You mean like a chest of doubloons?" He took another sip of his whisky and chuckled.

"I don't know what it is, but it could be a shipwreck. Last week, I was measuring out the crappy little slope the committee assigned me and Charlie came up out of the hole. He was doing a decompression stop, so that showed me he'd been down deep. Anyhow, he was carrying a plate or something, and it looked like it was gold."

"Gold, eh? Here in the Red Sea, this close to a tourist town? Sounds unlikely."

"I can't be sure, of course. But Charlie tried to cover it up, and why would he do that? He said it was part of Joanna's piece, but she's making a fountain, for chrissake, so the plate thing couldn't be for that. No, I'm sure it was from the ocean floor somewhere under Site 13. And if there's one gold plate, there's bound to be more."

Bernard leaned back and crossed his legs, as if listening to someone narrate a tale. "If you think there's treasure, why don't you go after it yourself? Why are you telling me?"

"Well, I did try to take a look, but I'm not that good a diver, and it seemed pretty deep. It's not something I want to do alone. Then later I got a little sidetracked by a personal disagreement, and now I'm, let's say, a little too short on time to dive for treasure. You're welcome to check it out yourself. If you find anything, you can let me know and we can talk about how you're gonna thank me."

"Sure thing. Under Site 13, eh?" Bernard held out the bottle again, offering a third shot.

Reluctantly, George withdrew his glass. "I'd love to, but I just had a very tough dive and I'm getting a headache. It's about time for me to head back. I've got a flight to catch tomorrow morning." He stood up and unwound the bath towel from his shoulders, draping it over the back of his chair.

"Well then, sorry to see you go." Bernard stood up and drained his glass. They shook hands and George headed toward the sliding doors. He was a little unsteady going down the narrow stairs to the stern deck but made it without stumbling. Draping his sodden wetsuit over his arm, he managed to get over the gangplank to the dock, but when he started the long walk toward the parking area, he began to stagger.

He glanced back once toward the yacht where Bernard stood reigniting his cigar. Exhausted and befuddled as he was, he sensed Bernard's contempt boring into his back.

Son of a bitch. Wasn't *anyone* going to cut him a break?

❖

The white dinghy floated ghostlike on the black water, still attached to the exhibit mooring, and they reached it after a few minutes of weary swimming. Without equipment on her back, Joanna clambered first over the side and then reached down to take hold of Charlie's tank. With her supporting its weight, he hauled himself inside the boat.

Too tired to talk, they motored to the end of the dock and climbed up the ladder. The row of yachts still looked the same, lined up in their indifferent luxury. Joanna nearly tripped over the dark bundle right at the edge of the dock and then realized it was her diving vest and tank. George had made it to land and had fled. She was glad he hadn't drowned after all. Professional jealousy would be such a stupid reason to die. With a grunt, she hefted the empty tank onto her back again and trudged beside Charlie along the dock.

"I wonder where he's gone," Charlie said idly.

"He almost drowned, and he knows he's going to be charged with smashing one of the artworks. He's probably headed back to his room, shaking with fear. Then I'm guessing he'll make a discreet and sudden departure without talking to anyone. Maybe his father can pay for the damage he caused."

"Mmm. I almost feel bad for him that we have to report it tomorrow. Almost."

"Yeah, but think of Khadija. She's got a broken statue now. All George is going to suffer is a little humiliation, which he deserves."

When they passed the *Hina*, the light was on in the salon, but Joanna forced herself to glance away and focus on Charlie. Kaia was a million miles away from what they'd just experienced, ensconced in her salon, learning her lines for a Christian movie. Joanna snorted softly with contempt and plodded on toward the car.

CHAPTER SIXTEEN

The headquarters of the Committee for the International Egyptian Underwater Exhibit of Ecological Art was located in one of the newer buildings at the center of the village of El Gouna. The village itself was an unassuming, not to say sad, little commercial center of souvenir shops, restaurants, and a feeble reconstruction of the traditional Arab souk. It seemed to exist solely for the tourists in the surrounding hotels when they got tired of the beaches and swimming pools. But its designers had vastly overestimated the ability of a fake Egyptian village to lure tourists away from their lounges and hotel bars. It was only eleven in the morning, to be sure, but the restaurants were completely empty and so were most of the shops.

By comparison, the underwater city, though populated with figures in concrete, seemed busy and alive. Joanna wondered, after the exhibit was open, whether the souvenir shops would sell tiny miniatures of the underwater sculptures. She smiled to herself, realizing it was almost certain.

They climbed the interior staircase to the second floor where Rashid Gamal had his office. He obviously wasn't important enough to warrant a secretary, but when Charlie knocked on his closed door, Gamal called out something in Arabic, which they took to mean "Come in."

Gamal stood up from his desk as they entered. "Good morning, Dr. Boleyn, Dr. Hernie. To what do I owe this pleasure?" He motioned for them to take seats in front of him.

"What a compliment, that you remembered both our names," Joanna said, as they both sat down.

"You may take it as a compliment if you wish, but in fact we know all the artists' names and the sketches of your works. The project is far too important for us not to. But please tell me, what has taken you away from your workshop and brought you to my dreary little office?"

"Actually, several things, Dr. Gamal," Joanna said.

He smiled, looking even more like Omar Sharif. "Ah, now it is you who are making the compliments. It is only *Mister* Gamal."

"*Mr.* Gamal, then. We want to keep you up to date on what has been happening at the site, though it appears that you also know some things that we don't."

Gamal's eyebrows rose in a sort of facial question mark, though he didn't reply.

Charlie added, "I believe you recall the three tablets I brought to you recently."

"Yes, of course. A fortuitous find, for which the Egyptian government is very grateful."

"Yes, I'm sure it is. Anyhow, since the tablets seem so valuable, we wondered at the lack of announcement from the committee about their discovery. They are, as you must be aware by now, in Akkadian cuneiform and almost certainly thousands of years old."

Gamal's handsome eyebrows had jumped again, seemingly of their own volition. The man would be a terrible poker player. "And how is it that you know what language they are in, Mr. Hernie?"

"I didn't know. But while Joanna was injured and my own work was finished, I took the liberty of photographing all three tablets and sending the shots to my colleagues in London. They informed us that the language is Akkadian and they have undertaken a transliteration."

"I wish you had let me know of this, Dr. Hernie. The artifacts are, of course, the property of the Egyptian people."

"There was never any doubt about that, Mr. Gamal," Joanna said cordially. "Which is why we surrendered them immediately. It was out of pure curiosity, a curiosity I am sure you share, that we took steps to have them examined and translated. And having deciphered their content, we returned to the site last night to see what other tablets could be retrieved for similar study. We discovered, as you can imagine, that all of the artifacts had been removed."

"Yes, we did that as soon as we were able, to guarantee their safety."

"Very wise, of course. We simply wonder why there has been no announcement of the find."

"That was a decision made by the committee, not by myself. We have not yet fully explored the terrain and there could easily be other artifacts. Surely you realize that announcing a trove in accessible waters could easily lead to pillage by treasure hunters."

"You mean by ruthless anthropologists, greedy to get their hands on cuneiform blocks?" Charlie scoffed.

"No." Gamal replied with exaggerated patience. "It is not the clay tablets that concerned us. You'll recall that gold objects were also among the tablets. With the exhibit opening in just two weeks, attracting—we hope—hundreds of divers, any announcement would be an invitation to visit the treasure site. It would both open the wreck site to theft and detract from the exhibit itself. Not to mention be quite dangerous."

Gamal scratched the edge of his mustache for a moment, as if finally grasping what Joanna had admitted a few moments before. "So you returned to the site yourself. At night. Why was that?"

Joanna was becoming slightly annoyed. "We told you, since the committee didn't seem in any hurry to look at the tablets, we wanted to retrieve them ourselves. And we went at night for precisely the reason you stated, to avoid drawing attention to the site. We certainly would have turned everything over to you. We've already done that."

"Quite so. You have. Is this why you have asked to meet with me today? To ask what became of the artifacts?"

"Actually, no." Joanna said. "It was to inform you that we discovered vandalism at the exhibit."

"Vandalism?" Gamal leaned forward on his elbows. "What sort? How do you know?"

"Last night, when we dove into the city, we came upon someone smashing a head from one of the statues in the Palestinian work, the one by Khadija Saïd. The diver fled when we came close, and when he turned off his torch, we lost him temporarily. We went down to the site of the tablets but came up as soon as we found nothing to retrieve. It was at that time that we found the vandal. In fleeing us, he had hidden in one of the buildings, the railroad station, in fact. He became trapped, and when we found him, he was running out of air."

"Good grief. What did you do?"

"What any diver would. We gave him air, of course. That's when we identified him as George Guillaume. We freed him, and I let him have my tank. For all I know, his own scuba equipment is still inside the station. He reached the surface before we did and swam to the dock, where he left my vest and tank. In any case, we thought the committee might want to be apprised of that."

"Have you informed Miss Saïd?"

"No, she wasn't at the hostel and we didn't pass her on our way here."

Gamal was already scribbling the information on a notepad. "While the coincidence, of all three of you being in the city at the same time at night, is extraordinary, I do thank you for that information. We'll contact Miss Saïd immediately and take the appropriate action. Now, please tell me again about these supposed transliterations you have obtained."

Charlie relaxed in his chair and crossed his legs, most likely to remove any suggestion of being confrontational. Charlie was good at that. "They are not 'supposed' at all. Two of our colleagues in the relevant fields did the transliterations, and they will be published shortly in the museum bulletin. It's very likely that they'll also appear in one or more scientific journals. But of course, in the meantime, you *have* all the tablets and you're free to translate them yourself, the old ones and all the others we haven't seen. Who knows, you might discover texts far more thrilling than ours."

"And what *have* you discovered, if I might ask?"

Joanna and Charlie exchanged glances. "You might, indeed. It was the story of Lot's escape from Gomorrah," she said neutrally.

"Ah, the one righteous man." Gamal considered for a moment and then winced. "Hmm. That might present a problem of interpretation, since our medina might be taken as a reference to one of those sinful cities. That would be unfortunate."

Charlie scratched his beard. "Only if you consider Sodom and Gomorrah to actually *be* sinful. Our tablets suggest something quite different. The writers talk about prosperous market towns filled with traveling merchants, multiple religions and languages. Pretty harmonious places, I mean as far as Bronze Age cities go."

"In fact, there *is* a very nice parallel with our own underwater scene," Joanna said. "It's a city on a plain, filled with international art and intended to attract people from all over the world. There's even a fountain just like the one mentioned in the tablet. One might go so far as to call the exhibit an 'underwater Gomorrah of art.'"

Gamal shook his head vehemently. "Good grief, no! I don't think we should even *consider* associating the exhibit with Sodom and Gomorrah, no matter what your tablets say. The religious community would be up in arms."

Joanna laughed coldly. "Ironically, that's the message implied by both the transliterations. That the two cities were not destroyed because of their innate evil, but because they offended the 'religious community' of the Jahwe fundamentalists. They called themselves the Angels of God, and were…well…terrorists, pure and simple. Genocidal terrorists."

Gamal sighed deeply. "You may be right, Dr. Boleyn, but even if what you say about the tablets is true, and you can establish a parallel, you do your cause no good by rubbing the faces of the Egyptian public in it."

"Cause? I have no cause, Mr. Gamal. I have only some tablets written thousands of years ago that give a firsthand account of what in the Bible has the status of legend. Fanaticism then was not much different from fanaticism now, and *you* do the modern world no favor by ignoring it." She took a breath. "Forgive me if that sounded rude, but I think you'll agree that religious fundamentalism is a destructive force in the world today."

Gamal stared up at the ceiling, then took a deep breath. "Unfortunately, Dr. Boleyn, religion is not an intellectual matter in Egypt, as it might be in the United Kingdom. The majority of Egyptians are poor, and for them, belief in the truth of the Quran is vital, their consolation in a puzzlingly cruel life. Whatever you have found, and however authentic it may be, you do not have the luxury of being 'right' here. You must be judicious and subtle."

"Subtle." Joanna turned the concept around in her mind. "Yes, we can be subtle. Will it be subtle enough if the tablet texts are published only in the United Kingdom?"

"If they contradict the story of Lot as radically as you say, then that would obviously be…judicious."

"And if Lot is hinted at in one of the statues but is not identified as such, that would be subtle?"

Gamal scratched the edge of his mustache again. "You really are pushing the boundaries, Dr. Boleyn, and you may get us both in great trouble. But it's true, if you make no identification, I should think it would be safe."

"Well, it looks like we've got everything settled then," Charlie said, standing up.

Joanna glanced at her watch and stood up as well. "I'm glad we could reach an agreement, Mr. Gamal. And we've taken up too much of your time. Thank you for seeing us."

Gamal shook their hands and walked with them to the door. "And thank *you* for calling our attention to the vandalism. We will contact Khadija Saïd immediately. I look forward to seeing your final work in our exhibit."

As the office door closed behind them and they strode toward the stairs, Charlie glanced toward her. "Civic duty accomplished. What do you want to do the rest of the day?"

In a sudden flash Joanna recalled the three of them, she and Charlie and Kaia, playing dive-school in the warm shallow waters at the end of Bikar road. Her guiding touch, hip to hip, their shared air, and afterwards, laughter. That's what she wanted to do. She forced away the thought.

"We're going to make us some pretty girls."

"Great idea. Can't wait to get started on *that*." He took her arm but it was cold comfort.

Chapter Seventeen

Kaia sat in the guest cabin of the *Hina*, turning her father's cane idly between her fingers. She brought it up to her nose, wondering if it held a residue of Joanna's hand lotion, but she detected only a faint whiff of old varnish.

Three days had passed since she'd quarreled with Bernard, two nights in which she'd slept in the guest cabin instead of the marriage bed. Bernard had spoken only the minimum, asking where the clean laundry was, warning that they were about to run out of orange juice. They ate dinner together but in near silence, and the rest of the time they avoided each other. He'd left without saying good-bye and now, thank God, he was on his way to New York to face the producers of the movie he was about to renege on.

Bernard's silence was ominous because she'd never experienced it before. Of course, she'd also never stood up to him before, and neither of them knew how to handle the unexpected rebellion.

The professional calculations ran through Kaia's mind constantly, and she was certain they were running through Bernard's as well. Her career was in his hands, but his very profitable agency depended almost completely on her celebrity. Now he had to negotiate his way out of a contract he had bludgeoned his way into, and it wouldn't be pleasant. He'd find a way to punish her and get her back in line, she had no doubt.

But it would not be in bed, of that she was sure. She cast her mind back over the twenty years they had been together. They had never had a real honeymoon, since the marriage had been one of convenience for both of them and passion had never reared its mysterious head.

As far as sex was concerned, it was rather like that of other couples, she supposed. Twice a week in the beginning, then once a week, and finally only on vacation when Bernard had no access to the starlets he managed. She was just as glad. Sex with him had never much excited her, though her naturally healthy body usually produced an orgasm from pure friction. Though he never actually hurt her, she always felt an element of force in the way he rode her, making her close her legs under him so he had to pump harder.

When their marital sex tapered off, it was clear where he directed his attention. The new talent on his roster was easy prey, and she could almost always tell by their behavior which of the bouncy young things had passed the bedding test. She also overheard him talking on the phone to the occasional Tracy and Tiffany and assumed they were high-priced escorts who'd let him do some of the kinkier things he liked. But as long as he never brought home any diseases, that was fine with her. The arrangement suited them both.

She'd managed it just as she'd managed the balancing act of career and family. Or had she? Kiele and Mei had tolerated him for a year or so, then seemed to actively avoid him, and she couldn't understand why. He'd plied them with gifts, expensive clothes, even a horse. But a coldness always pervaded the room when they were together. She'd asked once what the problem was, but they said nothing, so she decided they preferred their amiable but chronically unemployed Hawaiian father and let it slide. In any case, the situation resolved itself when they went off to college.

She laid the cane aside and wandered into the main cabin. If she was going to stay in the guest cabin, she needed to move her things. She gathered up her underwear and shorts from the drawer and shifted them to the empty drawers in the new cabin. On the second trip, she collected an armload of shirts from the closet and, as an afterthought, picked up the little plaster statue of the goddess *Hina*. It was a piece of tourist kitsch, which she'd bought long before they purchased and named the yacht, but it had sentimental value. She held it toward the light, studying the blue coral-studded dress that swirled around the goddess and the crescent moon in her hand.

She set the figurine on top of a set of drawers and hung her shirts in the cabin locker. Lethargy came over her and she dropped down again onto the bed, listening to the sounds of Abdullah making lunch in the galley. What was she going to do when Bernard came back? With no movie to begin in the fall, how would they keep up the various payments on all their property? She felt as if a heavy weight were on her chest that kept her from breathing. When had she last been happy?

Ah, she remembered exactly. It was under water, swimming in a circle in the shallow water near the beach off Bikar road, sharing air with Joanna. Joanna Boleyn, who never lost her head, whose lips were so soft, whose hair and cheeks and breasts Kaia wanted to touch. Was there nothing of that day she could recapture?

At least she could return to the water. The El Gouna diving center offered lessons, and all she had to do was walk up the dock to their office and sign up. Yes, she would do that today, before Bernard returned and tried to browbeat her. She would have a few new things in place before he came back. Permanent separate quarters, diving lessons, and a serious discussion of the acting jobs she would consent to in the future.

Revitalized, she sat up again and returned to the master cabin to fetch the last of her things. But where was her credit card? She'd left it with her watch on the night table a few nights ago, and now only the watch was there. She checked all her own drawers again, but no, she remembered distinctly leaving both card and watch by the bed. Bernard must have put it some place to keep her from using it. Typical of him to try to control her that way too.

Angry now, she began rifling through his drawers. The top drawer was full of his expensive underwear, with a side section for his male cosmetics. The second drawer held tee shirts and socks, the third drawer cashmere sweaters. The bottom drawer was a jumble of slippers, bathing suits, fishing and hunting magazines. Nothing.

Where would he have hidden the card so she couldn't use it? Then she remembered. Of course. How stupid she'd been. In the safe in the smaller of the two crew cabins that he called his office. He used his little lockbox for contracts, cash, his Rolex watch when he went diving, and other things she'd never asked about.

It had annoyed her slightly that it was *his* safe and not theirs, and that it was intended to be secure from her intrusion as well. Bernard was entitled to his safe, but he was not entitled to keep business secrets from her, especially since his business, by and large, was *her*. On the very first day he had brought the twelve-by-fifteen steel box home to have it fitted into the yacht, she'd discreetly obtained the code from the accompanying papers. She'd scribbled it on a tag and put it in her jewelry box and in five years had never looked at it. But she still had it, goddam it, and the time had come. She slid the lower drawer shut with a thud and got to her feet.

Once back in the guest cabin, she opened her jewelry box, though "jewelry" hardly described its contents. Five or six of her favorite earrings, a locket with her daughters' baby pictures, souvenir bracelets and chains that had slowly lost their sentimental value. And under the velvet lining lay the scrap of paper.

She hurried into the cabin that passed as his office and knelt before the tiny safe. She wasn't sure whether to feel guilty for trespassing or amused at her own cleverness and guile. If she hadn't been so angry at his attempt to control her, she might have enjoyed the role of safecracker. But this intrusion into the safe scarcely counted as cracking since the code worked smoothly and instantly. It was almost laughably easy to break into Bernard's sanctum sanctorum, and she didn't even have to do it quietly. "What a fool you are, Bernard," she said out loud.

She yanked open the door and peered inside. To her surprise, it was rather full. Several long envelopes held contracts, another thick one held two thousand dollars in hundred-dollar bills, and a tiny cardboard box held a man's diamond ring. Hmm. She hadn't known about the ring. No matter. She slid her hand inside again, groping for anything small and plastic, and…well, well, there it was. The bastard.

Disgusted with the whole procedure but pleased with herself for defeating him and finding her card, she began cramming the contracts back into the small space. But one of the envelopes, manila in eight-by-ten format, had been stored curved rather than folded and was harder to reinsert than the others. The envelope was eroded at the edges, either very old or very often handled. She opened it and slid out the contents.

Black-and-white photographs. About a dozen. Perplexed, she sat back on her heels and leafed through them, her confusion turning slowly to revulsion. It was children, mostly girls. Pre-adolescents in various sexual poses. Girls of ten or eleven, lying naked and spread-eagled, or standing awkwardly with their little-girl pants around their ankles.

Vague memories came back to her, of Bernard's oblique references to making shady movies that nonetheless provided the seed money for him to establish himself as a legitimate agent. He'd never elaborated and she was careful never to ask. Was this what he meant? Was he involved in kiddie porn? The thought sickened her.

She leafed through more of the revolting photos, disgusted and bewildered that Bernard would keep such a collection. The poses became more lewd as she went through the pile, more sexually explicit. Prepubescent girls with tiny budding breasts, their hands on men's erect organs or straddling men's laps, their erect penises jutting up through the childish thighs.

She dropped the pile as if it had stung her and recoiled so violently she fell back onto the floor. It wasn't possible. She had to be mistaken. Her heart pounding, she gathered up the last three, delicately and with disgust, scarcely wanting to touch their edges.

Her daughters, Kiele and Mei, naked, each one touching herself between her legs and both with uncertain, awkward smiles for the camera. The last one was Kiele, lying on her back with her knees drawn up and her legs spread, as if waiting to be penetrated. Yet her hairless, breastless body showed she was a child, no more than eleven.

Kaia recognized the room, remembered the season. It was the second year she and Bernard were married, when they vacationed for a month at a beach house in Tahiti. The girls had seemed happy at the beginning, less so at the end. And from that time on, the family atmosphere was never the same.

It began to make sense now. Bernard must have made his first fortune in the child-pornography business. The maggot. That would explain why he'd always been so evasive. Even if she had been able to overlook the pornography, and she wouldn't have, his encroachment on the innocence of her daughters was unforgivable. Were there more photos, she wondered, suddenly alarmed. What else had the sleazy bastard done? Had he molested them physically?

She had to talk to Kiele and Mei, but not on the phone. It was too delicate a subject, too long ago, too easy to suppress or deny. They wouldn't want to talk about it. No, it had to be in person. Her fiftieth birthday. She would pay to bring both girls to Egypt for the celebration. For some quality time together and for a quiet, serious talk.

She felt like she'd been hit by a truck, a garbage truck, and that it had hit her daughters too and covered all of them with filth. With nausea rising, she crammed the photos back into the envelope and curved it back into the safe. Then she staggered to the toilet and vomited.

CHAPTER EIGHTEEN

Fahimah and Fayruz stood by, all but dancing with anticipation, as Joanna broke away the two molds and exposed the concrete statues inside. Witnessing their own faces in the two heads cast the day before had delighted them no end, but now they were about to see themselves whole.

Both statues were up on the workbench in sitting positions, one inclining languidly on an elbow, the other bending forward, elbows resting on her knees.

Joanna placed each of the previously molded heads over their respective concrete torsos. The two girls giggled awkwardly at seeing themselves in stone.

Fahimah, the older, approached her likeness and ran her finger along one of the protruding irregularities on the drapery. "So many... uh...of these little bumps," she said. She looked up shyly through limpid black eyes. "And the hair is...not like me."

Joanna carefully set the head castings on the table. "Don't worry, it will be. I have tools to smooth out all the bad spots and make you look pretty. Of course you know that very soon your bodies will be covered with coral, don't you?"

"Yes, Charlie told us. But not the faces, right?" Fayruz anxiously stroked the stone cheek with a fingertip.

"Not right away, though they'll probably get a little green after a few months. But I promise you, before that happens, we'll take lots of photos of them under water that you can show to your friends."

"That's great," Fahimah said, then poked her sister. "Hey, I have work now, and you have school." The younger girl replied something in Arabic and, punching each other on the shoulder, they scrambled toward the door.

Joanna watched them for a moment, recalling her own teen years, which were not nearly so innocent, and wondered idly what it would have been like to have a sister, her own Astari or Aina by her side during the hard times. Would've been nice to have more people in the family. Or a family at all, now that both parents were gone. Well, she had formed her own life pretty well, solitary as it was. She took up her wooden mallet and number-two chisel. Tapping gently, she began to knock away the knobs and bubbles protruding from the concrete forms.

When she had removed the last of the irregularities with her chisels, she fitted on her goggles and dust mask. Locking the correct wheel onto the axle of the power sander, she ran it along the flowing stone fabric. After a few passes, the girls' clothing looked smooth, fluid. She loved this part of the process, refining the forms and bringing them ever closer to the person they were taken from. But it was messy business, and soon she was covered with a fine layer of grayish powder.

She carefully chiseled between the shoulders of the first statue, carving out a hollow. The head fit nicely into the spot and was ready to be cemented. Joanna studied the face of Fayruz-Aina, captured in the flower of her adolescence and felt a sudden swell of outrage at the very thought of Aina's rape by her own father.

Even in its original form, the myth of Sodom and Gomorrah had always disgusted her, but finding out it was real horrified her even more. Her mind wandered to the tablets themselves. Another transliteration was due. She fervently hoped it would be relevant and not some unrelated artifact: a cargo list, perhaps, or any of the million things that showed up in cuneiform.

The only thing that troubled her was that the committee still hadn't assigned her a site. She didn't fear losing a choice spot to a fellow artist; it made no difference where her fountain stood. But while she was in limbo, as it were, any perceived offense against the committee or against Egypt could still block her participation.

They would definitely publish the two testimonies. Their finding the tablets at all had been a fantastic coup, a gift fallen into their hands, and they had a deep moral obligation to reveal the truth. It would vindicate two innocent girls and rightfully condemn an Old Testament hero as a fanatic and a rapist. Inevitably, fundamentalist Jews, Christians, and Muslims would be offended. But how violently?

She hoped by then she'd have a fait accompli, an exhibit bolted together and imbedded securely on the floor of the Red Sea.

By the time she was finished with the first statue, her fingertips were raw. Though she'd covered her face and worn a cotton cap, the cement dust adhered to her sweat-dampened neck, and the itching between her breasts meant it had crept down with the perspiration. It was time to stop.

As if on cue, Charlie strode in. "Hey, you. It's six o'clock. Time to call it a day!"

"How do you like her?" Joanna pulled off her goggles and mask and felt the cool air on her face. "I've just now finished her."

"She's a beauty. I see you've already attached the head."

"Yes, but the cement needs to set. By tomorrow, she and her sister will be ready to go down with the fountain."

"Good, then all we've got left is the mother. Any ideas for her? You could ask Hanan to pose." The tentative note in Charlie's voice revealed that even he didn't much care for the idea.

"She's not really what I have in mind, but let me think about it."

"Why don't you think about it at the Sun Bar? The others will have arrived by now, and you look like you could use a few cold ones." He scratched a bit of powder off her chin. "And a shower too."

"Ya think?" She brushed her shirt, sending a cloud of cement dust into the air. "Sure, a cold beer or two is just what I need. Meet you there in half an hour."

The Sun Bar was already busy when Joanna arrived. Though it was still bright afternoon, the end-of-the-day drink was such a well-established custom that half the hotel population showed up and the bar was always full.

The artists' table was also already occupied by most of the project artists. Someone had left a knapsack on the floor by the table and its straps lay dangerously underfoot. Joanna stepped over them carefully, then nudged them with her foot back under the table and sat down.

In a circle made up of Yoshi, Sanjit, Japhet, Faisal the Saudi, and Rami the Moroccan, Khadija sat hunched over her lemonade narrating the story of the attack on her sculpture.

"The bastard," the Congolese Japhet said. "Are they sure they know who did it?"

"Of course they're sure," Khadija shot back. "Didn't you get the same message from the committee that we all got?"

Japhet shook his head.

"Well, they said it was George. In fact, I knocked on his door this morning to confront him, and he was gone."

Charlie, Marion, and a moment later, Gil arrived and added more chairs, and they all sat elbow to elbow. The handsome young man who was their usual waiter hadn't bothered to take orders and simply brought half a dozen glasses of beer. Along with the others, Joanna reached for one of the glasses.

"What was he so upset about, anyhow?" Yoshi asked.

Sanjit opened his hands, as if displaying the obvious. "The work was critical of Israeli soldiers. Probably he didn't like that. He's an American, after all."

"Maybe he's Jewish," Faisal suggested. "That would explain a lot."

"Not necessarily," Colombian Eliezar said. "I'm a Jew and I think Khadija's work is spot-on. All she did was portray what happens every day in the West Bank. And even if it didn't, even if it *was* propaganda, which it isn't, the proper reaction would be to lodge a protest with the committee, not smash the work."

"What are you going to do now," Rami asked. Can you bring the statue up and put another head on it?"

"No, I'm going to leave the work as it is. The smashed head of one of the Palestinian women is a bigger political statement than the work itself could ever have made. The work is done and I'm done. I'll let people's reactions speak for themselves."

"There's no way to predict anyone's reactions. There are way too many works in the exhibit, and each one tells a different story," Yoshi said. "I'm just glad my dragon is done and I can stop worrying about it."

"Everybody is finished now, *nicht*?" Marion said. "Except for Joanna." She turned to the side. "How goes it? Do you need any more hands?"

Joanna shook her head. "Thanks for the offer, but I'm almost done too. All that's left is to find a model for the mother. I need a really striking face to go with the girls I already have."

"What about that actress who was taking care of you?" Yoshi asked. "That Kaia woman."

Joanna avoided her glance. "I'm not really in touch with her at the moment. Besides, her husband is her agent, and he'd never allow it." She chuckled bitterly. "Or he'd demand royalties."

"What a shame," Yoshi said. "Her movies are big, even in Japan. She has a face that could start a Trojan War."

"Mmm," Joanna murmured noncommittally. What would the Japanese think of Kaia's next movie—the crappy propaganda film for which she was learning her lines at that very moment? Suddenly, Kaia's own assessment of the Hollywood life came back to her, and she was disgusted.

The handsome waiter was back with another tray of beers and a few glasses of the bar's dreadful local wine. "Thanks, Hassan," someone said, handing the glasses around the table and dropping a large bill on his tray.

"You know, maybe I'm a little giddy because my work's all done, but I love this group. I love this bar." Sanjit smiled and frowned in rapid succession. "Is that naïve?"

"Naw," Charlie said. "I feel the same way. This place is like a little United Nations, without the bickering. Wouldn't it be nice if there was a whole city like this?"

"A lot of cities aspire to be that way," Gil said. "Big ones like New York, London, Berlin, Paris."

"Mumbai to some extent," Sanjit added. "On a good day."

"Tokyo?" Yoshi thought for a moment. "Well, it *wants* to be cosmopolitan, but it's not really. The Japanese keep to themselves around foreigners."

"Weimar Republik, Berlin," Marion added. "But look what happened to that."

"What happened to it?" Sanjit asked.

"Nazis." Marion knocked back the last of her beer.

"Oh, right. Sorry, my German history isn't so great."

Charlie shook his head. "Seems like there's always Nazis. I mean extreme nationalism, us-versus-them forces lurking in the recesses, everywhere."

Yoshi nodded. "Skinheads, religious fundamentalists, racial purists. Something in the human heart afraid of the 'other.'"

"That's what I love about our underwater city. It's full of the 'other,'" Gil said, unusually talkative.

Marion laughed. "That's what the purists hate, too much 'other.' They call it Sodom and Gomorrah."

Joanna started to get up from her seat but caught her foot in the strap of the knapsack on the floor. "Whose bag is this?" she asked, holding it up. It was heavy, filled with books or something.

No one answered.

The waiter was just coming back with another round of drinks. "Hassan, I think someone left their stuff here. Maybe you should take this to the bar in case someone comes back later. It's sort of in the way here."

"Yes, miss," he said, collecting the empty glasses onto his tray, then hooking the knapsack over his shoulder.

Joanna turned back to the group. "As I was saying, it's damned difficult to keep an open society. Marion's right. The Weimar Republik was about as liberal as it could get in early twentieth-century Germany, but it fell apart. That undercurrent of resentment and racial arrogance just seeped out, like a disease. I don't know what—"

The boom was deafening. Then came the chaos of screams, cries for help.

The center of the mayhem seemed to be the serving bar, now a heap of splintered wood and, beside it, scatterings of bloody limbs and scraps of clothing. Something hideously round still rocked on the floor and Joanna looked away, nauseous. Blood trickled from her forehead into her eye and she became aware of the bright pain in her scalp. Finally, realization dawned.

The knapsack, the tray of glasses, Hassan.

The glass fragments had exploded outward in a deadly sphere, slicing into whatever they hit. Beside her, Charlie grimaced, holding his forearm, and Marion too grasped her shoulder, blood seeping through her fingers. The others at the table were just moving from stupefaction to fear and trying to get out of the booth. She wasn't sure whether she fell herself or whether the others had pushed her, but she found herself on her knees among glass shards. Charlie grabbed her by the arm and pulled her to her feet again. Not daring to look toward the carnage at the bar, she hurled herself toward the door along with the fleeing crowd.

CHAPTER NINETEEN

Joanna woke up at seven, unrested after a fitful night. She sat up and rubbed her face, and the sudden sharp pain from her scalp wound reminded her of the previous evening. She had fled, along with all the others, to the periphery of the hotel, returning to the square in front of the bar when the police and ambulances arrived.

By then, Charlie and Marion had both determined that their wounds were superficial, and so all three made statements to the police but declined to go to hospital. Traumatized and agitated, they stayed together in Charlie's room until nearly midnight when, emotionally drained but reassured, she and Marion went to their own rooms.

Now, by the cold light of morning, she wondered what the fallout would be. How many had been killed and...oh! The image of Hassan's dismembered body flashed in her mind, and she shook it away, forcing herself to think of more mundane things.

The committee. Would they delay the opening of the exhibit or change the rules? The only way to find out was to carry on and wait for official announcements. She dragged herself into the shower, dressed, and went down to the workshop.

By eight she was laying out the tools for the day, determined to work, at least until exhaustion caught up with her, probably some time in the late afternoon. Fifteen minutes later Charlie marched in from the doorway, holding up an English-language newspaper.

"Three dead," he said. "Hassan and two other Egyptian workers. Nineteen cut with flying glass, three seriously, but no other fatalities. And it looks like they identified the bombers."

"Really? That's incredible. It only happened yesterday."

"Yeah, the bar manager actually knew them, fanatics who used to stand outside the bar and insult the patrons. He saw them pass through with the knapsack earlier but didn't notice that they'd left it behind. The police arrested them in the middle of the night and they confessed. They were proud of it, the bastards, even though all they killed were their own good Muslim countrymen."

"Not so good if they worked in a bar. But that means they left that bomb specifically at our table." She dropped her voice to a murmur. "For us."

"Yeah, looks like."

"My God." She exhaled horror, pressing her hand against the Band-Aid at her scalp line. "What about the others in our group?"

"Seems like only the people on the left side of the table got it. You and I and Marion."

"And you? How are you feeling this morning?"

He patted his upper arm where the thickness under his shirt suggested an improved bandage. "I'm fine. You look like hell, by the way. Not the cut but the bags under your eyes."

"Yeah, I can feel them. But no one ever died of baggy eyes. I wonder if this will affect the project."

"I can't imagine it. Way too much money's already invested, and now the world is watching. I think they'll just put security all around. And that reminds me, I got this from the office just now. A letter from the committee." He handed over an envelope that had already been opened.

She glanced at the front and saw it was addressed to both of them, but Charlie didn't wait for her to read it.

"They've offered you George's site, the one on the slope. I think we can work with that, don't you? I mean, the fountain can go at the bottom and the statue of Lot's wife on the slope above it. That's in keeping with the story, too."

She perused the letter briefly, nodding. "Lot's wife. I always hated that Lot had a name and she didn't. But yes, you're right. The slope's fine. Do they want us to confirm?"

"It would be the polite thing to do. I'll go and call them now and get it out of the way." He turned toward the door.

"Thanks for taking care of that," she called after him. Brooding for a moment on the irony of the tragedy, she fished around in her pocket for a dust mask and clicked on the sander. The hum of the sander motor and the grinding of the stone muffled all other sounds, providing a comforting white noise she'd grown accustomed to.

What could the assailants have possibly found so offensive in the underwater project that they wanted to kill its artists, half of whom were fellow Muslims? Was it simply the reactionary's fear of the new, of things damaging to their tradition?

Or did they have a real beef and no one was listening to them? She tried to think what the anger and resentment might be about, but it all seemed so complex that she tired of it and focused her attention instead on smoothing the arms of Astari.

They would be covered with live coral within a year, but something in her wanted to start off with the girl in all her beauty. Not only the head, but also the hands were cast in dense, smooth stone and would resist growth longer. Let lovely Astari have more time to remain herself before nature claimed her. The hair, too, would be swept back, as if by an underwater current. As she sanded, she began to hum something vaguely resembling the chorus of Beethoven's Ninth Symphony.

She worked with her back to the sunlit doorway, only slowly becoming aware of a long shadow creeping along the floor beside her. It approached slowly, then stopped, phantom-like and ominous.

She turned off the sander, her heart pounding. Was it another terrorist, back to finish the job? Who was trying to hurt her anyway and why? What could she do to defend herself, and would Charlie come back in time? She slowly pivoted around to face the intruder.

The figure was silhouetted against the blinding exterior, so it took a full two seconds for Joanna to discern who it was.

"Kaia?"

"I was worried about you." Kaia stepped into the workshop with the grace of a dancer. She wore the same white cotton pants and blue shirt she'd had on when she arrived at the hospital, and Joanna suddenly recalled the innocence and anticipation of their first day together. A time before humiliation and rejection and terror. A wave of longing washed over her.

Kaia stepped closer, hesitantly, hands in her pockets, as if she could think of no other place to put them. "I heard about the bombing and I knew the artists always met in that bar. My worst fear was that you were there."

Joanna stood nonplussed, the sander hanging in her hand at her side, then snapped back to reality. "I *was* there. Uh, but I'm all right." She touched the Band-Aid with her gloved hand. "Just a small glass cut."

"You poor thing." Kaia swept to her side. "First sharks and now this." She reached out a tentative hand, then let it fall again. "You must feel like fate is out to get you."

They stood face to face for an awkward moment and Joanna could smell Kaia's sun-warmed skin and hair, a hint of perfumed soap. She vaguely recalled she was supposed to be angry, but with Kaia in front of her, in the corridor of sunlight that radiated from the doorway, she could think of nothing to say except, "How have *you* been?"

Stupid, bland remark. *Have you missed me? Have you thought about me? Do you still want to kiss me?* That's what she really wanted to know.

"I've been busy."

"Learning your new role?"

"No, I told Bernie I wouldn't do it. I refused to sign." Kaia seemed relieved to have something to talk about and spoke in a stream. "He's back in New York now talking to the film company and his lawyers. The contract he hashed out isn't valid without my signature, but he's lost a lot of credibility by negotiating it in the first place. He's trying to cut his losses and save his reputation as an agent by offering them a younger actress he also manages, at a quarter of the price. The producers will probably go for it, but I don't care any longer, I really don't, and…well, a lot of things are changing." She stopped for air.

Joanna set the sander down, brushed grit from a bench, and motioned for Kaia to take a seat. "I'm glad. I mean about your standing your ground. You're too good for religious-propaganda films. I hope this doesn't cause any great financial hardship for you." Joanna sat down on the same bench, a safe two-and-a-half feet away.

"I'll live. I've got some good working years ahead of me. And I'm about to make some changes. I have to talk to a few people though."

They were chatting now and Kaia showed no signs of wanting to leave. *So far so good,* Joanna thought. She dragged her fingertips nervously through the stone dust then brushed them clean, annoyed, and clasped her hands in her lap. "So, what else have you been doing?" Damn, could her conversation be any more banal?

Kaia brightened. "Well, you'll appreciate this. I've started taking diving lessons. One of those quick courses they give at the dive center, but the last lesson was in deep water. I'm pretty confident now, and I've even bought my own vest and regulator, just like Bernie's. I thought you'd be proud."

"Oh, I am. You'll be able to see the exhibit now. That'll be nice."

"Yes, that's what I was thinking." Kaia smiled helplessly, the subject having reached its end, and then swept her gaze around the workshop. "Those are your exhibit?" she asked, glancing toward the statues of the two girls.

"They're part of it. There's also the fountain over there." Joanna pointed toward the corner where the trapezoid blocks of concrete were piled up. "Once they're below, we'll bolt them together to form a hexagon. The bowl and air reservoir will go in the middle."

"Ah, I see. The girls will be seated on the fountain." She stood up and went to kneel on one knee in front of them. "They're quite beautiful," she said, running her finger delicately along one of the concrete arms. "It's uncanny seeing such human faces on a statue. I really want to see everything in its final place."

"You will if you're still here next week."

"Yes, I will be, of course."

The subject ended with another awkward silence as Kaia stood up and turned directly toward her. She bit her lips. "Look, last week ended in such an ugly way. I'd...um...I'd like you to come back to the boat again. At least until Bernard gets back."

Joanna let a moment of silence pass. The thought of being alone again with Kaia made her heart pound. But the memory of Bernard throwing her off the boat was painfully fresh. What would be the point? Whatever the invitation meant, it would only be an evening or two, and then things would be back to the way they were. Kaia and Bernard with their strange adversarial marriage, and Joanna, back at her workshop with Charlie and the others. No, she wasn't going to be some straight actress's walk on the wild side.

"I'm sorry. We're nearing the end of this project and we're pressed for time. We've got more statues to make, and then we have to take everything down to the sea floor."

Kaia looked away, obviously embarrassed by the rejection. "Yes, of course. This is what you came to Egypt for. Silly of me to forget.

Well, now that I know you're all right, I'll let you get back to work." Ducking her head as if she feared being struck, she hurried along the column of sunlight to the doorway and out of the workshop.

Joanna stood motionless at her workbench facing empty space, a tightness in her chest. "God damn it," she muttered, and coughed to dispel the threatening tears, then yanked her goggles back on. "Where the hell are my gloves?" She continued swearing until she found them, slapped them against the workbench to remove the powder, and picked up her sander.

She resumed sanding the already smooth statue, fearing to turn off the motor since only the rasp of the wheel against stone kept her from crying. What had she just done? What should she have done? How had she gotten herself into this state?

With a moan of despair, she turned off the sander and set it carefully on the workbench. She had to get out, get away. She needed air, space, perspective. She yanked off her gloves, tossed them next to the sander, and stormed out of the workshop.

The commercial part of El Gouna was empty of customers as usual, and many of its shopkeepers stood outside smoking. Joanna avoided passing them and swung into a side street.

Crap, out of the frying pan into the fire. She was in the souk, the long row of stalls and kiosks filled floor to ceiling with pharaonic junk, or beach equipment, or tall display baskets of dried and dicey-looking vegetation. Here too, the scarcity of buying public brought the owners out into the street to cajole her, offering the widest selection, the finest quality, the best possible deals. She brushed past them with her head lowered, muttering "No, thank you" over and over, sorry now she'd ever left the quiet of her workshop, then stopped abruptly with a grunt to avoid bumping into a man.

He turned around at the sound, surprised, and she stared at him for a moment before she recognized the muttonchops.

"Abdullah! Uhh, hello. I didn't expect to meet you here on dry land."

"Hello, Miss Joanna." His thick lips parted in a wide smile. "You come to shop here, with Egyptians? That's good."

"Well, not exactly. I was really just taking a walk. Obviously you *do* shop here."

"Yes, sometimes, but today is just this," he held up a package wrapped in brown paper, "from my brother. He has a tea shop." Abdullah gestured with his hand behind him toward a tiny shop with two round tables in front.

"Shafik, come," he called to the man standing in the doorway. "This is my friend Joanna." The portly Shafik, who, with a round face and normal-sized nose, bore no resemblance at all to his brother, offered his hand. "Ah, a friend. Please come and have a cup of tea. No charge for a friend of Abdullah. Really, I'll make you a nice cup and you can relax." He pulled out a chair from one of the tiny tables.

Seeing no way to refuse without giving offense to Abdullah, who had always been kind to her, she acquiesced. She glanced toward him, expecting him to sit down as well, but he merely bowed slightly and said, "Have a good afternoon, Miss Joanna," and left.

Slightly annoyed at having been entrapped, she took a seat on the rickety chair. Well, after a morning of sanding stone and walking half an hour in the Egyptian sun, she *was* thirsty. A cup of tea wouldn't hurt.

A moment later, Shafik was back with a small tin teapot and two glasses. He poured out the fragrant tea and sat down across from her, pushing a battered sugar bowl toward her. Obviously she was going to also have to have a conversation. Defeated, she dropped in a sugar cube and sipped from her glass.

"Oh," she exclaimed softly. "It's Earl Grey. You carry Earl Grey."

"Of course I do. I drink it myself. An agreeable habit I picked up in London," he said in perfect English.

"You were in London?"

"Yes, for two years. I drove a taxi and learned that English drivers are just as crazy as Egyptians."

"I suppose they are. Why did you come back?"

"Homesickness, of course. And to get married. Besides, I couldn't have stood it much longer. All that bloody rain. After two years of it, I almost changed skin color." He sipped his own tea and seemed to take note of her cut. "I hope you're being careful with that. In this heat, things infect quickly. Did you see a doctor?"

"Yes, briefly, at the hotel. He examined me and said the same thing. It's from broken glass."

"Broken glass? Oh, my god. You're one of the victims from the Sun Bar. Oh, I am so sorry. I apologize deeply for my country. We are a reasonable people, but we have our fanatics. They think they are saving Egypt, but all they do is shame us."

"I'm glad you feel that way. So maybe you can tell me why they do it. What's so threatening about us that people want to kill us?"

He blew out air. "Lots of reasons. Take your pick. A long history of bitterness at Western colonialism and greed for Arab oil. Euro-American politics that keep our own dictator in power. Israel's swallowing up of Arab Palestine with the full support of America. Western business and commercialism undermining our culture. A sense of being treated as inferior. I suppose it's a stew of all of them."

Joanna found herself nodding. "Yes, and all of that spiced by the toxic myth of religious martyrdom. So what's the solution? If you had your way, and it wouldn't bankrupt Egypt, would you want to have all the tourists go home and leave Egypt to itself?"

"No, of course not. All foreigners are welcome to drink tea in my shop. Completely aside from Egypt's dependency on tourism, *no* country can exist in a vacuum in the twenty-first century. As for religion, I don't have answers to my country's problems, but I know that Islam does not have them either."

At that moment, a young couple, both in Bermuda shorts and tee shirts, stopped in front of the shop. "Can we buy some tea here?" the woman asked. The man said nothing but cupped his hand protectively over his wallet in his side pocket. Joanna smiled to herself. Domestic financial conflict in microcosm.

"To be sure. The best tea in Egypt." Shafik sprang to his feet. "Dozens of flavors and very fresh," he said as he guided them skillfully into his shop.

Joanna swallowed the last of her now-lukewarm tea and checked her watch. She'd been pouting long enough.

"There you are. I've been looking all over for you." Charlie appeared in front of her and sat down in Shafik's place.

"How did you know I was here?"

He lifted off the cloth bag that had hung on a strap diagonally over his chest. "Hanan told me you were headed toward the village, and I met Abdullah just as I came to the square. He said you were here."

"What was so urgent it couldn't wait?"

"This." He reached into the bag and drew out a packet of several pages, folded in half. "The transliteration of the last tablet."

Joanna's mood lightened abruptly. "Fantastic. Read it to me. I need some good news."

"I figured as much. That's why I hunted you down." Charlie unfolded the fax, patted various pockets until he found his reading glasses, and slid them on.

"Here be the words of Gebreel, son of Hed, which bear witness to the suffering of the daughters of Lot. With this testimony I proclaim that which they were not given to see and which the people of Abraham were not given to know. On my soul before God, this is what came to pass o'er the cities of the plain.

Hed was a servant of Abraham who was possessed of God and with an iron will, and I was born into his household. Abraham's love of God was so great that he made to sacrifice his son Isaac upon God's altar. He came within a breath of doing so, but for a sudden vision that stayed his hand. My father was of equal zeal, and with harsh rule, he raised me to be a servant of God.

In such a household, I longed to join with them whom Abraham anointed as Angels of God, who pledged with sword and fire to make the One God lord of all the lands. Though too young to lend my sword in their chastisement of Sodom, I reached my fourteenth year in time to stand with them at Gomorrah.

With a score of others of our tribe already secreted within the pagan city, three of us betook ourselves to the gates. Thereupon our leader Mesoch did proclaim before the people, saying they had offended God and were commanded to repent their ways. But the people did mock us and turned away from us. Abraham's kinsman Lot came before us then and bade us sup with him and we went in. While we broke bread, the elders gathered before the house and called us out to justify ourselves, on account of Mesoch's admonition. But Lot did gnash his teeth at the people and threw his daughters in amongst them for their pleasure, if they would but renounce their interest in us.

The people of Gomorrah were perplexed by this and brought the maids unharmed unto their father's door, but Mesoch threw the embers of the hearth into their faces, whereby they fled to tend their injuries.

All the while, within the house I cast my eyes upon Atiyah. How full of grace and tenderness was the wife of Lot, as she embraced her weeping daughters. I knew not my own mother, who had died aborning me, and so I sorely longed to share in that embrace.

But with great haste, Yassib brought Lot's women to the stable and gave them to know God's Will, that His Angels would smite Gomorrah that very night. He bade them thus to flee into the hills. They were sore afraid, for they knew not that the Angels were ourselves, the men of Abraham.

While Lot and his women fled, a host of other Angels joined us and Mesoch gave out the tasks: one to slaughter livestock, one to set the fires and ignite the granary, another to pull down the houses, and yet another to smash the idols in the temples. The most zealous were to enter the houses of the elders and slaughter them and their families in their beds.

I swung the sword alongside of them as we went through the streets, though it was more butchery than battle, for the people had no defense. Even I, with boyish arms and growing doubt, smote many a man that night. When we returned to the house of Lot, his servants and kinfolk still lived. One of the women they called Tiamat held an infant. Yassib ripped the babe from her arms and dashed it against the stones. Tiamat made to flee but I blocked her way in my confusion, and when she halted, Yassib plunged his sword into her back. Then he set his torch to the beds and curtains and to the beams of the house.

Heavy with remorse, and with the wrathful smoke at my back, I hastened after Lot's family to assure their escape from the ruin of Gomorrah. Shortly I came upon them, stopping midway up the hill. The maids were fled, but Lot and Atiyah were in dispute, for Atiyah repented of her decision and made to return to the burning city.

"Wife, do not look back," Lot shouted. "This is God's retribution on Sodom and Gomorrah for they were as offal that breedeth vile creatures."

"Liar!" she cried out. "Men of good heart tended Gomorrah's olive groves for generations and welcomed you when you came as a stranger, despising us. I lament the day I left my father's house and joined your monstrous faith, for look what it has done!"

"Be silent, wife. I will forgive your blasphemy as the One God has forgiven you and brought you out of Gomorrah. But only this once. Do

not foreswear this mercy and fall back into sin." He reached out a hand to her, yet she recoiled.

"I do not want your forgiveness. I will return in search of Tiamat, wherever she is fled, for I loved her more than ever I did you."

Lot did rebuke her and swelled with wrath. "Behold Gomorrah's iniquities: the wildness of women, the lusts of men and boys, the mixing of races, the prayers to false gods. But the boil is cleansed. Tiamat is dead now, with all the others. Our Angels have seen to it."

"Tiamat, dead? You monster! You swine! I curse your angels and I curse your God." She spat before his feet and, weeping, turned her face toward the burning city.

"Daughter of Eve. You are a poison to my house!" Lot called out, and took up a rock and smashed it upon her head. She fell onto the stony ground and did not move.

Lot gathered the stones and blocks of salt that lay around him and piled them up to conceal her. Then he made haste to ascend the mount and shortly he was out of sight.

Torn by grief, I knelt before the mound and pulled the stones away from Atiyah's bloody countenance. I kissed her, tasting the salt of the rocks and of her tears, and something broke in me. I wept for her and for the mother I had not known, and for all the mothers we had killed. I tarried on the hill beside her for two nights, weeping, and on the morning of the third day I gave her an honorable grave in a hidden place. Then at the place where she was struck, I gathered up a block of salt and set it on its end, a monument to Atiyah, the wife of Lot.

Bitter was my heart when I reached the cave where Lot had housed and came upon his daughters packing the beasts of burden. Seeing me, they trembled and I comforted them saying, fear not. I will not harm you. Go you to Zoar, unto the house of Bessem, who is of your tribe and full of kindness. Tell him that Gebreel has tarried at Gomorrah. This they did and so were spared greater harm, and they stayed within the fold.

As for myself, I wandered many days through the ruined cities of the plain among the scorched remains of man and maid. I searched for signs of God's approval and found none, only fountains stopped with ash and jackals and vultures feeding off the innocent.

Whosoever shall read these words, in whatever generation, let no man say this was the will of heaven, for it was brutish men that *extinguished Sodom and Gomorrah. What God there is must surely have looked upon it with revulsion, and if He did not, He is malevolence itself.*

Joanna sat back, slack-jawed. "I can't get my mind around this. An eye-witness report that religious fanatics, not God, destroyed Sodom and Gomorrah."

Charlie took off his reading glasses and tucked them into his shirt pocket. "I don't know why you're so upset about all that. The Bible is full of genocides, scores of them, of just about any tribe that worshipped other gods. It was a primitive time. And whether myth or history, what was righteousness then is terrorism now."

"Ancient Hebrews as al Qaeda. Now there's a comparison you'd never expect."

Charlie shrugged. "The Persians and the Greeks and the Mongols all did the same. Some behaviors repeat forever and only change their names. And speaking of names, we have them now for all the women. I kind of like Atiyah, don't you?"

"Yes, and Gebreel too. The modern Gabriel. The assassin who came in from the cold."

"A lot of good it did the girls," Charlie mused. "They still lost their home and their mother, bore their father's children by rape, and married men who shamed them. Frankly, I find the whole story disgusting."

Joanna stared into the middle distance for a moment. "I'm going to put Lot in the exhibit. I want to record the outrage. The design's already been approved with five statues. All I'm doing is adding identity to them. Identity and a story. Would you stand as the model for Lot? I know he's a bastard, but with the beard and all, you're perfect."

Charlie stroked his chin and stood up from the table. "I thought you'd never ask."

"You're getting good at this," Charlie remarked as Joanna troweled the second coat of plaster over his lower body. "You've done this whole thing in record time."

Joanna snorted. "I think I could do a casting in my sleep now." She thickened the coating over his chest and then carefully smoothed another layer over his upraised right arm. "You need to hold that arm up for an hour, so let's put a support under it," she said, fetching a six-foot length of doweling. She measured off the correct height and then clipped off the top and nailed an inch-wide platform at the upper end. Slipping it under the heel of his upraised hand, she maneuvered the arm until she found the right angle.

"Now we just need a rock," she said, folding several rags into a tight round wad and laying it on his hand. "Curve your fingers around it. Perfect. I'll shape it with the sander later."

With the remaining quart of plaster, she coated his wrist, fingers, and the wad at the center. Then she stood back. "Looks good, Charlie. Now you just have to hold the position for," she looked at her watch, "forty minutes."

"Piece of cake," he said. "Except, um, can you please scratch my nose?"

"Anything for a friend." She scraped her nail around the tip of his nose until he moaned relief. Then she occupied herself with the cleanup, such as it was. She washed out the bowl and miscellaneous other instruments, wound the loose cord around the sander and stowed it under the table, and quickly inventoried the remaining cloths. With luck and care, she'd have enough for the final statue.

Charlie dared not turn his head, but he followed her with his eyes. "Nigel and Judy want to publish the transliterations right away in the museum journal. What do you think? It will have all our names on it."

"That's fine with me. I'm assuming the museum will also make a press announcement. We can give them a call tomorrow, right after we've done your head." She swept the floor around his feet, collecting all the dried pellets of alginate and plaster into a dustpan.

"It's a shame we have to be so circumspect about who your statues are. I don't think a generic man with a rock is going to get the message across."

She dumped the refuse into a bin and set aside broom and pan. "We promised Gamal we'd be discreet. I won't go back on my word. But..." She nodded to herself. "I'll find a way. Just give me a day to work out how. But listen, we've got a very tight schedule now. Everything's got to be at the drop lot by Sunday."

"Well, you still need Lot's wife. I mean Atiyah. Who do you have in mind?"

Joanna knew what was coming, and a beat later, it did. "Why don't you ask Kaia? Are you in contact with her since you, um…departed from her yacht?"

She glanced away. "Yeah, she was here this morning to make sure we were all right. Her husband's gone to New York again and she invited me back to the boat."

"Great. If that means what I think it does. You *are* going, right?"

"What's the point? In a day or two her husband will return and claim his property, and we'll be back to square one. I'm not up to another humiliation."

Charlie's expression registered slight impatience. "Humiliation, schmuliation. This may sound crass and male, but if a beautiful actress invited me to spend the night on her boat while her husband was away, I'd be there in a minute. With clean underwear and a toothbrush."

"It doesn't bother you that she's married?" Joanna tapped lightly on the plaster on his chest. The muffled sound told her it was still too soft.

"According to you, she's married to a bastard."

"A bastard husband is still a husband." She felt along his arm where it was slightly harder, but only a little.

"Suddenly you're an evangelist for fidelity? Look, Kaia is a grown-up woman, and she's married to a creep. If she decides to have an affair, that's her decision, not yours. You have no business deciding her morals. Do you know how many millions of men, not to mention women, would jump at the chance she's offering you?"

"A chance of what? Meaningless gratification?"

"Not everything has to have meaning. Go have fun. Give her an experience she'll never forget. Maybe one you'll never forget either. Stop waiting for the magic prince, or princess in this case, to come and wake you from your slumber."

"Would this be the Sleeping-Beauty-in-the-castle slumber or the Valkyrie slumber on the burning mountain?"

"Actually, I was thinking more of the Snow White poison-apple slumber. That would make Gil and Marion and the rest of us the seven dwarfs."

"Charlie, for a grown man, you know way too much about fairy tales. But I'll give it some thought. I do need an Atiyah. Soon." She tapped on his chest again and heard the satisfying thud she was waiting for.

"Ah, finally."

❖

Joanna and Charlie stood back and admired the still-headless casting of Lot.

"Fabulous, wonderful, excellent, and other superlatives," Charlie said. "But really, it's a beautiful piece of work."

"Yeah, it is, if I do say so myself." Joanna ran her hand along the upraised arm of the statue. "The rock still looks like a bundle of rags, but I'll sand that down later today, along with the other rough spots. Meanwhile, I'm starved. How about going over to Falafel Ali's for a bite?"

"Sorry, dear. I'd love to, but first I'm enjoying a long hot shower and then I'm taking a snooze. This old man does have his limits and, well, these last couple of days…"

"Okay, fine. I'll just grab something and come right back." Joanna waved him off and washed her hands in the workshop sink. With the pleasant sense of achievement, she set off again for El Gouna village and Falafel Ali's. Maybe some of the other artists would be there too. She was in a mood now for company.

Though it was well past lunchtime, Joanna was pleased to note that Marion was at one of the outside tables in the shade of a canopy. She pulled up a chair across the table from her.

"How's the war wound?" Joanna asked, pointing with her chin at Marion's thickly bandaged shoulder.

"Not so bad. Doesn't hurt, but I can't dive for a couple of days. Good thing I'm finished with the project, *nicht*? What about you?"

"Almost finished, but I'm working on a theme now. I never liked just having generic figures at my fountain, so now I'm giving them identities."

"Really? Who?'

"That's actually a long story."

"So? I've got time, lots of time. Talk to me." She held up two fingers to the man behind the counter, the eponymous Ali, indicating two falafels.

"Well, I don't suppose there's any harm in telling you. Let me try to summarize." Joanna thought for a moment. "Okay. At the bottom of the crevice where my display was *supposed* to be, Charlie and I found some artifacts that were probably from an ancient shipwreck." At Marion's expression of amazement, she amended her tale. "Well, we saw no sign of a ship, but we did find some gold objects and some tablets. We gave them to the Egyptians, of course."

The falafels arrived and they put off discussion while they both bit in.

Marion chewed thoughtfully for a few moments and then swallowed. "How do you know they are ancient and not dropped from some tourist boat?"

"Because the text on them is in cuneiform and because it tells the story of the destruction of Sodom and Gomorrah."

"Oh, those myths. Just anti-gay *Scheisse*."

"Well, they were anti-gay, for sure, but they weren't myths. The tablets give an account of the destruction and the aftermath from the perspective of Lot's daughters, and they seem to be authentic. You can tell by the style and the language." She set down the pita bundle and held out both hands for emphasis. "Marion, they seem to be proof that those cities actually existed and were burned to the ground. Can you appreciate the importance of that? It's staggering."

Marion chewed silently for a moment. "Impossible."

"I don't think so. Of course we'll find out when the clay of the tablets themselves is finally dated. But we can't do that right now because the Egyptians have them. We, that is, Charlie, just took photographs and sent them to London for translation."

"But even if they are three, four thousand years old, they could still just be more versions of the same myth, like the *Evangelium*. Don't know the English word."

"You mean the gospels. No, they're not at all like the gospels. Those are all told in the third person, the way myths always are. But the tablets are all first-person accounts, and they seem very real. And they describe how religious fanatics set fire to both cities, wiping out everyone and everything. God, I can't imagine…"

"I can," Marion murmured. "A city burning." She pushed aside the rest of her meal and took a breath. "My family is from Dresden. My father was in the Dresden firestorm and I spent my childhood hearing about it. So I can imagine it very well."

"How awful for you." Joanna recognized the blandness of her remark but could think of nothing stronger.

"Yeah, you know how some people are so traumatized by something they never want to talk about it? My father was the opposite. He couldn't think of anything else. When they rebuilt the city after the war, he moved the family near the Elbe River, you know, just in case it happened again. It was the way we could save ourselves, you see, by jumping into the water. And anything could start him talking. He would get this distant look in his eyes and start talking about the sound and smell and feel of a burning city."

"Please, I don't want to hear," Joanna said.

"I didn't either. But you can't close your eyes to history, he said. So he talked and we had to listen. Everyone should have to listen. About human torches trapped in the molten asphalt, the roar of the wall of flames, the screams from adults, children, even animals in their cages as the zoo burned. Dresden was a big city, but I think the suffering was the same in Sodom and Gomorrah. All people burn to death in the same way."

Joanna stared into unfocused space for a moment. "You know, when you read about the Old Testament genocides, you never really think about the physical suffering. Biblical stories you simply take at face value, as detached moral lessons. But when you accept that Gomorrah's firestorm was as real as Dresden's, you begin to sense the horror of it all. You imagine the people burning to death in their homes or running with their children and infants, only to be struck down in their streets. Familiar streets, with shops and fountains, all a blazing inferno."

She thought of the mysterious Tiamat and her infant and shook her head. "All for having the wrong gods or the wrong lovers. It makes you physically sick."

"*Ja, ja.*" Marion nodded helpless agreement. "And some do it still." She touched her bandaged shoulder.

"So what do we do to stand up to that?"

"Tell the truth, I guess. And not be afraid to love. Very important to not be afraid." Marion shrugged with her good shoulder. "But what do I know? I am just a stupid person who makes statues."

Joanna snorted softly. "Yeah, me too."

Chapter Twenty

Joanna pulled into the lot in front of the dock and stepped from the car, strangely self-conscious. Did she look all right? Well, she was wearing her favorite moss-green shirt and freshly washed cargo pants, so it wasn't going to get any better than this.

She stood for a moment staring up at the evening sky, calming herself and collecting her thoughts. There it was, Orion, in only a slightly different position from where she'd seen it two weeks ago. Orion, the hunter, or the Fool, depending on your culture. She took a deep breath and started down the path onto the dock.

As she passed the other boats she heard the casual evening conversations of workers and boat owners in Arabic, French, English. A quiet night in the neighborhood of the very rich. But while she walked, something seemed to evolve in her. The uncertainty she'd felt in the workshop talking to Charlie had worn off and been replaced by determination. She was tired of being at the mercy of other people's decisions. She would be the actor now, not the acted upon.

There it was, the *Hina*, looming darkly against the cobalt sky. Only at its center on the upper deck, a warm amber light shone like a hearth from the salon. Curiously, the gangplank still connected the stern of the boat to the dock, as if she was expected. But that was hardly possible.

She stepped on board, climbed the stairs to the main deck, and paused in front of the double glass doors. It was ten at night. Surely they'd be locked. But when she laid her hand on the handle, they slid open smoothly.

Kaia sat at the small table at the far end of the salon. At the sound of the opening doors she stood up but remained motionless. Then she brought her hand to her chest.

Joanna paused, not from uncertainty, but because the instant was precious. Kaia waited for her, a vision in white and blue, with summer skin longing to be touched. The air between them was electric because she knew, they both knew, that everything was about to change. There would be no sweeter moment than this one, of anticipation and certainty, the crossing of a gulf to a new land.

Joanna strode the length of the salon. Momentum brought her hands up to caress Kaia's face, then to pull her forward.

The kiss, at least at first, was not so much passionate as it was an act of laying claim. But as Kaia's arms encircled her and as their two bodies pressed together, Joanna felt her whole body heat.

How wonderfully she kisses, she thought, feeling Kaia's lips sliding lightly across her own. It wasn't at all like in the movies, in all the scripted kisses she had seen her do with Hollywood's dashing men. She didn't bite, or moan, or seize Joanna's head. She seemed instead more cautious, tentative, and then she broke away.

For a second, Joanna feared rejection. But Kaia simply ran her thumb over Joanna's mouth and said, "Not here. Come downstairs. I don't want us to grapple like teenagers on a sofa. I want it to be in bed."

Bed? She said "bed"? Joanna yielded wordlessly when Kaia took her hand. This did not correspond to her resolve to be the initiator of events, but things seemed to be moving along well, so she followed Kaia down the circular staircase and into the guest cabin.

Kaia turned on the low bed lamp, then faced her again. "I was afraid I'd lost you," she said. "You were here, and I let you slip through my fingers and I thought I'd never get you back."

Dazed, Joanna stepped out of her sandals and moved again into the embrace, burying her face in the thick brown hair. "I'm here now. As long as you want me." Then, with sudden alarm, she drew back. "Your husband. He's not going to walk in, is he? He's got a talent for that."

Kaia undid the top button of Joanna's shirt and kissed the spot just above her breasts. "No, he won't. Stop talking. Just be with me."

"Yes, oh, yes." Joanna grasped handfuls of Kaia's dark mane and kissed her hair, her brow, her eyelids. Like a blind animal moving across a foreign terrain, she explored with her lips the way along Kaia's cheek and ear down to her throat, inhaling the fragrance of her skin, her shampoo, the perfumed detergent of her clothing.

The soft, washed-out denim shirt awakened memories, of comfort at her hospital bedside, of strength and rescue, of her own stolen glances at the swellings beneath. And now she could uncover them.

She covered Kaia's mouth again and they dropped awkwardly together onto the bed.

Resting on one elbow, she unbuttoned Kaia's shirt and kissed downward in a line to her breasts, then drew the shirt back freeing her shoulders, finally her arms. Only the bra remained and, with a deft movement, Kaia rid herself of it.

Kaia's breasts were all that Joanna had imagined. Small and round and not at all the way they appeared in her films, they had been little harmed by age. "Beautiful, so beautiful," she murmured, not minding the cliché. She brushed her cheek and lips over the coffee-and-cream skin of Kaia's chest, down to the earthy brown of her nipples. A shiver of arousal went through her as she encircled one with her tongue. It still seemed forbidden and dangerous.

"I want to touch you too, your wonderful young body." Kaia laid her hand on Joanna's still-covered breast, and Joanna felt the warmth of her palm seep through the fabric. With her eyes shining as if she opened a gift, Kaia finished unbuttoning the shirt and exposed the pale flesh of Joanna's chest.

"Look at you, you don't even wear anything underneath." Kaia pulled the moss-green shirt out of her trousers. "Come here."

Joanna stretched out over the length of her, and kissed the pulsing throat. "Is this 'here' enough?" she murmured as Kaia slid hands inside her pants and tugged them down. The cool air on Joanna's naked buttocks caused her sex to tighten suddenly. She rolled to her side and gave a little kick, freeing her feet from the pants' legs.

"Now you," she said, unzipping Kaia's white cotton pants and sliding them along her hips. She studied the soft womanly belly, the beginning of pubic hair. *This is the forest primeval.* Then she drew them farther down, exposing the full dark mystery of Kaia's sex. There was the awkward, faintly comical moment of seizing the pants by the cuffs and pulling them over Kaia's feet, but then Joanna fell back next to her, studying her naked form.

Kaia seemed to blush. "Don't look at me that way. I'm not used to being so exposed."

Joanna laughed gently. "What? After all those hot movie love scenes, with the cameras revealing every inch of you? How is that possible?" She trailed gentle fingers from Kaia's throat down between her breasts to her belly.

"That wasn't me. I mean of course the kissing scenes were with me. But for the sexy stuff, they used a body double."

Joanna sat up. "What? All that time people were drooling over your luscious tan flesh it was…?"

"Someone else's luscious tan flesh. Yes. Actually several people's. It was never me."

"So that means I'm not sharing this with anyone?" She bent forward and brushed her lips along Kaia's midsection.

"Well, hardly anyone. But no, it hasn't been on the big screen." She took Joanna's hand and kissed her palm. "And you are the first woman. It's strange…how much I want you. And I don't even know what it is I want. Just that I want it with you." She pulled Joanna over her again and they shared the first long kiss of deep arousal. "I want you to do everything. Teach me everything, Kaia breathed."

"Nothing to teach. You know already, I'm sure." Joanna slid her tongue along the valley between the warm swells of Kaia's breasts down to her belly and to the mysterious dark triangle. She grasped Kaia around the hips, then covered the moist crevice below with her mouth and finally knew the wonderful lemony, earthy taste of Kaia's sex.

"Yes, oh, yes. Do that." Kaia threaded her fingers through Joanna's hair, lifting toward her, offering herself.

Joanna massaged the pliant flesh under her hands, then gripped the warm thighs. With her thumbs she spread the vulva, allowing her tongue to enter the wet cavern, and felt the hardened clitoris. There could be no play-acting here.

Her tongue intruded and began its dance, in the soundless, wordless communication of their passion. She slipped one finger inside, then two, and thrust with a steady gentle rhythm. Kaia murmured incoherently, her body swallowing up the invaders in the slow hula of their lovemaking. Joanna was relentless, but when Kaia pressed against her hungrily, Joanna slackened, drawing out the torturous climb.

"Oh, God…on fire," Kaia, panting, whispered into the air as Joanna drew out the final tension. She grasped Joanna's hair, arched off the mattress, then called out suddenly as the climax seized her.

Joanna waited until she felt her soften into languor, then withdrew and slid up to lie under Kaia's arm. She wanted to whisper something tender in her ear, but the joy that filled her at that moment was wordless, their lovemaking the gratification of some animal want that did not need speech.

Kaia's chest still rose and fell with the deep breathing of satiation, but finally she turned sideways and stroked her face.

"I want to make you happy like that, but I don't know yet…I've never…"

Joanna reassured her. "It's all right. You know all the places. And I'm so excited that you only have to touch me a little. See?" She pressed Kaia's hand into the wetness between her legs.

Kaia's touch was electric. Tentatively at first, then obviously learning the landscape of Joanna's sex, she stroked with skill and confidence. Then she began to tease, slowing the movement of her fingers, caressing every place but the hot, hard spot that yearned for it.

Joanna closed her eyes under the exquisite torment, and a shimmering scenario coalesced behind her eyelids. Circles spiraled within glistening circles, laughter sounded over the rushing of a stream from deep below. The water rose and fell and rose again, and the circles turned more tightly, spiraling the silver liquid upward pulse by pulse until it was unbearable. For the briefest instant it stopped her breath; then all erupted brightly, and she was the water and the fountain and the joy.

She lay spent for a moment in the sticky sweet air of the adulterous bed, then murmured into Kaia's hair, "I could almost face the sharks again if I knew it would end in this."

"Don't talk of sharks. Let's never talk of sharks again. Just tell me that you care for me."

"You know I do. How can you doubt it?" *I want to spend the rest of my life with you*, Joanna thought, but dared not say it. The woman in her arms still belonged, at least legally, to a man. And he was due back.

Kaia was falling asleep. She murmured something in return, something incoherent, but Joanna thought it could have been the word love.

Joanna awakened abruptly at some sound but then realized it was only the boat thrown against the dock by a wave from a passing powerboat. She slipped quietly from the bed and went to use the charming nautical bathroom she had grown to love in the week it had been hers. Its glass-enclosed shower and tiny polished wood cabinets were luxury in miniature. She stepped inside the shower to rinse the stickiness from her thighs, but a moment later Kaia stood in the doorway, her thick dark hair gorgeously disheveled. "You were going to shower without me?"

"I was just warming it up for us," Joanna said, adjusting the temperature. Then she drew Kaia into the tiny space and they stood in a slippery embrace as the warm water poured down, over, and between them.

They lathered playfully and then kissed again, tongues dancing in the same wordless language they'd used the night before, and the combined sensations of water and each other brought immediate arousal. Kaia broke away.

"Stop, before I collapse and break my neck in here." She took hold of Joanna's wrist and pulled her back to the bed where they began anew, their soapy bodies sliding against each other. Joanna once again invaded the sweet space she had learned the night before, and they climbed together the breathtaking steps of newly discovered passion.

Afterward, they lay damp and half dozing in each other's arms until Joanna asked, "What time do the crew arrive?"

"Jibril comes at ten and the others at noon. When we're in the dock, there's not so much for them to do. She twisted sideways to glance at the night-table clock. "Eight fifty-five. Come on. I'll make you a nice breakfast."

"Let's make another try at that shower first, okay? This time separately."

It was the same breakfast at the same sunlit table they'd had a week before, yet the world had changed. As she cleared away the plates, Kaia hummed something that sounded operatic and remarked about the scarcity of fresh pineapple in El Gouna. Joanna watched her while she squeezed oranges to make another round of fresh orange juice for them, as if they were a family. The thought brought a twinge, because they were not a family. They had different lives and responsibilities, and hers was to be in the workshop making the last statue.

The last statue? Uff. She all but slapped herself on the forehead. She hadn't yet even brought it up.

"Kaia, would you stand model for our fifth statue? Of Lot's wife?" She gathered up the remaining dishes and carried them to the galley.

"You mean the one who turns into a pillar of salt?" Kaia took them and set them in the sink.

"Uh, yes, that's the one. Her name was Atiyah, and she was much wronged. Murdered, in fact. I want to bring her alive again and your face is perfect for her. You've seen how we make the cast. It's not so nice being inside a mold, but it'll just take a day."

Kaia answered without hesitation. "Of course I would. I'll come any time you want." They returned to the table and Kaia poured the new orange juice into their glasses.

"How about today? We're very close to deadline."

"Well, why not? What should I wear?"

"Just something you don't mind leaving on the workshop floor. We'll wrap you in drapery for the mold."

"Oh, a costume drama. I love it. Let me change then. I'll be back in two minutes." With a quick kiss to the top of Joanna's head, Kaia disappeared down the staircase to the lower deck.

Joanna relaxed against the cushioned bench and let her gaze wander around the warm, sunny teak interior of the yacht, unable to decide whether she loved it or hated it. It was Kaia's yacht, but also Bernard's, and had become a symbol of what kept her tied to him. Being there this time felt like trespassing. Or maybe being the third party in adultery always felt like that; she didn't know. She had never loved a married woman before.

Loved? Did that word actually float by? She examined the thought, but then Kaia suddenly reappeared at the top of the stairs in very old jeans and a brassiere, holding a shirt in each hand. "Which do you think is more chic, the blue one with the paint or the green one with the grease? I have an image to protect, you know."

Joanna took the blue one and examined it. I think this one is—"

"What the hell are you doing here? I thought I made myself clear that you were not welcome." Once again Bernard Allen marched through the salon doors like the buffoon in a French farce. But he was no clown.

He stared for a moment at Kaia's naked shoulders and brassiere, then directed his glare at Joanna. "You fucked my wife, didn't you?"

Joanna stood speechless, as she had done before, paralyzed by fear, guilt, and a growing sense of banality.

Strangely, Kaia seemed unfazed. With a defiant calm, she took the paint-stained blue shirt from Joanna and slid one arm, then the other into the sleeves. She began buttoning from the top. "Twice actually. The best sex I've had in twenty years."

The insult caused an alarming change in Bernard's expression, from a scowl of suspicion to ice-cold rage. He focused on Joanna again. "I told you to stay the hell off my boat," he snarled.

Kaia rolled up the sleeves of her shirt. "It's *my* boat, Bernie, not yours. We bought it with the earnings from my films. I can invite anyone on it I want."

"You bitch. I could ruin you for this. You'd never be offered a contract again."

"Ah, a threat to my career. That was inevitable. Divorce won't do it any good either, I suppose. Well, obviously we've got a lot to talk about. For starters, I know about the pictures in your safe."

"My safe? What the hell are you talking about?"

"The pornography. The girls. You slimy bastard."

Bernard took a step backward at the sudden game change. Joanna did too, though she had no idea what the discussion was about. Obviously something deadly serious, for Bernard's voice dropped in volume and menace. "Do you really want to discuss these things in front of a stranger?"

"She's not a stranger. But, no, I don't want to discuss our shame in front of her." Kaia turned to Joanna. "Please excuse my husband's bad manners. But he's right. We have unpleasant matters to talk about in detail and in private. Don't worry. I'll come by the workshop around noon. I promise."

"You're sure?" Joanna asked, reluctant to leave. Did Hollywood agents beat their wives? She looked nervously at Bernard, but he appeared more shaken than threatening.

"Yes, I'm sure. Don't worry. It'll be fine. If I'm not there by twelve, you can come back and pick me up."

Joanna was not sure if the "come back" remark was a practical suggestion or a hint to Bernard that someone would be looking out for her. Either way, Joanna agreed. She dared not lean in to kiss Kaia good-bye so merely stepped around Bernard. She walked with deliberate, casual steps through the salon and down the stairs to the stern deck. As she stepped onto the dock she passed Jibril, who was just coming to work. She had never warmed to the dour crewman, but now she was relieved.

Or would a rigid Islamist simply make things worse?

CHAPTER TWENTY-ONE

Joanna stood at the workshop doorway and watched the road.
"Stop worrying," Charlie said behind her. "She'll be along.
We only need about four or five hours to do both head and body, and
we'll still be able to finish today."

She returned to the workbench with him. "You don't understand.
It's Bernie I'm worried about. You should have seen the look on his
face, like he could have murdered us both right there. The only way
I know he's not beating her up is that one of the crewmen is there,
probably all of them by now. So I suppose—" The sound of a car motor
made her hurry to the doorway.

Kaia stepped out of the rented Mercedes and waved. "I'm sorry if
I'm late. I had to settle a few things before I could leave." She stopped
in front of Joanna, somewhat flushed from exertion. "I'd have preferred
to stay there while he packed his things, but I knew you were waiting
for me."

"Packed? What do you mean?"

Leading the way into the workshop, Kaia lifted her shoulder bag
over her head and looked around for a place to set it down.

"I told him to leave. We've got two residences he can choose
from, a penthouse in New York and a house in Los Angeles, but I
suppose he'll go to New York and talk to his lawyer again." She smiled
a greeting at Charlie and dropped her bag on the floor out of the way.

Ever the model of discretion, Charlie made no comment, but
gestured toward the modeling stool. Kaia sat down and went on talking.
"In addition, he's got an office in West Hollywood, so he might end up
there. It's all part of what we have to work out in the divorce."

Joanna was about to pour water into the alginate for the face cast but stopped, holding the beaker suspended in midair. "You're divorcing him because of...of last night?"

"No, of course not. I mean, last night was absolutely amazing, but even if you hadn't shown up, I was going to tell Bernie that it was over between us. It has nothing to do with you. I mean, it didn't. There are... other matters."

"Ah, I see." Joanna didn't see at all, but sensing that it wasn't the time for such a conversation, she held back asking further and turned her attention to the mixture.

Charlie also seemed unsure whether to react to the announcement and simply held out a plastic shower cap while Kaia tied up her hair. After inserting a few large clips to hold it all in place, he laid the cap over the entire mass.

But Kaia was obviously feeling talkative. "Anyhow, I called my daughters," she said, even as Charlie inserted plastic tubes into her nostrils. Unfazed, she continued while Joanna applied the first layer of alginate over her forehead and crown. "They've agreed to fly here for a week, for my birthday. I've got important things to discuss with them in any case. Of course, I want you to meet them. I'm sure you'll like each other."

Daughters. Right. Kaia had a life of her own, Joanna remembered. She would go back to the States soon, and life would go on. Without Bernard, apparently. At least there was that. She shook herself back to the present.

"Ah, yes, well. As soon as you're ready, I'll paste up your eyes and mouth. And then you can't move your lips for forty-five minutes."

"Okay. I've cold-creamed up my face. Go ahead and smear me. I can take it." Kaia closed her eyes. "I can take anything, now."

Ignoring the enigmatic remark, Joanna scooped up a dollop of the thickening alginate batter with her spatula. "All right then. Here it comes. I'll start with the right eye." She laid it on, then scooped again. "Now the left one." She scooped a third time. "And this is for those lovely lips."

"Ummph," Kaia commented.

"Yes, I thought so, too," Joanna said.

Charlie laid on netting and Joanna slathered on a second coat of the mixture. "If you have any problems under there, trouble breathing, or an anxiety attack, just grunt twice and we'll let you out," Charlie called into one of the thickly coated ears.

Kaia grunted once. "Ummph."

"We're finished applying the goo, so now you just have to relax," Charlie added. "It's going to seem like a long time, so we'll try to entertain you."

"Oh, dear. We forgot to ask whether she preferred show tunes or poetry readings."

From underneath the mask Kaia emitted a distinct moan of despair. "All right. We'll skip the show tunes."

Kaia made a gesture of writing on her hand and Charlie fetched a pencil and pad of yellow lined paper. She scrawled across half the page, "Tell me about you."

"I think she means you, Joanna," Charlie said. "Or do you want to hear *my* life story?" he shouted at the creamy white head with nose tubes.

"Um umm," the head answered, and the hand scribbled, "Some other time, Charlie."

Joanna pulled up a bench to sit in front of her mute model. "Well, I don't know how much is worth talking about. I work at the London Museum of Natural History, with Charlie, though he's been there a lot longer. Before that I was at UC Santa Barbara, in California, teaching marine biology. I started diving while I was in graduate school at Stanford, and when I was at Santa Barbara I dove all along the Pacific Coast."

"Ugh. Cold," Kaia scribbled.

"Yes, it was cold, but we explored some nice shipwrecks off the Channel Islands and occasionally saw gray whales. But once I started diving in warmer waters, I became interested in coral, which is notably absent off the California coast."

"London?" Kaia wrote.

"Well, I published a few papers on corals and how they were endangered, and the museum offered me a job. People asked me how I could leave California for rainy London, but I guess it's in my blood and I need rain for at least half the year to stay properly English. Otherwise I get too cheerful. What about you?"

The white head, which Joanna's gentle poking revealed was beginning to harden nicely, chuckled softly.

"Nothing to say? Well, I'll let Charlie talk while I prepare everything for the next stage." Joanna stood up to collect the packages of gauze and rods for the larger body cast while Charlie took over the entertainment, describing life at the museum.

A short time later, a final tap on top and side revealed that the mold was formed. Joanna incised a line from the right shoulder tip along the side of the head and down to the other shoulder. When she was satisfied the cut was clean, she and Charlie pulled the mold apart.

"Ah, finally." Kaia panted, as if she'd been running. "It was pretty awful in there. If you hadn't been rambling on and on, I might have panicked."

Charlie examined the inside of the face and handed it back to Joanna. "Nice work. This one's going to be the best yet."

Joanna scrutinized the hollowed-out face, turning it back and forth. "I think you're right. But let's not waste time flattering ourselves. We've got to do the body now, and that will take a little posing. So, everyone who is about to be stuck in plaster for an hour should take a quick potty break." She pulled a tiny ball of alginate from Kaia's perfectly shaped eyebrow. "I think that means you."

Bernard seethed as he knelt on the deck of the tiny cabin and emptied the contents of his safe into his briefcase. Getting to his feet, he knocked an ashtray from his desk. He kicked it furiously out of the way but felt no satisfaction. What he really wanted was to pound his fist through the bulkhead. Or into Kaia's face.

How the hell had she broken into his safe, the bitch? It was his private space, a supposedly secure place where he could store any goddamn thing he wanted, including his pictures. He didn't look at them often, but every now and again, when Kaia was away, he couldn't resist. It was like an addiction. Sure, he was a normal guy and could get his rocks off with any woman, but the thought of those smooth little bodies and their tight little pussies made him crazy.

He wasn't a perv. He'd never raped any little girls; force wasn't his style. But he sure liked looking at the little peaches between their legs and beating off to the thought of them. And sure, maybe once or twice, he'd done a little touching. "So shoot me!" he demanded of his invisible accuser. When he was the same age, he'd been fingered and jacked off by his uncle plenty of times, with no harm done. There was no reason for such hysteria.

And it wasn't like he was alone in the world. Christ, there was a whole market for kiddie porn. He ought to know; he'd made a small fortune off peddling it. He only stopped when he found some real talent and a beautiful woman he could market legitimately.

Okay, it *was* asking for trouble to have kept the pictures of Kiele and Mei all those years. But they were the ones that got him really hot. All he had to do was recall the time he'd cajoled them into stroking his dick, and it gave him a major woody every time. Dumb to bring them along on the yacht, though, he had to admit.

"Goddamn it!" he growled, as he crossed from the tiny cabin to the master suite. He yanked his suit bag out from under the bed and folded his business suit and all his clean shirts into it. Then he hauled out his Louis Vuitton rolling luggage and crammed in his vacation clothing, shaving kit, and hair products.

Things were going along so well, and then suddenly it had all turned to shit. Oh, the marriage had gone cold years ago, but the business partnership had continued. He always had plenty of young women to fuck—would-be actresses looking for an agent, the occasional bar meetings and hired escorts—so he was never hard up. And if need be, he could still sometimes get Kaia drunk enough to let him have a quick poke at her.

But that was rare. He'd already lost his lust for her when she'd turned forty. He liked his women young and vivacious with tight little pussies and mouths that knew how to suck. Kaia had never shown much interest in anything kinky, so he began to look for it elsewhere. If he'd known she liked girls that might have extended his interest in her.

Still, she was big box office, and they'd made a lot of money together. More money than he ever expected. This fucking divorce was going to be a disaster. With his main star gone from the roster, his office would be reduced to pushing the careers of perky, talentless twits and queer pretty-boy actors.

He snorted, cramming the last of his clean underwear into the corner of his luggage and zipping it shut. The screwing you get for the screwing you got. Well, it wasn't over yet. No, it definitely wasn't over.

"Jibril!" he shouted. When the crewman appeared, Bernie pointed to his luggage. "Take that up to the end of the dock, will you? And call me a taxi."

"Yes, Mr. Allen," Jibril replied mechanically, and began wrestling the bulky objects up the spiral staircase. Bernard had already turned away to snap his briefcase shut. He'd worry later about his diving and fishing equipment, but everything he'd need for the short term was packed, so he quickly perused the cabin. Nothing of interest was left.

Had Kaia stolen anything from him? She'd broken into his safe, so he wouldn't put anything past the bitch now. He kicked open the door of the VP cabin and glared down at the still-unmade bed with its several damp spots. The sight aroused him, provoking an image of them doing what lesbians did—and he'd made enough porn to know what that was. For a brief moment, he fantasized fucking them both but then turned away, disgusted.

There on top of the bureau stood Kaia's silly plaster figurine of the goddess Hina. He knocked it onto the floor with his fist and stepped on it, crushing it.

He climbed up to the salon deck, checked the dining table for keys or other things he might have forgotten, then strode through the glass doors. On the stern deck he spotted Kaia's new diving gear, faintly registering annoyance that she was diving now with equipment just like his.

"I hope she fucking drowns in it," he muttered, kicking her buoyancy vest in passing. Then he stopped and stared back at it for a long moment before turning away.

An idea took shape gradually as he made his way along the dock toward the path where Jibril stood with his luggage. He dismissed the crewman with a mumbled thanks but no tip and waved at the arriving taxi. He was changing his afternoon's plan by the second, and by the time he was seated in the taxi, he'd altered his destination from "airport" to "Sheraton Hotel."

Bernard propped himself up on pillows piled against the headboard of his hotel bed, stirring the ice in the remains of his scotch. His plans were beginning to gel, and he was feeling rather good now. He took a sip and winced. It wasn't Johnny Walker Blue, but it was all the minibar had. He set it aside, lit a cigar, and made the first of several preparatory calls.

"Hello, Linda? Yeah, it's me. Everything okay at the office? Good. Listen, we're having some work done on the boat, so we're staying for a while in a hotel. The Sheraton Miramar. Let me give you the number." He recited the numbers of the hotel telephone and his room.

"Yeah, yeah. We're fine. Kaia's got a new hobby and is going nuts for scuba. Who'd a thought, huh? I keep warning her how dangerous it can be. It's not like snorkeling. But you know how headstrong she can be."

He grunted agreement with the cheerful platitudes coming from his secretary. "Anyhow, I just wanted to check in and see if I had anything urgent on my desk. No? Great. You'll let me know if anyone calls in, right? I'm always reachable. Oookay. Bye for now."

And it was done. He leaned back and took another puff on his cigar, calculating how to proceed. He was getting a clearer idea now and even made a sort of mental calendar, with all the steps and specific tasks for each day. They're right, he concluded. Revenge is best served cold. He took another slug of the inferior scotch and felt in control again. And control made him horny.

It was time to put on an expensive suit and go down to the bar. He'd never met a hotel bar in any country that didn't have at least one woman who suddenly became available when he let slip that he was a Hollywood agent. He knew how to spot them, too, and he always chose the youngest one, the one with the firmest tits and tightest little ass. Oh yeah. He was feeling better already.

Chapter Twenty-two

Seven o'clock and the sky was just turning from whorish orange-fuchsia-pink to respectable blue. Joanna resolved to dive more often in the early morning. More of the larger fish were visible, and in general, it did the soul good. This morning her soul was doing very well indeed, since all the pieces of her exhibit were in place, and Kaia was by her side. It had been a long, hard haul in the last few days, but with Charlie's help, she'd cast a beautiful Atiyah and made her deadline. Now she had only one small addition to make before the opening the next day.

A pleasant breeze wafted through her hair as she stood on the lower stern deck pulling on her new wetsuit. Next to her, Kaia struggled with hers, becoming familiar with the deceptive tightness of neoprene. Jibril came onto the stern with two fresh bottles of compressed air and stood expressionless over them while they connected the cylinders to their buoyancy-control vests.

Joanna closed her weight belt and hefted on her vest-cum-tank, glancing at Kaia who, with Jibril's help, succeeded in doing the same. She patted her pockets to check she had the necessary tools: tubing, underwater adhesive, cutter. She spit-cleaned her mask to prevent fogging, then wiggled her feet into her fins. Together they flapped the last two steps to the edge of the deck.

They knew the routine. Guarding their masks and mouthpieces with one hand, they leapt together, submerged briefly, then bobbed to the surface. "Everything okay?" Joanna asked. Kaia signaled *fine*, and they descended slowly, feet first and face to face.

In a few minutes they were at the underwater site, just above the train station. Joanna hovered awhile, giving Kaia time to scan the buildings and objects that made up the City on the Plain. There was no diver's sign for *wow*, but Kaia invented one, spreading the fingers of both hands and holding them out in front of her. Seeing the exhibit through Kaia's fresh eyes, Joanna couldn't help but feel proud of the collective achievement by artists of a dozen nations

Kaia swam first around Gil's locomotive, running her hand along the rim of the smokestack, then paddled a short distance into the middle of the city square and made a circle. She returned to Joanna and once again made her *wow* sign.

Joanna had seen most of the exhibits, either in the holding lot or under water, but she hadn't seen Charlie's wall, and he'd been very mysterious about it. She motioned to Kaia to follow her and paddled toward the arcade.

A long building with a solid wall along the back and a series of eight columns running along the front, it housed several works. Joanna led the way past Rami's acrobats at one end and Japhet's *Band of Brothers* at the center. Then they reached Charlie's wall.

Under the roof of the arcade the light was much reduced, and Joanna shone her flashlight on the display. In the murky half-darkness, a skeleton rested on an elbow, one bony hand clutching a tablet and the other a stylus. Its skull, thrown back and facing the onlooker, was startling. The slightly open jaws seemed to laugh. More disturbing were the eye sockets that should have been hollow, but instead held pupil-less white balls that caught the light and stared up at them, blind and shimmering.

Joanna gazed for a few moments upon the eerie memento mori, then raised her light to illuminate the wall. She read only the first two lines of the text chiseled in lovely calligraphy before memory tightened her throat.

> *Full fathom five thy father lies;*
> *Of his bones are coral made;*
> *Those are pearls that were his eyes:*
> *Nothing of him that doth fade*
> *But doth suffer a sea-change*
> *Into something rich and strange.*

Joanna hadn't read or even thought about Shakespeare's *The Tempest* in decades, and she had completely forgotten Ariel's little song. But now the recollection came to her from over a quarter of a century and struck her hard. Prospero was her father's last role, and the celebration of the play's success had marked the last night of his life.

She'd told Charlie of his drowning, as she had told Kaia, simply in passing, but she had never made the connection with the song. Her lips trembled around her mouthpiece. So like Charlie, to hold on to a little detail like that and give it back to her as a gift.

Kaia also seemed moved by the verse, for she drifted down near the skeleton and studied it until Joanna nudged her shoulder. They emerged then from the colonnade and Joanna led the way past the works of the other artists—the Israeli soldiers and Palestinians, the Saudi stallions, Sanjit's animal gods, Yoshi's dragon, Marion's underworld balance. They'd study them in detail on another day. Today she had a final job to do.

After curving around the periphery of the exhibit, they arrived at the fountain at the northwestern corner. Seeing it again, Joanna was all the more grateful that George had rejected the slope. The two levels suited the drama of her scenario perfectly, with the murder of Atiyah high on the slope and the fountain and girls at the foot.

Kaia paddled up the slope and hovered in front of the statue of herself. Joanna joined her, noting with pleasure the shafts of sunlight that penetrated the water and sparkled around it like a blessing.

Presumably bored of admiring her own image, Kaia let herself sink down toward the two girls at the fountain, and Joanna seized the opportunity to inspect the last-minute alterations she had made to the statue. Her final idea, of a way to bring Atiyah "alive" once more, had been an inspiration, but it had taken all her skill and hours of work to execute it. And there was no way to test it before opening day without ruining the surprise. Everything did seem to be in place, though. The fine plastic tubing and the holes she'd drilled were all discreet.

Satisfied she descended to the foot of the slope to prepare her final coup.

She circled the fountain, her chest nearly on the seabed, and brushed the sand from around its base until she located the pipe leading to the internal reservoir. Coming to a halt, she withdrew a six-inch length of fiberglass tubing and a syringe of underwater adhesive from her pocket. With deft movements, she smeared a collar of the glue around one end of the tubing and thrust it into the pipe. Once the bonding agent had set, the tube would sit firmly and would not be dislodged by the constant handling of divers.

Still lying on her chest in the limestone sand, she searched along the base of the fountain with her fingers for the end of the duct tape she had attached in the workshop. Ah, there it was, still holding tightly. It would certainly stay in place until opening day.

All tasks accomplished, she lifted herself from the sea floor and prepared for the ascent. Suddenly a hand on her arm swung her around, and before she could react, Kaia removed both their mouthpieces and pressed a brief kiss on her mouth.

Given the steel tanks on their backs and the buoyancy vests protruding from their chests, an embrace of any sort was impossible, but the kiss was not. Kaia flicked her tongue into Joanna's mouth, along with a shot of salty water. Playful and emboldened, she tugged the two of them together and entwined her legs in Joanna's.

Joanna used her free hand to grab Kaia by the buttocks, and inside her own neoprene suit, she felt the sudden warmth of sexual awareness.

The kiss quickly reached its natural end, as their oxygen depleted, and they once again sucked compressed air. But they still hovered playfully with legs entwined, neither one wanting to separate from the other. Then Kaia pointed to her own heart, crossed her arms, and touched the center of Joanna's chest. The universal sign for *I love you*.

❖

Bernard took one final look at his list and his calculations before tearing the paper into tiny pieces and flushing them down the toilet.

It seemed foolproof. He had been watching the yacht for days, noting the rhythm of the two women. They generally dove early in the morning, then left the water around ten to go to the workshop. They presumably took meals with the other artists, because they never returned to the boat before eight. A visit to the yacht one afternoon on the pretense of collecting forgotten items revealed that only Jibril was working, and that his last duty each day was to fill their air tanks at the compressor before leaving about five.

Bernard knew what to do now, when to do it, and, most important, how. He needed only a length of hose of the right diameter, and he had already measured for that. A quick rummage through the locker and through the engine room the day before had yielded nothing useful, but with a few brief inquiries, he had located a marine-supply shop.

Allowing himself another cigar, he headed for the commercial street in El Gouna.

A few tourists wandered among the shops, buying the pharaonic kitsch, or jewelry, or souvenir beach towels that had EL GOUNA DIVER embroidered across the bottom. A few people, not many, sat at tables on the various restaurant terraces drinking beer or cola. He was perspiring, more from nerves than exertion, and could have used a beer himself, but he didn't have any time to waste. The opening ceremonies for the underwater city were the next day so this was his last opportunity to pull everything together. He spotted the marine-supply shop and flicked his half-smoked cigar into the street.

The shop was empty of customers and the proprietor himself was absent, so Bernard searched out the relevant aisle and rummaged among the boxes of plastic and rubber tubing.

A slender man of about forty with deep acne scars came through a rear door with a glass of tea. He set it down on the counter and approached Bernard. "Can I help you, sir?"

"Yeah, I'm looking for tubing. About five centimeters in diameter."

The shopkeeper bent down and drew two hoses, both of plastic, from a lower shelf. "What length? We have three, five, and ten meters."

"Three meters will be fine. And I need a collar clamp to hold it in place."

"Right here," the man said, fishing the item from a box of miscellaneous hardware.

"Not much business today," Bernard observed as they walked together to the front counter.

"Not much business any day. Too many shops and not enough tourists. Nobody buy anything."

"But a shop like this isn't for tourists. All those yachts in the marina need stuff like this." Bernard tilted his head in the general direction of the harbor.

"No. They bring everything themselves. They need maybe screws, nails, some oil, or a little hose like this." He held up Bernard's purchase. "Maybe after the underwater city is open, things will get better. *Inshallah*." He added the usual appeal to God.

"You think it's going to make that much of a difference, a bunch of statues?"

"Statues and treasure. Everybody is hoping for a big treasure."

"Treasure? What do you mean?" Bernard suddenly thought of George something-or-other, the pathetic diver he'd shared a late-night whiskey with. Could it be the same thing?

"Everybody is talking about the treasure, but nobody knows where to find it."

"I don't understand. How do you know about it then?"

"The cousin of my wife works for the committee, and he saw things in the committee office. Gold cups, plates. They said they were from under water. But nobody knows where. He's not a diver, so he asked someone to look but nobody knows where. Maybe the committee knows but is not telling. Everybody waits to find out the story. Maybe tomorrow when all the divers are go down."

"When all the divers go down? Oh, right. The opening ceremonies. They're at noon, aren't they?"

"Yes. Cousin of my wife asked someone to go look, but I think too many people all at once is not good. So for my shop, I just hope many more boats to come to El Gouna."

"Yes, thank you," Bernard said, scarcely paying attention as he handed over a wad of Egyptian pounds for his purchase and wandered out of the shop into the evening sunlight. *Damn*, he thought. George was right. What was it he said? Oh yeah, it was at the bottom of the drop-off under the sign for Site 13. Right behind the dragon.

This changed the schedule somewhat. He'd planned to carry out his strategy in the early evening, then go to the hotel bar for a celebratory dinner and, with a little luck, find himself some late-night nooky. He'd already checked out the bar and seen several likely candidates among the hotel clientele. But now he'd have to hurry to finish the preparations in time to dive while it was still light. That would be a bit more complicated. Celebration and bar conquests would have to wait.

But it was a great plan in which he'd never be a suspect. He imagined Kaia losing consciousness under water in front of a hundred people, her lezzie girlfriend unable to save her. It would be her best performance yet. Then he'd stand on the shore, holding gold artifacts and gloating, while the emergency services hauled her body in a plastic bag into an ambulance.

But now he had to set it all up, step by final step. He snorted a short, bitter laugh. Would make a cracking good screenplay for a movie.

Chapter Twenty-three

Slouching against the door of his second rental car at the far side of the parking area, Bernard checked his watch. Ten after five. If Jibril kept to the schedule of the last three days, he'd be stopping work now and locking up the boat.

It was still unpleasantly hot, and Bernard plucked his shirt from his damp chest. Damn, where was that sand nigger, anyhow? Ah, finally, there he was, just coming up the path from the dock. Bernard stepped back behind the car until Jibril was out of sight. Then with his tools in a brown paper bag, he hurried down the dock toward the *Hina*.

The salon doors were locked, as he expected, but he still had his key, of course. He called out, on the off chance that one of the other crewmen was still there, but no one responded. Man, this was going to be so easy.

He continued forward to the bow where the air tanks were lined up. Two were at the forefront, already attached to buoyancy vests and regulators, obviously for Kaia and her girlfriend. He opened the valve on both tanks and checked the pressure gauges. Both indicated just over two hundred bars, ready to go. He closed the valves again and hauled a third tank from the locker, setting it up next to the compressor.

It took a while to cut the hose to a convenient length and attach it to both the air-intake valve of the compressor and to the exhaust pipe of the compressor motor, and by the end, he was sweating profusely. He fit the original tubing from the compressor to the intake of the air tank and started the motor.

Watching the gauge on the new tank, he could follow the rate at which air was being compressed into the tank. It seemed to take longer than usual, probably because the intake pipe on the compressor usually sucked in clean air from overhead, and now it sucked it from its own motor. *From its own ass,* he thought, smirking.

Odorless, tasteless, and deadly, carbon monoxide was perfect for the job, even greatly diluted. Ideally it should merely cause a sort of vague malaise at the beginning of the dive. He knew Kaia. She'd never admit she wasn't feeling well and would soldier on, being a good sport. She wouldn't ask for help or share someone else's oxygen, because she wouldn't know what was wrong. She'd just keep breathing, and her hemoglobin would suck up the carbon monoxide instead of oxygen and keep circulating until critical mass was reached in the brain and she'd lose consciousness. Deep under water. Then even shared air wouldn't help her; she couldn't suck air from a regulator when she was unconscious.

When the twelve-liter tank had finally reached a pressure of a hundred bars, he removed the exhaust connection and added the remaining amount of clean air. He watched as the pressure gauge slowly climbed to the same two hundred bars as before, then closed the tank valve.

Now to make sure the deadly tank was attached to Kaia's buoyancy vest and not her girlfriend's. Though it would have been satisfying to dispose of the interfering bitch, it would still leave Kaia to humiliate him, and who knew what crap she'd leak to the tabloids? He unfastened Kaia's vest from the original tank and attached it to the newly filled one, letting the two women's tanks rest against each other as they had been before. He even made sure the vests hung in the same way, although he doubted she would notice.

Would he come under suspicion, once Kaia's tank was found to be polluted? No, he was fairly sure Jibril would take the rap for that, since he was the one who filled the tanks every afternoon. The small gas-run compressors were always a bit hazardous, and careless handling could allow exhaust to creep into the intake pipe even under normal circumstances. Once he'd gotten rid of the connecting hose, nothing would point to him.

He glanced at his watch again. Six o'clock. Almost two more hours of light left. Christ, that'd been easy. And now that the job was done, he'd get rid of the hose far away from the yacht. It meant a simple ten-minute hike up to the trash bins at the rear of the closest beach hotel.

He had a moment's misgiving about leaving the deadly tank unmarked, if only to himself. There was a miniscule chance of a mix-up, and he certainly didn't want to risk using the poisoned tank himself. He searched through the locker again until he found a roll of duct tape and tore off an inch-wide strip. The bottom of the tank was the least conspicuous place, so he pressed the strip onto the black foot of the tank and smoothed it with his thumb.

Job done, he stood up and rubbed his back. The sense of accomplishment was making him horny again, and he toyed with the idea of hitting the hotel bar to look for some willing young thing. But no, his next fast-fuck could wait until evening. He had something more important to do once he'd dumped the hose; he was going to dive for sunken treasure.

He rolled up the hose, shoved the hose clamp into his pocket, and hurried off the boat.

Jibril ruminated as he stood on the curb waiting to catch the jitney van to Hurghada. Najjid and Mazhar had been such honest and pious boys. But now they were in jail, awaiting trial, and they faced long prison sentences. How had it come to that? He struggled inwardly, trying to interpret what they'd done. Had they been fulfilling what the Quran commanded and been arrested by infidels who were doomed to hell anyhow? Or had they misunderstood the Holy Scripture and acted in un-Islamic ways? They had tried to drive away the infidel but had ended up killing Muslims. Yes, they were Muslims who worked in a bar, but was that much different from what *he* did—work for two rich white people, even taking them their wine? Was the attack holy jihad or terrorism?

Daily praying for understanding had not helped, for both of the two possibilities—of ever-increasing subjugation to the infidels or murder in the cause of Islam—seemed equally appalling to him. He had fallen back on the primary principle of his life; the cure for not understanding Quran was to read more Quran.

And then he realized that he had left the precious book on the boat. Imbecile! He'd decided to take it to Najjid during visiting hours and search out passages with him but had simply walked off the boat without it.

He did an about-face and began the march back to the dock, this time hurrying. When he reached the *Hina*, he was distressed to find the salon doors unlocked. Had he forgotten to secure them? That was terrible; he could lose his job if someone broke into the boat. Thank God he'd come back to discover the problem.

But maybe someone *was* on board stealing something. He tiptoed in, wincing at the *whoosh* the doors made as they closed behind him. He crept farther inside, sweeping his glance from side to side in case someone was hiding, although there were few places to conceal anything on that deck. Downstairs maybe.

As he reached the spiral staircase, he was startled by the sound of a motor. It alarmed him at first, but then he recognized the sound of the compressor motor coming from farther forward. Puzzled, he let himself into the pilot's room, where he could overlook the bow.

To his surprise, he saw his employer. His immediate inclination was to go out and greet him with the usual deference. But was he still the boss? Who was in charge now?

While he struggled with the dilemma, he noticed the other anomaly. Mr. Allen had just turned off the compressor and was attaching Miss Kapulani's vest to the diving tank he had apparently just filled. Why was he doing that? Was he going to dive with it? If so, why wasn't he using his own vest?

With the increasing conviction that something was not right, Jibril watched for a few more moments while his boss tore off a segment of duct tape and bent over the newly filled tank. Then he crept away from the window and went below to one of the cabins.

He waited silently, with the door closed, his heart pounding. If Mr. Allen came downstairs and found him here, he could tell the truth, that he had come back for the Quran. He had done nothing wrong. But then why was he hiding?

After ten minutes of fearful uncertainty, he ventured out again and saw no sign of anyone on the bow, or on any of the decks.

The compressor was still there, in its original place. But which tank had just been filled? He touched all the tanks lined up on the side, and when he laid his hand on Kaia's tank, the residual warmth told him it was the one. Why had Mr. Allen removed the vest from the tank that Jibril had filled and attached it to another one? And why had he done it in secret?

Then he remembered the piece of duct tape his employer had used. He upended the tank and saw the little strip of silver tape. Yet another puzzle. Why had he taken pains to identify the new tank when all three on the deck were filled and ready for use?

Whatever was going on, Jibril didn't like it. He was a good worker. He had never once made a mistake in filling the air tanks for anyone. If they didn't like his work, they should tell him. To simply negate the task that he had diligently carried out was an insult to his honor. The longer he thought about it, the greater became his sense of outrage. Honor was all a poor man had, honor and faith, and he would not allow anyone to take either one away from him.

He sat back on his heels, exasperated with the whole lot of them. Mr. Allen for treating him like a servant or even a dog, Miss Kapulani for tempting him with her body, and the other woman for—he couldn't think of a specific offense, but he did not like the way that she watched him. He wished he could be free of all three of them.

But then, what was the right thing, the Islamic thing, to do? He fingered the prayer beads in his pocket for a moment. Then he decided.

Kiele Palea halted at the gangplank connecting to her mother's yacht. "God, how vulgar," she muttered loud enough for the others to hear.

"My sister, the anti-snob," the younger Mei said. "Can't you simply enjoy a little luxury when it's offered?"

Kaia laid a hand on each of their shoulders. "Kiele has a point. It *is* vulgar, and I've thought that same thing ever since Bernard convinced me to buy it. I'm planning to sell it, as a matter of fact. But we'll talk about all that later." She herded her daughters and Joanna onto the stern.

"Don't sell it right away, Mom. Not until I've had a little fun on it," Mei said as they climbed the stairs to the salon doors. "It's seriously cool."

"That's what I thought when I first came on board, Mei. Way cool." Joanna immediately liked the younger of the two sisters. But as they passed through the salon, she fell silent, sensing the complicated family dynamic that she had no business upsetting. Better to simply let Kaia set the tone of the family reunion.

"Let's take care of practicalities," Kaia said, leading the two girls down the spiral staircase to the cabins. "You'll have to draw straws between the master suite and the crew cabin. One's twice as big as the other, of course, but someone's got to rough it."

"How come *you* don't sleep in the master cabin?" Kiele asked.

"I used to, but that's all changed, and I'll tell you the whole story as soon as you're settled in."

"I'll take the crew cabin, then. I don't want to sleep anyplace where Bernard has slept," Kiele announced.

Kaia gave a wan smile and touched her daughter's forearm. "I know what you mean. But don't worry, had clean linens put on all the beds."

"Nonetheless, I'll be happier here," Kiele said, pushing open the door to the crew cabin with one foot and dropping her valise on the floor.

"You're such a drama queen, Kiele," Mei brushed a swath of long straight hair over her shoulder. "As long as it doesn't smell of cigar smoke, I'll be fine."

"It doesn't. He never smoked inside. I'll give him that." Kaia stood in the doorway while Mei unloaded her backpack.

Peering over Kaia's shoulder, Joanna was amused to see what she pulled out of the nylon rucksack. A bathing suit, a sweatshirt, a blue Navy work shirt, tee shirts, and shorts. Clearly a no-nonsense kind of woman. Joanna wondered if she was gay.

"Do you want to take a nap first? You must have terrible jet lag, coming all the way from Los Angeles. There's nine hours' difference in time."

Mei shook her head. "Actually, we slept on both the big flights, and only the Cairo to Hurghada flight was exhausting. And customs was chaotic. It'll probably hit me this afternoon, but right now I'm up and ready. What about you, Kiele?" she called across the corridor.

"I'm too travel-dizzy to be able to sleep now. Don't worry about us, Mother. When fatigue hits, we'll let you know."

Kaia put her arm over the plump shoulders of her oldest daughter. "All right, then. Drop off your stuff and come on up to the galley to have some brunch. Abdullah, our cook, has prepared something for us. The opening ceremonies are at noon, so we have a couple of hours to just relax."

Kaia herded her family around the breakfast table, which already held a platter of sandwiches and a pitcher of lemonade. Not knowing which was more polite, to leave or to stay, Joanna simply occupied herself close by, slicing tomatoes. From her position at the cutting-board counter, she studied the two girls, trying to get a sense of their personalities and of the family tensions.

Kiele had her mother's natural beauty—enormous eyes and full, sensual lips. But her dark-brown hair was blunt cut at shoulder length and drawn back in a short ponytail. With some attention and a very little bit of makeup, she would have been stunning, but for the fact that she was overweight and drably dressed. The tan blouse and long brown skirt would have better suited a fishmonger than a woman in her twenties. She also slouched, both when she walked and when she sat, giving the impression that she preferred not to be noticed.

Mei seemed the polar opposite. Her stronger and flatter Hawaiian features bore no resemblance to her mother's, and Joanna guessed she took after her father. But the wide Polynesian face was rendered attractive by its animation and by the ease with which she laughed. Her hair hung long and loose, so that she had to constantly brush it back behind her ears, but she seemed to enjoy running her fingers through it. Her clothing too was lighthearted, a yellow tee shirt with the periodic table on it, tucked into black denim jeans. She sat with one sandal-clad foot drawn up on the seat of her chair, her arm around her knee. "I'm really liking this place," she announced, glancing around. "I hope we get to spend a lot of time here."

"We can be here as much as you like. After the opening dive, I'm sure you'll both want to rest in your cabins for a few hours. Or loll around on deck. But then tonight, we'll have a sort of party with some of our friends from the project."

Mei brushed her hair back. "Like the parties you and Bernard used to throw for your fake filmy friends? That doesn't sound like too much fun."

"Oh, they're not at all like people in film. I haven't met their families, but Gil and Charlie and Marion themselves are all down-to-earth people. They're not Bernard's friends. They're mine. I know you'll like them."

The older daughter seemed to have no interest in the party plans. With her arms folded guardedly under her bosom, she let her gaze wander around the salon and return to her mother. "You told us on the phone that you and Bernard had separated. Why finally now, after all these years? Is he out of the country, or is he going to show up at some point?"

"As for why we've separated, I don't want to go into that now, but on the question of where he is, I actually don't know. I expected him to fly back to New York, but one of the crewmen said he saw him in the village. If he comes back, it will only be to collect some of his things and I won't let him stay. In any case, it's not only a separation. I'm going to divorce him."

"It's about time," Mei exclaimed offhandedly, then bit into one of the sandwiches.

Kiele frowned. "How are you going to manage that? I thought he was your agent and the one who got you all your work."

"He is, I mean, was. But I'll find another agent. I may be unemployed awhile, but I have other friends in the business and I'll be all right." Kaia didn't sound terribly convinced by her own optimism, but the announcement was made.

"Why now? Why didn't you dump the creep years ago?" Kiele repeated.

"Because everything's different now, and anyhow, I'd rather we talked about that later in the week when we've got more time."

Mei would not be so easily put off. "What's different? Seriously, what's changed? Why can't we discuss it now? You've got me curious."

Kaia fell silent for a moment. "Because…" She took a long breath. "Because I only now found out what he did to you," she said, her voice breaking.

"I don't want to talk about that." Kiele dropped her sandwich back on her plate. "I didn't take a week's leave from my job and fly all the way here to drag out ancient history. It happened a long time ago and has no relevance to anything now." She slid her chair back and stood up, but Kaia laid a gentle hand on her arm. "Please, darling" she said. "We do have to talk about it, but only for a while. Then we'll be done with it. It's already over for you, but not for me." She drew her daughter back down onto her chair.

Mei glanced back and forth, seeming confused, at her mother and sister. "What are you guys talking about?"

"He kept photographs in his safe." Kaia paused again, then quietly, as if hating the words, said, "Of child pornography, and of you too, as children. But I just found them and I don't know how far it went. I *have* to know what happened and try to understand how I could have not seen it all those years."

"I don't understand what the big deal is." On the other side of the table, Mei threw up both her hands. "He just shot a few stupid pictures of us taking off our bathing suits."

"No. It was more than just the photos." Kiele stared into the distance. "You've obviously forgotten. It wasn't a few pictures. It was a lot of them. And he touched us. He made us touch him. The bastard," she muttered, closing her eyes as if willing the memory away. Then she came back to life.

"How could you have been so blind?" she snapped at her mother. "That whole year, he was after us all the time. You didn't see any of that? I began to lock the door to the bedroom when we went to bed."

Mei winced. "I don't remember that much any more. Just that I didn't like it when he made those 'photo shoots,' as he called them. They made me feel a little dirty, and then guilty."

"Why didn't you come to me and simply tell me? I would have believed you." Kaia was close to tears.

"I don't know, really." Mei shrugged. "Maybe there just wasn't any time when we could get to you. On the rare occasions you were home, you were always on the phone talking to this or that important person, arranging interviews, photo shoots, worrying about your weight, your wardrobe. And he told us never to bother you because you were busy working on your movies. We knew that he was the one who got you all your jobs, and we were afraid that if we caused trouble, it would harm your career. It sounds stupid now, but we were kids, and it was easy for him to mess with our minds."

Kiele took up a clean butter knife and absentmindedly traced a pattern on the tablecloth. "He made it pretty clear. We could keep on playing along and being his 'sugar girls,' as he called us, or we could go back to being poor in Hawaii. I didn't like being poor. I liked dressing up and having nice things." She drew a line through the pattern she'd made. "But after him, I stopped caring about that."

"Then he bought us the horse," Mei added.

"Yeah, the horse." Kiele snorted. "First the threats and then the bribery."

"We named him Wind," Mei said wistfully. "It was Kiele's idea, but I liked the name too, because riding him made me feel free. Although 'riding him' mostly meant wandering around the paddock. Still, he was this wonderful, beautiful, powerful thing, and he belonged to us."

"I liked him too, but I knew why we got him." Kiele laid down the knife and stared through the salon window out at the sea.

Kaia wiped her eyes with her napkin. "Did he…" She choked out the words. "Did he rape you?"

"Rape?" Kiele snorted again. "If you mean in that big melodramatic way where they tear off your clothes and stick it in you, no. Nothing like that. But he still messed us up. Me, anyhow. He taught me shame and disgust."

She chewed her lip and it seemed that she'd spent her anger, but after a breath, she continued. "Do you remember when we were little and you read *Peter Pan* to us? You told us that in Neverland there were not only the Lost Boys, but Lost Girls too, so we could enjoy the story more. You married that creep years later, but I remembered, and even when I was sixteen, I wanted to run away and be a Lost Girl. That's how much I hated him." She paused again in her tirade.

"Imagine. When other teenagers were already shagging boys, I was dreaming of bloody Tinkerbell. I'd see a shrink, but I'd have to tell him the guy who molested me is the agent and husband of the Great Actress Kaia Kapulani." She took a short breath. "God, how I despise him." Her mouth began to tremble and she finally fell silent.

"I'll bring charges against him." Kaia embraced her daughter. "There's no statute of limitations on child molestation. I'll put the bastard in jail for life."

Kiele disengaged herself. "What's the point? It was over fifteen years ago, and charging him won't change anything." She bit off the corner of her sandwich, as if eating would soothe her rage. "It'll just stir up all the dirt. I have a good job and I love teaching young kids. I don't want people at my school to look at me with pity."

"But I can't bear the thought of his getting away with that. What if he molests other children?"

"If he didn't all those years after we left, he probably won't now," Mei said. "Kiele's right, Ma. Accusing him might make you feel a little less guilty, but really, it'll just make life miserable for all of us."

"But it was criminal of him, and criminal of me to have not seen it because I had my head wrapped up in my career. I feel like I have to make it up to you somehow."

"Well, you could buy us another horse," Mei quipped.

"What?"

"Sorry, it was a joke. A bad one. But listen, Ma. Just get rid of the bastard and never talk to him again. Get another agent. I mean, you won't be unemployed. You got an Academy Award, for God's sake."

"Of course. I'm not worried about work. But it won't be that simple to ignore him. If he doesn't get what he wants in the divorce settlement, he'll try to ruin my career. It's easy for him to start a whisper campaign around the studios. He just picks up a phone, and by the next day it's the universal gossip. Making and breaking stars is his métier."

"How can he smear you? You haven't done anything," Kiele said.

"No, I haven't *done* anything, but he knows about Joanna and me."

"Joanna and you…what?" Kiele glanced back toward Joanna in her discreet corner, who had continued cutting the tomatoes into ever-smaller bits, then back at her mother.

"That we're…that I love her," Kaia said.

After a moment of tense silence in the salon Mei burst out laughing. "My mother is a lesbian! How cool is *that*?!"

Kiele still frowned, but seemingly more out of consternation than disapproval. "Seems a little weird to me, I mean after so many years?" She glanced again furtively at Joanna, who had remained silent throughout the whole family discussion. "At least it's someone who won't try to control you."

"I don't know how 'cool' it is, Mei. It's just what happened. I've never been so happy, and I love her enough to take the chance of the public disgrace it might bring."

"Public disgrace? Oh, c'mon, Ma. This is the twenty-first century. It's no big deal any more. Certainly not in Hollywood. Look at Ellen and Martina and Melissa. No way can he shame you with that."

"Well, he'll certainly try."

"Let him." Mei poured herself another glass of lemonade. "Even if we don't jail him, karma will come round and bite him in the ass. You'll see."

Behind her countertop of butchered tomatoes, Joanna glanced at her watch and spoke up for the first time. "I'm sorry to interrupt, but it's almost time for the opening ceremonies, and we really should get ready."

Obviously relieved at the change of subject, Kiele stood up from her chair. "Great. Just tell us what we need to take with us. Mom said we could snorkel while the two of you were diving. Is that true?"

"Yes, we'll be paddling all around the site taking pictures, but you should be able to see us at least part of the time," Joanna said. "Most of the exhibition is about twelve meters down, so you won't see any of the details, but you'll have an overview of the city. Fortunately, the upper part of my exhibit—which is where your mother's statue is—stands at about nine meters, so you'll get a pretty good view."

"I've got masks and snorkels for you already. They're right here." Kaia opened one of the lockers under the running bench in the salon and pulled out two net bags. "They're identical, so don't fight now over which one gets the green one and which one the blue." Kaia smiled for the first time that morning, playing at being mother again, as her two daughters took their respective kits and traipsed down the staircase to get ready.

Joanna came out from the galley and embraced her cautiously. "They're wonderful, your daughters. Smart, attractive, real survivors. They seem to take care of each other too."

"Yes, they do. Thank God, since obviously I didn't take good enough care of them. And I can't even protect them now."

"What do you mean?"

"I mean, what happens now? I didn't want to dwell on it with the girls, but I don't see how things can turn out well. Charges or no, if I reveal Bernard's sleazy past, the press will eat it up. It will make major headlines that will taint the girls *and* me. Who wants to have people look at them and think instantly of child molestation? They just want to have normal lives, and I just want to go on making movies."

She shoved her hands into her pockets, a sign of helplessness. "And if we say nothing, he's won. He's already so angry that I'm sure he'll try to hurt me. He'll find a way, I know."

Joanna embraced her again. "Look, you can rebuild, no matter what happens. You have your daughters and the air is cleared. You're gorgeous and talented, and people will still want to make movies with you. In the meantime, you can take a few months off and let the dust settle."

"Mmm." Kaia nodded hesitantly. "You know, earlier this year I got two invitations to do live theater. One was to do Ibsen at the Mark Taper Forum in Los Angeles and the other was for a *Macbeth* in New York. Bernard refused both of them. He said they didn't pay enough and kept me too much out of sight. If the offers had just come a few months later, I might have a job."

"You're really so determined to do theater again."

"Oh, yes. I just have to figure out how to get through the door and—"

"Okay, team, let's get this show on the road." Mei appeared at the head of the stairs. She wore shorts, but the top of her bathing suit was visible in the opening of her Hawaiian-print shirt, and her snorkel jutted out of the small knapsack she held on her shoulder.

Kiele came up directly behind her, still drab and dumpy in a loose blouse and fat-girl skirt, but she carried a mask and snorkel in her shoulder bag as well. "You did say it started at noon, and it's half past eleven now. Where's it taking place, anyhow?"

"On the barge right over there," Kaia said, pointing through the salon window. "We'll go in our own dinghy, since we'll need it later anyhow. Jibril's already loaded it with our diving gear."

"Okay then, let's get going." Mei said, as if she were one of the organizers of the afternoon. They marched single file through the salon and down the steps to the stern deck, where Jibril held the guide rope to the inflatable.

They climbed in, and once they'd distributed themselves and their gear, he started the outboard motor.

"This is going to be a great day," Mei exclaimed.

Jibril smiled, coldly, it seemed to Joanna, and muttered, *"Inshallah."*

CHAPTER TWENTY-FOUR

Within moments, they were at the barge that had sent down all the objects of the exhibit, and Joanna smiled at the sight. Having completed all the heavy lifting and lowering of the objects, its powerful crane no longer held a steel hook but simply flew the flag of Egypt. The work was well and truly over.

The artists had been instructed to arrive on the barge before noon. The ceremony would last about an hour, and at its conclusion, several official dive boats would collect the divers and their equipment from the barge and ferry them the five hundred meters to the exhibition site.

But Joanna knew how those things went in Egypt. Rather than deal with confusion and delay and problems of where to store their diving gear during the ceremony, she chose independence. They would arrive at the barge by dinghy, and Jibril would simply wait for them on the water with their gear. At the end of the ceremony, he'd take them the final distance to the underwater city and they'd be among the first in the water.

When they pulled up at the rear of the barge, the number of small passenger boats jockeying for space at one of the two ladders made it clear that others had come up with the same idea.

They climbed the portside ladder onto the barge, and Joanna noted that many of the lockers, winches, and other machinery had been unbolted from the deck, and rows of benches had been installed in their place. At the forefront stood the inevitable podium, where various dignitaries would give their official blessings. Cameras were set up on rolling tripods on both sides, and press already occupied the front-row benches. Clearly the committee had prepared well for publicity.

At the rear of the barge, where they had boarded, an area had been blocked off for people to line up so passenger boats could collect them and ferry them to the buoys over the exhibit. It was a reasonable and well-thought-out system, though Joanna was glad she'd prepared an alternative.

The majority of the audience was made up of divers, and their tanks—some thirty of them—lay in rows along the two gunwales of the barge. Family members and snorkelers made up the next group, and another dozen-or-so apparent tourists. Only a very few people—presumably officials and politicians—arrived in suits.

Joanna surveyed the wide deck until she located the other artists in a cluster, most with family members. Khadija was there with her husband, and a quick glance around also revealed Sanjit, Japhet, Yousef, and Rami, as well as a row of Egyptians who she thought might be the original architects of the buildings. Three rows farther along she spotted Marion in close conversation with the woman she'd danced with in the Sun Bar before its destruction. Well, well. Good for her.

Gil sat directly in front of them along with his wife, two sons, and a child about five, presumably his granddaughter. Noting that the bench in front of the Collins clan was "reserved" with towels, Joanna led her own clan along the row. "Is this for us, I hope?"

"Of course it is. Did you think we'd forget you?" Gil pulled away the towels and balled them up, until his wife took them out of his hands and folded them.

Once seated, Joanna twisted around to talk to them.

"This is Jacqueline, my wife…" Gil tilted his head toward the woman at his side, who stopped folding the towels and offered her hand. Under simply coiffed gray hair, her wide face held the same amiably squinting eyes of her husband. "She'll take care of our granddaughter while we're under. And these are my two boys, Oliver and Peter."

The young men, both in their thirties, shook hands with the new arrivals. Oliver, athletic and with black buzz-cut hair, said "helloo there" with great warmth, but his attention shifted away quickly when the little girl climbed onto his lap. Peter was physically softer and plump, and the image of his father. But while Gil's hair was white, Peter's was shaggy and red. He offered a quiet, self-conscious smile.

"These are my daughters, Kiele and Mei," Kaia said, and the four Collins adults nodded in lieu of yet another set of handshakes.

"Are you going to dive?" Peter directed his question toward Kiele. Mei answered for them both. "No, we're still at the snorkeling stage."

"Yeah, we're not into the heavy-metal stuff," Kiele said with atypical wit.

"Oh, that's too bad." Peter's glance lingered on Kiele a fraction of a second longer than it should have.

Was it Joanna's imagination, or did Kiele notice it too and lower her eyes?

"Anyone seen Charlie?" Joanna asked.

"I'm right here," he said, moving into the bench row where they sat. "Just got here. I had to stow my gear in the dinghy we're using. This, by the way, is my lovely wife Viviane." An attractive woman in her early sixties and wearing a Harley-Davidson tee shirt nodded greeting to everyone just as the piercing whine from the speakers sounded, indicating that the microphone on the podium had gone live.

When the public quieted down, the government liaison with the committee—Joanna couldn't remember his name—spoke a few banal words of congratulations and then introduced the president of Egypt.

To polite applause, Hosni Mubarak stepped up to the podium. His speech, in English, was brief, merely articulating the theme of the ceremony and the exhibit. Egypt, land of monuments and antiquities was taking its place in the modern world of art and ecological concern. He made only an oblique reference to the bomb attack in the Sun Bar by saying, "Egypt moves ever forward, and the forces of ignorance and extremism will never pull us back." Then he surrendered the podium to Rashid Gamal.

"Thank you, ladies and gentlemen," Gamal said in the same self-congratulatory vein as the two other speakers. With its collection of foreign artists, he gave the world to know that the city was both Egyptian and international, in the same way that the pyramids were. He hinted that other announcements about the site were forthcoming, and Joanna guessed that meant a press release about the horde of tablets. If that was the case, had his office obtained any transliterations and thus knew how explosive at least some of the texts were?

A series of other speeches followed, from the minister of the interior, from a representative of USAID, and from a seemingly endless line of committee members. Finally the announcement came that divers wanting to see the exhibit should suit up and get in line for the small craft going to the site.

"That doesn't mean us, does it?" Kiele asked.

"Nope, we're ready to go. Just follow me." Joanna gave a quick departure kiss to Gil and Charlie and began to guide the family to the port-side ladder. Kiele held back for a moment in conversation with Peter and was in danger of disappearing in the crowd that surged toward the stern.

"Come on, dear. We don't want to lose you," Kaia said, linking arms with her.

"Okay, okay," Kiele said, then called back over her shoulder, "I'll be over the train station, whatever that is."

Jibril waited impassively out on the water, and when Kaia caught his attention, he motored directly under the ladder and tied up. Ten minutes later, they were at the familiar buoy where Joanna and Kaia wrestled on their wetsuits. Boats began arriving after them and tying up at the five other buoys, distributing the divers over the surface of the whole city.

"Okay, here's the program," Joanna said. "Kaia and I are going to make the rounds with the camera. You should be able to see us when we're on this side of the exhibit, especially over the fountain. Everyone's wearing a black wetsuit, so it's going to be hard to tell people apart, but remember Kaia's suit has the turquoise arms and her fins are light green. My fins are yellow. But if you lose sight of us, don't worry. Just stay close to the dinghy and...well...have fun. Jibril will help you back on board whenever you want."

"We shouldn't be down for more than thirty or forty minutes," Kaia added. She clipped on her weight belt and threaded her arms into the buoyancy vest, while Jibril held onto the heavy air tank.

"What's this?" Joanna asked, taking hold of a tip of the duct tape on the bottom of Kaia's tank.

"Just a marker, miss, to show the tank is full," Jibril said, avoiding her glance. He peeled it off and dropped it into the bottom of the dinghy.

Joanna made a brief check of mask fit and flow of air. "We ready?"

Kaia nodded agreement, and when it was clear that no divers were underneath them, they toppled backward into the water.

After the pleasant shock of submersion Joanna surfaced again for a moment, in time to see Kiele and Mei splash into the water with their snorkels.

They sank slowly, allowing ears and sinuses to adjust to the doubling of atmospheric pressure, and in a few moments they hovered in front of the railroad station near the locomotive. Joanna confirmed that the two girls were floating spread-eagle directly overhead and peering down at them. Kiele waved and Joanna waved back but noticed with amusement that one of the other divers near the locomotive was waving as well.

It was apparently one of Gil's sons, since Gil was close by, his gray hair floating in a halo around his head. He was posing by the locomotive while the other of the two boys took pictures with a large underwater camera. Joanna palmed over next to him and snapped a few photos with her own little Canon 100. Then she and Kaia began the counterclockwise circle of the city.

She led Kaia first toward the long gallery, and as they swam under the arcade she saw Charlie kneeling on the floor next to his fiberglass skeleton, posing for pictures under his Shakespearean quotation. Two other divers, whom she didn't recognize, were studying the text with their lamps.

Rather than disturb Charlie's star-turn, she drew Kaia along to the other statues under the arcade, Rami's acrobats, and the daring set by Japhet. Labeled "Band of Brothers," it depicted four men in a sort of chain embrace. One stood loosely embraced from the rear by a second man, who leaned back cheek-to-cheek with the third man, who in turn was held by the arm of a fourth.

She snapped another picture, laughing inwardly. The naïve might imagine it was a family of particularly affectionate brothers, but a more jaded eye could recognize it as an homage to queer love. Japhet, that sly dog, had smuggled in a work of gay art, in much the same way Michelangelo had smuggled it into the Sistine Chapel, with the full approval of the authorities.

They passed through the center of the city and Khadija's semicircle of Palestinians, one of them headless. A curve to the right brought them to Yoshi's dragon goddess, hunched over itself with gaping jaws and outstretched wings. Joanna took her next photo.

Kaia was already ahead of her at an archway that led to a walled enclosure and Eliezar's group of musicians. A violinist, cellist, and flutist silently performed some piece of chamber music. She imagined it to be Vivaldi.

Emerging from the court, they swung again to the right to a field of animal sculptures, Sanjit's smuggled-in Hindu gods: Ganesh, Vishnu, Hanuman. They did an about-face to confront two splendid Arabian horses sculpted in bronze by Faisal. Other divers were drifting down to straddle their backs to be photographed riding under water.

Kaia was already paddling toward the next exhibit that stood between two pylons—the iconic "Great Balance" weighing the heart in the underworld that Marion had created. The Balance was half again the height of a man, and the two dishes, one holding a heart and the other a feather, swung slightly in the current. Attending the balance was a rather ferocious jackal-headed Anubis and a slightly comic ibis-headed Thoth. Off to one side, as a detached observer, sat the blue-tinted figure of Osiris.

As Joanna took her photos, Charlie swam up behind them and, after waving recognition, he tugged on one of the dishes. To Joanna's amusement—and apparently that of half a dozen other divers—the dish dropped down half a meter and the other dish rose, revealing that it was a functioning balance. Coral growth, if not careless tourists, would soon bring an end to that, though the frozen-faced blue Osiris didn't seem to care.

They swung around, completing the circle, and Joanna glanced back at Kaia, who seemed to be fatiguing. As a precaution, she swam close and made a quick check of her pressure gauge, but her tank was still at half.

They had arrived at the fountain now, where other divers were already gathered around the seated girls. Joanna moved up the slope to the figures of Lot and Atiyah. Sunlight still penetrated at the shallow depth and seemed to dance around the two statues. *Ironic*, she thought. It suggested a benediction, but the scene was one of murder.

More people were arriving, some of them with cameras in hand, and it seemed like a good time to spring the surprise. Joanna turned in a circle, searching for Kaia, but didn't see her among the divers. Then she glanced downward toward the sea floor.

To her horror, Kaia was on hands and knees with her head lowered, and she swayed sideways, thrashing, as if losing consciousness. For a brief second, Joanna was rocked by horror and disbelief. How long had Kaia been without air?

Then training kicked in.

With a flick of her fins, she was at Kaia's side. Pulling free her auxiliary mouthpiece with one hand, she seized Kaia by the shoulder with the other and spun her around. But Kaia's mouthpiece was still in place, and bubbles rose normally through the outlet valve. Only her mask had come off and her eyes were pressed tightly shut against the bite of the super-salted water. It was clear now why she was thrashing. She had been groping blindly in the water in front of her searching for the mask. And there it was, lying on the sea bed beside her.

Other divers were arriving, ready to help, but it appeared the problem was only the displaced mask. Joanna stroked Kaia's cheek to reassure her, then took up the mask and stretched it over her head again, brushing loose hair from under the soft plastic. Once it was in place, Kaia nodded and blew air from her nose to empty it of water. She opened her eyes and, though her chest still heaved, signaled that she was fine.

At that moment, a diver, by the size of him a young teenager, arrived with one fin on his foot and the other in his hand. He mimed striking Kaia on the head, and it was clear then that in the crush of people, he had inadvertently knocked her mask off with a clumsy fin-stroke. He slid his foot back into the fin, then paddled over in front of Kaia, making prayer hands in an apparent apology. Kaia seemed to have regained composure by then, and her outstretched hands gestured conciliation. When Joanna pointed toward the surface, Kaia signaled *no*.

As the cluster of alarmed divers began to dissipate Charlie suddenly appeared, looking puzzled. There was no way to explain what had happened, but also no need, for the three of them hovering together seemed to re-establish normalcy and calm. Joanna decided to carry on with her surprise.

Leaving Kaia at Charlie's side she paddled back to the fountain and, after a brief search at the base, located the hidden hose. She pressed her auxiliary mouthpiece against the opening and filled the reservoir with some ten bars of compressed air, the maximum the hidden cylinder could hold. A moment later, a string of little bubbles rose from the center of the fountain. The hovering divers watched the ascending stream of air, apparently amused. A few of them waved others over to witness the trick.

But there was more.

Joanna tucked the hose back into its place and beckoned Kaia to follow her up the slope. Charlie came up behind them, followed by several others, and she brought them all to a halt before the figure of Atiyah.

The effect was all she could have hoped for.

Atiyah lived again. Though she stood just before her execution, she too gave forth bubbles of air from between her parted lips. Cameras flashed and video cameras scanned across the scene, and Joanna was elated. Though her own hands had added the hidden conduit from the fountain reservoir, she could almost imagine that the troubled spirit of Atiyah had come to rest and breathed again through the lovely mouth of Kaia Kapulani.

Charlie squeezed Joanna's shoulder in congratulations. Kaia clasped her hands in front of her face and was clearly stirred.

But Joanna had still to end the tale.

Leaving her companions on the slope, she descended again to the fountain and located the tip of the duct tape she had attached in the workshop. The fountain was bolted to the sea floor now, and it was safe to reveal its message. So, before the eyes of half a dozen divers and photographers, she drew back the tape, exposing the deeply carved inscription that ran along the base.

BELOVED GOMORRAH.

Winding the tape into a little ball, she allowed herself to drift away, letting the others move in to examine the enigmatic words. Few would make the connection with the story of Lot. It would remain a puzzle until knowledge of the tablets filtered back to Egypt. Even then, if the declaration stirred religious anger, there was little anyone could do about it. An inscription was not like a statue's head and could not be smashed so easily with a hammer. Only nature would cover it with coral, in its own good time.

But Charlie understood and brought his palms together in silent applause. Seeing him, Kaia water-clapped as well, though she knew only part of the story. Then, oddly, a half dozen others joined in the gesture. Joanna spotted Marion among them and realized that at least some of the crowd were her fellow artists who remembered the conversations in the Sun Bar and got the joke.

Joanna returned to Kaia's side and crossed her forearms in front of her, signaling, *Let's go up.* It had been a good day.

❖

When she broke the surface, Joanna felt a twinge of guilt for dwelling on her own success and not checking on Kaia's welfare. As soon as Kaia appeared next to her in the water, she removed her mouthpiece. "Are you okay?" she called out. "Seeing you on your knees that way gave me a real fright."

"Me too, but you did everything right. Actually, I think I did too, staying calm and all that. But I can tell you I was pretty relieved when you arrived and found my mask."

"Well, you were a trouper yourself, clearing the mask and carrying on without a whimper. I was proud of you."

"Hey, Ma! Joanna! Over here!" Joanna followed the sound and spotted Mei waving from their dinghy among the half dozen other inflatables close by. Jibril sat next to her, upright and tense, as if waiting for his next order.

Kaia waved back and they paddled together to the boat.

Following protocol, Joanna handed up her weight belt first, then removed her vest and air tank for Jibril to lift aboard. With a heave from the water, she clambered over the side of the dinghy and turned to help Kaia climb in behind her.

Mei gave her mother a hug. "That was really cool, Ma. I had a great time and I could see you both when you came back to the fountain. But it looked like you had some trouble there toward the end."

Jibril was suddenly attentive. "You had problems with the air, missus?"

"Nothing like that. There was a crowd around the fountain. Then some kid struck me in the face with a fin and knocked my mask off. But it was nothing, really, and Joanna came to the rescue. Forget about that."

She relaxed against the gunwale and pried off her fins. "I want us all to remember how wonderful today is. Could you make out Joanna's fountain scene? Could you see the air bubbles coming from my statue?"

Mei shook her head. "Not really. From this angle, it was like looking down into a huge aquarium. You guys were like big humpback black fish swimming around toy castles. I really have to learn scuba now, Kiele too. Snorkeling just doesn't do it."

"Where *is* Kiele?" Kaia glanced around.

Joanna pointed over Kaia's shoulder to where, less then ten meters away, Kiele was in animated conversation with a diver. She kept afloat by lying on her back and hanging onto his inflated vest. Her snorkel was tucked up near her forehead, and it was clear that the conversation held her interest more than the underwater spectacle.

"Looks like someone found other entertainment," Joanna remarked.

"For God's sake, don't tease her, either of you," Kaia commanded. Whoever it is, the more friends she makes the better."

"It's Peter Collins, and he *is* nice," Mei said. "He works in an animal shelter and he's studying to be a veterinarian. He's really shy though, and says he likes animals better than people."

"You found out all of that while we were under water?"

"Yeah, well, you guys were down there for a long time, and he popped up a couple of times to talk to us. Well, mostly to Kiele. They seem to have hit it off."

"Sounds like a perfect match." Kaia beamed maternally.

"Well, don't get any ideas, Ma. She'd hate it if she thought you were watching her."

"Don't worry, I'll be discreet. We'll all be discreet, won't we, Joanna?"

Joanna puckered her lips and turned an imaginary key in front of her mouth. Minutes later, when Kiele arrived back at the dinghy and Mei pulled her in, Joanna took pains to be looking elsewhere.

"Ah, there you are," Kaia said, as if she had just noticed there was another person in the boat. "Could you see Joanna's fountain?"

"Only the tops of everyone's heads. But I spotted the statue that was supposed to be you. The one about to be bonked by her husband."

"Not bonked, dear. Murdered."

Was it Joanna's imagination, or did Jibril flinch at the word murder? She couldn't tell.

"Yeah, what's up with that, Joanna?" Mei lolled next to her mother, one hand trailing in the water as they motored back to the yacht.

"It's a portrayal of Lot, killing his wife. A Bible story, but it's not the one you're probably familiar with. Anyhow, I just used your mother's face because it's beautiful and I wanted to immortalize it."

"Until it's covered with algae." Kiele snickered.

Joanna smiled. "Ah, someone's been doing their research. Yes, you're right. After a year or so, it will be. Thus passes glory."

"Don't remind me of passing glory." Kaia kicked her playfully. "I'm fifty years old today, remember?"

They arrived at the stern of the *Hina* and stepped up one by one while Jibril handed up the equipment. When he finally hoisted himself onto the deck, Kaia faced him.

"Thank you, Jibril, for all your help preparing the dives, and for the birthday party too. I need you to work this evening if you can, but of course I'll pay you for the extra time. You've been very good to us and I don't want to take advantage of you."

Jibril looked away. "Yes, missus," he mumbled, and hauled both of the steel air tanks up the stairs to the higher deck.

Joanna watched him, more puzzled than ever. What bleak thoughts were simmering in the man's mind?

CHAPTER TWENTY-FIVE

On the upper deck of the *Hina*, Joanna and Kaia leaned against the railing and watched the sun fall below the horizon. The searing yellow ball suddenly flickered out and left a salmon-colored sky, while in the east, a scattering of stars was already visible.

Kaia stroked Joanna's forearm then reached down to her hand and let their fingers entwine. "I'm so proud of you. Your talent, your courage. That's a wonderful thing you've made down there. Several wonderful things, in fact." She pointed with her chin toward the exhibition site. "I wonder what people will think about the inscription."

"I suppose a few will run and check their Bibles to see what they might have missed. Later, when people learn about the tablets and get the reference, who knows? In any case, I'm done with it for now. I'm here with you and that's all I care about tonight." Joanna lifted Kaia's hand and brought it to her lips, tasting a faint saltiness on her skin.

"I love being with you and my girls. I wish we could stay like this forever." Kaia exhaled wearily. "And I dread the next few weeks. Divorce proceedings, fighting Bernard, looking for an agent, avoiding the press."

"Just take one day at a time. I hate clichés, but that one is true. I'll help you get through it. The girls will help you too. You've got them back again now and they both seem very resilient."

As if on cue, Mei emerged from the stairs and joined them, taking her place at the railing. Kaia shoulder-bumped her. "Where's Kiele?"

"In the galley helping Abdullah make dinner. She's learning how to cook, Egyptian style."

"Oh, dear. Abdullah's galley is his private domain. I hope she isn't hurt if he throws her out. He throws me out all the time."

"Apparently he hasn't," Mei said. "When I left them, they were getting on like a house afire. Although I think the last thing she needs is to learn how to make food taste better." She perused the darkening sky. "Nice night. No light pollution, tons of stars."

Kaia gazed upward. "The last time we sat out here looking at stars, Joanna pointed out the Hunter. I thought I could spot him, but I don't see him now."

"Orion, you mean," Mei said. "No, by now Orion has set."

"You know the constellations? Since when?"

"Since I studied science at the university. I mean, duh! Cosmology, after all, *is* the study of the stars, along with particle physics, of course."

"Of course." Kaia mocked her gently. "So, Miss Cosmology-pants, name the constellations that *are* up there."

"Hmm. I'm more used to the sky over California, but let's see. Over there to the north are the easy ones, Ursa Major and Minor or, as you normal mortals say, the Big and Little Dipper. Toward the west is Leo, that little cluster in the southwest is Sagittarius, and right in front of it, more or less trailing behind Orion, is Scorpio."

"Isn't there a myth about the scorpion killing Orion?"

"I don't keep track of all the myths that go with the names, and astrology is a joke. We only learn the constellations to identify the neighborhood of a given star. Everyone knows that star clusters are not on one plane, so the zodiac images are simply patterns projected by superstitious primitives."

Joanna smiled at the blithe way Mei dismissed a field of study that had occupied several cultures for thousands of years. She was right, of course, but time would probably teach her to temper her contempt. Or maybe not.

The sound of people talking on the dock below interrupted her. "Oh, right. We told our guests to be here at eight. We'd better go down."

Charlie and Viviane had already come aboard and Jibril was just leading them into the salon. After a round of air kisses, Charlie handed over a bottle in a crumpled paper bag. "It's champagne. You have no *idea* what I had to go through to get any quality stuff here. We refrigerated it before we came, so it's already cold."

"Oh, thank you," Kaia gave him a second kiss. "We've got plenty of wine and beer aboard, but I didn't think to ask the men to buy champagne." She stepped back and gave Charlie's wife an admiring glance. "Viviane, I love your Harley-Davidson shirt. With the pants and jacket, it's a real Johnny Cash look. You'd be right at home at an agent's party."

"Well, I was going more for Marlon Brando, but Johnny Cash will do," Viviane laughed. Joanna led them toward a table with several wine bottles and began to fill their glasses. At that moment, Gil and tribe arrived and came up the stairs for another round of greetings.

Standing at the head of his family, Gil made the presentation. "In Ireland it's customary to give flowers for birthdays, but there's not much of a floral industry here, so we got you these." He flourished an oblong box, which seemed to be three-quarters filled with tissue paper. Reaching in carefully, Kaia uncovered a bouquet of glass flowers: roses, tulips, and what might have been petunias surrounded by glass greenery.

"Oh, it's exquisite," she exclaimed. Much better than the kind that die. Thank you so much."

Peter stepped forward awkwardly. "We also have something for Kiele and Mei." He presented envelopes to the two girls, giving each one a kiss on the cheek, then stepped back, his face turning pink.

Mei tore hers open with unashamed haste. "Hey, it's a certificate for an introductory dive at the dive center. The beginning of a course!" She beamed.

"Yeah, we thought you were really missing out by staying at the surface," Oliver added. "If you like the 'baptism' as they call it, you have time to learn the basics for a dive down to the exhibit before you leave. After you finish the course, they'll let you go to fifteen meters with a monitor."

"Oh, yay!" Mei exclaimed. "I was thinking about it, you know, but wasn't sure it was possible. So cool to find out it is." She hugged both boys with obvious glee.

Kiele held her unopened envelope to her chest. "Thank you for this. It's perfect," she said directly to Peter.

"Glad you like it," he replied, exhausting his repartee.

"Come on, everybody, sit down." Kaia waved her guests over to the table, diverting attention from the two.

"Does anyone know where Marion is?" Joanna pulled out chairs.

"Don't worry about her," Charlie said. "She'll be along later. She took her girlfriend on a night dive to the city."

"Her girlfriend's a diver?"

"Yup, two stars. On vacation here with her brother. Why do you think Marion snapped her up like a seagull would a French fry? Anyhow, if everyone's arrived, I suggest we open the champagne while it's still cold." Charlie stood at the foot of the table while everyone found a seat. After urging the cork from the bottle to a well-controlled pop, he filled each glass, and the company raised a toast.

"To Kaia," Charlie said.

"To good friends," Kaia replied.

"To good friends at the Red Sea," Joanna amended, and everyone drank.

When all were seated again, Joanna leaned across the table toward Viviane. "I want you to know, Charlie has been a lifesaver. Literally, of course. I don't know how much he told you about the accident, but he not only saved me from the sharks. He stood by me like a trooper afterward."

Viviane glanced affectionately at her husband. "That sounds like him. The trooper part, I mean. The shark rescue was a first."

"Do you dive with him?" Kaia asked.

Viviane shook her head. "No, that's not my thing. Charlie says I have claustrophobia, which makes it sound like a sickness, but basically I prefer to get my air from the air and not sucked from a tube. I also like traveling at a higher speed than you do down there. But we ride our Harleys together. I'd much rather have bugs on my goggles than seaweed in my hair."

Conversation stopped for a moment as Abdullah and Jibril came from the galley bearing steaming tureens of seafood and rice. "Egyptian paella," Kaia announced, and passed the first of them to Gil's wife Jacqueline.

Catching Viviane's eye, Mei asked, "Do you have a real Harley-Davidson?" She scooped seafood onto her plate, adroitly avoiding the mussels.

"Yes I do. We both do. You ever ridden one?"

"No, but I'd sure like to. Are they expensive to maintain?"

"Hey, now don't lure my daughter into motorcycles." Kaia laughed, "At least not until she's finished school."

"Oh, you're a student? What are you studying?" Viviane's question allowed motorcycles to drop from the conversation.

Mei's fork stopped midway to her mouth. "Particle physics, with a specialization in cosmology. I'll start graduate school in the fall at Stanford, to work with their linear accelerator. It's an antique though. What I really want to do is work at the LHC in Geneva."

"The LHC? What's the LHC?" Oliver asked.

"A particle accelerator, built to look for the Higgs-boson particle." The fork made it to her mouth.

"Higgs boson particle?" Oliver was still at sea, and Joanna suspected everyone else at the table was as well.

Mei chewed for a moment. "The one missing part to the Standard Model of sub-atomic particles. You know, quarks and neutrinos, and other teensy-weensy things. They also call it the theory of almost everything."

Oliver looked up through his eyebrows. "Riiiight," he said, and began eating in earnest.

Joanna redirected the conversation. "Jacqueline, what do you think of Gil's project? You've seen it, of course."

Jacqueline brushed back a strand of white hair and beamed like Mrs. Santa Claus. "Not under water, but of course I watched the whole thing develop when he made all the drawings. And today I saw the top of it from the boat. I'm so happy for him. He's always loved trains."

"Yeah, you should have seen all the train sets he built for me and my brother." Peter set down his glass. "Little wooden ones when we were babies, then electric ones when we were older. But the one he made here is the biggest toy train he's ever played with."

"Can I play with the train too?" Gil's granddaughter asked, her little face just rising above the level of her plate.

Jacqueline took her napkin and wiped a piece of rice from the child's chin. "As soon as you know how to swim, Grandpa and Daddy will teach you how to snorkel, and then you can play with it."

"Fnorkel. I want to fnorkel."

"Yes, sweetheart. Here, drink your juice," Jacqueline said.

For the next ten minutes, the main sounds were the clattering of cutlery on porcelain and the murmuring of compliments. The paella was in fact excellent, and Joanna remembered the breakfast Abdullah had prepared for her on her first day. The man really had culinary talent. Any hotel in El Gouna should want him.

When the last sets of knives and forks were laid across plates, Abdullah appeared again to collect them and take them to the galley. A few moments later, he emerged bearing a chocolate cake, and Joanna stood up from the table.

"Ladies and gentlemen. Please raise your glasses for another toast. We are celebrating Kaia's birthday, of course. But I'd also like to announce the coming publication of an article in our museum journal, a transliteration of three clay tablets Charlie and I found on our first dive. There's no small connection between the tablets and the exhibit, and someday the world may recognize it."

"You might have to explain that a little," Charlie said.

"Well, in a nutshell, the tablets tell the morality tale of Sodom and Gomorrah. In reverse! That is, Sodom and Gomorrah were, in their time and place, as multicultural and colorful as our undersea City on the Plain, and religious fanatics destroyed them."

"To Sodom and Gomorrah then." Gil laughed, and everyone drank.

Charlie tapped the side of his glass with a spoon. "Yeah, yeah, all very well and good. But this is first and foremost a birthday party for Kaia. So, all of us, your friends, would like to present you with a gift." He stretched out his hand toward Gil's granddaughter. "The sacred object, if you please."

Beaming at her new office, the child handed a small box across the table toward Kaia.

Obviously bemused, Kaia took up the box and turned it in her hand for a moment, then tore it open. "What's this?" She lifted out what looked like a digital watch with an extremely large face. "Oh, my gosh. A diving computer!"

"Do you know how to use it?" Gil asked.

"No, of course I don't. I only know that it's supposed to tell me the depth and dive times. But don't worry, I'll learn. Joanna will teach me." She caressed the face of it with her thumb.

"We have something too, Ma," Mei said, and handed her another small package. Kaia fumbled with the wrappings and then held up a silver chain. Dangling from the bottom was the silver figure of a diver with all four limbs articulated, a tiny mask, mouthpiece, hose, air tank, and long curved fins.

"Oh, it's exquisite," Kaia said, holding it up. "Here, help me put it on." She handed it back and lowered her head while Kiele draped the chain around her neck and closed the clasp. Stroking it with her fingertips, she turned to Joanna. "Does this count toward accreditation?"

"Oh, I'm sure." Joanna laughed as she reached into a pocket. "I also have a gift. It's really only a possibility, so you're free to refuse without hurting anyone's feelings."

Kaia looked perplexed. "Refuse a gift from you? What *are* you talking about?"

"You remember when we talked about theater? You said you wanted to do Shakespeare one day, and I said I had relatives in the British theater. Who I meant was Michael Boyd, the artistic director of the Royal Shakespeare Company. He's my uncle on my mother's side. I called him and said you were interested in doing something and that you'd performed Shakespeare as a drama student. He was thrilled at the possibility of having a big name like yours in one of his productions. This is the fax he sent me yesterday."

She withdrew a folded single page and presented it uncere-moniously.

Speechless, Kaia unfolded and read it. "He wants me to play in the second cast of *The Tempest*," she said, awestruck. "As a female Prospero." She stared incredulously at the paper, reading it a second time.

"Do you think you might want to do it? I mean, learn all that Shakespearean English and be stuck for six months in Stratford-on-Avon and then London?"

"Of course I would. How can you doubt it? It's the perfect place to weather the coming year."

Mei cleared her throat conspicuously. "Excuse me, but I believe there is a chocolate cake getting old on the table. Has anyone got a knife?"

Abdullah, who still stood by the table, produced one from his apron pocket, and Joanna began the critical surgery.

At that moment, Jibril appeared at Kaia's shoulder. "Missus, can I talk to you privately? Outside?"

Puzzled, Kaia looked around at her company, clearly reluctant to leave the table. "Uh, well, yes. I suppose so." Consternation registered on her face as she followed him onto the stern deck. Charlie had begun to tell an anecdote, and the laughter coming from the salon was cut off as the glass doors closed behind them. Jibril motioned for her to sit on one of the fishing chairs.

"What is it, Jibril? Can't it wait until tomorrow?"

"I'm sorry, missus, but I have a very bad feeling."

"About what? What's wrong?" She glanced back at the salon doors.

"Well, you know I always fill your air tanks, yes?"

Kaia nodded, frowning.

"Okay. But yesterday, ah no, evening of the day before, I came back to the boat and saw Mr. Allen with the tanks. He was filling a third tank from the compressor."

"Hmm. I don't like him coming on the boat when I'm not here, but he still has a key so I shouldn't be surprised. He must have been filling a cylinder for himself."

"No, missus. The strange thing was, he exchanged the new tank for yours. He put your vest onto it and took your tank for himself. He even marked the new tank, with a small piece of tape. I don't know why."

"So what are you trying to say? I still don't see what you're worried about."

"I worry because I ask, why did Mr. Allen give you a new tank? I did not like that. It was a dishonor to me because I am always very careful, and with *my* tank I know you are safe. I was angry, and to save my honor, I changed them back."

"This is getting a little confusing. I dove with the tank that had the tape, and it was fine."

"Yes, because I gave you the good tank again, *my* tank. I put his little tape on it to fool him. If he looked, he would think you had the new tank, the third one. But I put the third tank to the side. And now I fear something terrible happened because of that one. I think I am guilty, but I don't know for what."

"What happened to the third tank? Is it still there?"

"That is why I am so afraid, missus. When I collected your equipment this morning, the third tank was gone and so was Mr. Allen's diving vest. I think he went into the water."

❖

Marion Zimmermann tied up the four-person inflatable to the buoy, feeling exceedingly lucky. Lucky that the committee had left the various personal boats at the disposal of the artists even after the opening ceremony of the exhibit, lucky that the opening had gone well and that the press had taken a lot of pictures of her work, and lucky most of all that she had met Maryke Vaal. What generous fate had brought the woman from the rich waters of South Africa to vacation, of all things, at the Red Sea? Lucky also that she could convince the woman, who had been keeping her at arm's length for a week, to forego the opening day dive in order to enjoy a private tour at night. If this didn't get Maryke into bed, nothing would.

Maryke sat across from her, snapping together her own buoyancy vest and checking the pressure valves on both their tanks, obviously professional enough to know the safety drill. They both had underwater lamps plus a backup light, full tanks, and a diving plan.

"I showed you the seabed sketch, so you know the where we go. We start at Gil's railroad, swim left along the train cars to Joanna's fountain. We'll take a quick look at the figures in the middle of the city and then go to my piece, the 'Great Balance.'"

"Sounds good."

"After that, we make a circle and pass through the gallery where we'll see a poem on the wall from my friend Charlie."

"Uh huh." Maryke clicked her underwater torch on and off, testing it.

"If the current is strong, we head back sooner, okay? Remember, we also have a birthday party to go to."

Maryke slid on her fins and then snapped together her weight belt. "Okay, you're the boss."

"Ah, I love it when women say that to me." Marion laughed, making her own final safety check. She turned on the tiny twinkle light in the dinghy that would act as a beacon for them when they emerged. One less thing to worry about if they surfaced some distance away. "All ready?"

"All ready."

"Okay. Let's go!"

They toppled backward from opposite sides of the inflatable and popped up in front of it. Double *fine* signs showed everything was working, so they began the descent.

In a few moments they were on the seabed in front of the train station. They shone their lights inside but were disappointed to find nothing but exposed steel rods and a single fin wedged between two of them. The outside of the station was more realistic, and hovering on the platform, they studied the schedule carved in the concrete station wall and then swam among the passengers who waited to board.

The locomotive was impressive, and Marion ran the beam of her torch along its metallic side, still fresh enough to send back a reflection. Signaling that Maryke should stay in place, she swam to the other side and shone her torch on the smokestack, creating a hazy steam-like halo over it, which, with a bit of imagination, might suggest smoke.

They paddled the length of the train, shining their lights into the car windows as they passed. The seated concrete passengers looked out at them with empty eyes, like drowning victims, and Maryke signaled her discomfort by hurrying away. They passed the caboose and Marion led the way upward to the next objects on a slope of dead coral.

Maryke halted in front of the two uppermost figures and illuminated Lot, about to crash a stone against the head of his wife. Marion directed her attention downward to the fountain, and while Maryke knelt before one of the two girls, Marion found the reservoir tube and sent a shot of air through it from her regulator mouthpiece. A moment later, a series of silver balls burbled up from the center of the fountain. Marion directed her flashlight beam up to Atiyah, revealing the smaller bubbles that rose from the statue's mouth. Maryke's enthusiastic *fine* sign showed she was greatly amused, and it seemed increasingly likely that she would succumb to Marion's charm that night.

Anxious to present her own work, Marion wove in and out of the other figures in the city, not dwelling on any particular one. To increase the drama, she signaled Maryke to turn off her lamp and follow close behind her.

Thus they made their way in the dark, with only the small sphere of Marion's light sweeping slowly along the base of the first Egyptian pylon. Finally they came to the opening, guarded by the majestic figure of Osiris. Marion brought them to a kneeling position on the sea floor. Then she raised her torch.

Maryke jerked away from her suddenly, and Marion heard her sudden outcry through the mouthpiece. Marion froze in horror.

The arms of the "Great Balance" were tilted at a forty-five-degree angle, as if in final judgment. The higher dish, containing the feather of Maat, swung gently in the current. But the other dish had fallen to the floor, weighed down by the body of a diver caught in its chains.

After a moment of terror and paralysis, Marion approached to investigate. A man in a wetsuit lay face-up, his outstretched arms rising and falling puppet-like with the movement of the water. His regulator mouthpiece dangled in the water next to him. He wasn't tangled in the chains so much as caught by them, as if he had floated past and simply snagged.

Maryke shone her light on his pressure gauge. The needle still showed half a tank. She pressed the purge valve on the mouthpiece, and the rush of bubbles from it showed that it, too, was working properly.

She shook her head, puzzled. Diving theory offered half a dozen explanations for the death, but only a medical examiner could determine the cause for certain. But she'd had enough. She signaled *end of dive* and they ascended.

They were both silent as they hauled themselves back into the inflatable. She started the motor while Maryke shivered at the bow, muttering, "Horrible, horrible."

Shaken also, Marion couldn't bear to look down toward the black water and stared instead at the night sky. The constellations that sparkled overhead seemed silent witnesses.

CHAPTER TWENTY-SIX

Mei sprawled on the bottom of the dinghy clutching her flotation jacket while her mother steered the outboard motor. "What a shame you're selling the *Hina*. I've had the time of my life on it this last week. I mean, once the police inquiry was over and Bernard was buried. We're a family again here, away from the press, and we can invite who we want on the boat. It's our little home. "

"Is it because you need the money?" Kiele, sitting next to her with knees drawn up, looked anxiously at Kaia.

"Well, I'm not poor." Kaia concentrated on finding the correct buoy. "But it *is* a bit of a monster and very expensive to keep. I never wanted anything that grandiose. But don't worry, I'll get a smaller one, just for us, once I get all the finances straightened out."

Mei pressed. "How are you going to sell it if you're not here?"

"Darling, people don't sell their yachts in person, not when they're this size. A broker does it. Hamad will take it to Sharm el-Sheikh tomorrow, where there's a company that handles that sort of thing for a commission. It's all done by Internet these days."

Joanna glanced up from the diving vest she was adjusting. "It's a shame you can't also do the inheritance stuff in absentia, instead of flying all the way to New York. It would be so much nicer to spend the next two weeks getting settled in London before rehearsals begin."

"Yes, but the legal issues in this case are daunting, and I've got to face them personally. I have to meet with tax lawyers about the inheritance, business lawyers about selling the agency, and finally the entertainment lawyer who's going to be my new manager." She chuckled softly. "I'll be a major financier of the legal industry."

"Is that going to be a problem, selling the agency, I mean?"

"I doubt it. Bernard and I were the sole shareholders. ICM has been trying to buy us out for ages and should be happy to take over, especially since it means they'll be getting me. But it's definitely something you want to do with lawyers in the room."

"What about your contract with the Royal Shakespeare?"

"That's an agreement I made personally, and whatever happens in the next weeks doesn't affect it. I've agreed by fax to the contract they sent me. The New York lawyers would laugh at the salary anyhow. I'm not doing it for the money."

"What about the New York press?" Kiele said. "I'm sure they're going to be all over you about the *tragedy* last week. You'll have to play the grieving widow, but at least you're not under suspicion."

"No, thank God for that. With Jibril's testimony, the Egyptian police had no trouble declaring it an accident, from careless filling of the tank. Nobody has to ever know it was an attempted murder that backfired."

"The bastard," Kiele muttered. "Well, what goes around comes around."

Kaia bumped shoulders with her. "Let's talk about more cheerful things, shall we?"

"I've got something cheerful," Joanna announced. "I've applied with the Saint Tropez Art Museum to do another piece of underwater art. This time off the Côte d'Azur. Underwater art exhibits seem to be all the rage now. If they accept, it'll be in September."

Kaia drew the boat up to the buoy and turned off the motor, while Mei tied up to one of its rings. "That would be fantastic. What piece did you propose?"

"Something to do with Atiyah. I'm not finished with her yet. For most people, she's still only Lot's wife, even after all these thousands of years. I want the world to know her name and her story. I want her to have justice."

"Justice," Kiele murmured. "Definitely satisfying, even when it's a long time coming."

"Haven't you had enough controversy? I mean about the tablets," Kaia asked, opening the valve to her tank.

"Oh, I surely have. The museum managed to publish the translations on the day of the opening of the exhibit, and *The Independent* carried the news the next day. The speed of the reaction was astonishing. The day after that, people were screaming that the museum, if not science in general, has embarked on a war against the Bible." Joanna checked her pressure gauge, then slid on her fins.

"Well, let's not dwell on that right now," Kaia said. "This is our last day together in Egypt, and I want us to enjoy it. Kiele, Mei, you know how to get back in the dinghy from the water?"

"Ma, of course we do. We've been snorkeling from the boat all week, and we even made those little dives from here with Peter and Oliver. We'll be fine."

"Everyone's done the safety check? Air tanks open, vests inflated, weight belts in place? Don't want to lose anyone today." Joanna waited for all three heads to nod.

"Okay, over we go." Four somewhat awkward backward plops brought all of them into the water. As they descended, Joanna monitored the two younger women making the slow descent and equalizing of ear pressure.

She felt a vague and deeply comforting sensation, and it took her a moment to realize that it was the sense of family. Not the typical dynamic of parents and children, because they were all adults. It was simply a sudden awareness of cohesion and caring, of planning a future around the hopes and needs of several people, not just herself.

Joanna led the way to the slope where Lot was just about to fell Atiyah with his rock. Lot, with Charlie's face, and Atiyah with the face of Kaia. She wondered for a moment if it wouldn't have been more accurate to use the face of Bernard for Lot. Certainly their characters were parallel. But after reflection, she realized she would not have wanted to immortalize the face of a thug.

While the girls scrutinized the stone copy of their mother, Kaia had already lost interest in her alter ego and was paddling toward the fountain. Joanna joined her in locating the tube to the air reservoir and pumped air into it from her regulator.

A moment later, a stream of bubbles gurgled from the statue's mouth, to the amusement of the girls. Signaling their approval, they paddled down to sit with their mother on the rim of the fountain. The water was unusually clear, and from their vantage point, Joanna could see the entire city. In a moment, they would make the tour, seeing it all again with two fresh sets of eyes.

Kaia suddenly gripped her arm and Joanna glanced up. Three dark forms were just emerging from behind the Egyptian temple. Joanna froze.

She recognized the largest shark immediately by its torn dorsal fin. It was *her* shark, she was sure. Two others flanked him, like gang members.

A dozen thoughts shot through her mind: could they evade them by remaining motionless, could they fight them with a blow to their snouts, how hideously ironic for them to reappear on this final day, which had seemed so triumphant. In her terror, she was breathing faster and expelling more bubbles than usual. They all were. Could the sharks detect their fear?

The largest of the predators passed directly in front of her, and he seemed almost to recognize her, for he paused, one of his small, cold eyes focusing on her. Then he slid by, made a circle and returned, this time over all their heads, his companions swooping by in opposite directions.

They repeated their tour, round and round, in varying ellipses, changing the angle of their orbits. It seemed a game, a shark theme-and-variations to a terror-captive audience. Then, as if completing a dance, all three curled briefly over the fountain in a sort of triple helix and swam off.

Joanna took Kaia's hand, and gratitude settled over her like a blanket. They had come close to death before, she from Bernard's carelessness and Kaia from his rage. Yet they had both survived and had brought Kaia's daughters home as well. They were united now by a new secret, the knowledge that fate itself had come around and brought them justice.

Moreover, Kiele had met her own "lost boy," Mei was set to plunge into the mystery of subatomic particles, and Kaia was about to become the magician Prospera, as if to prove that the best kind of father was one who was a mother.

And to top it all off, she herself had made a damned good sculpture. She ran one hand along the still-smooth surface of the fountain rim. The underwater fountain of air was an inversion, a variation of the normal, even as her love of Kaia was, but the scene was also a declaration of truth, finally granting justice to three grievously wronged women.

Joanna removed her mouthpiece and signaled Kaia to do the same, for a final lover's kiss at the fountain of Gomorrah. Then the four of them ascended together.

About the Author

Recovered academic Justine Saracen started out producing dreary theses, dissertations, and articles for esoteric literary journals. Writing fiction, it turned out, was way more fun. With seven historical thrillers now under her literary belt, she has moved from Ancient Egyptian theology (*The 100th Generation*) to the Crusades (*Vulture's Kiss*) to the Roman Renaissance. *Sistine Heresy,* which conjures up a thoroughly blasphemic backstory to Michelangelo's Sistine Chapel frescoes, won a 2009 Independent Publisher's Award (IPPY), and was a finalist in the Foreword Book of the Year Award.

A few centuries further along, WWII thriller *Mephisto Aria* was a finalist in the EPIC award competition, won Rainbow awards for Best Historical Novel and Best Writing Style, and took the 2011 Golden Crown first prize for best historical novel.

The Eddie Izzard inspired novel, *Sarah, Son of God* followed soon after. In the story within a story, a transgendered beauty takes us through Stonewall-rioting New York, Venice under the Inquisition, and Nero's Rome. The novel won the Rainbow First Prize for Best Transgendered Novel.

Her second WWII thriller *Tyger, Tyger, Burning Bright*, which follows the lives of four homosexuals during the Third Reich, won the 2012 Rainbow First Prize for Historical Novel.

Waiting for the Violins, her work in progress, tells of an English nurse, nearly killed while fleeing Dunkirk, who returns as a British spy and joins forces with the Belgian resistance. In a year of constant terror, she discovers both betrayal and heroism and learns how very costly love can be.

Saracen lives in Europe ("where History comes from") in an adorable little row house on a winding street in Brussels. Her favorite non-literary pursuits are scuba diving and listening to opera. She can be reached by way of www.justinesaracen.com, through FB justinesaracen, and at Twitter as JustSaracen.

Books Available from Bold Strokes Books

The Princess Affair by Nell Stark. Rhodes Scholar Kerry Donovan arrives at Oxford ready to focus on her studies, but her life and her priorities are thrown into chaos when she catches the eye of Her Royal Highness Princess Sasha. (978-1-60282-858-2)

The Chase by Jesse J. Thoma. When Isabelle Rochat's life is threatened, she receives the unwelcome protection and attention of bounty hunter Holt Lasher who vows to keep Isabelle safe at all costs. (978-1-60282-859-9)

The Lone Hunt by L.L. Raand. In a world where humans and praeterns conspire for the ultimate power, violence is a way of life…and death. A Midnight Hunters novel. (978-1-60282-860-5)

The Supernatural Detective by Crin Claxton. Tony Carson sees dead people. With a drag queen for a spirit guide and a devastatingly attractive herbalist for a client, she's about to discover the spirit world can be a very dangerous world indeed. (978-1-60282-861-2)

Beloved Gomorrah by Justine Saracen. Undersea artists creating their own City on the Plain uncover the truth about Sodom and Gomorrah, whose "one righteous man" is a murderer, rapist, and conspirator in genocide. (978-1-60282-862-9)

Cut to the Chase by Lisa Girolami. Careful and methodical author Paige Randolph falls for brash and wild Hollywood actress, Avalon Randolph, but can these opposites find a happy middle ground in a town that never lives in the middle? (978-1-60282-783-7)

More Than Friends by Erin Dutton. Evelyn Fisher thinks she has the perfect role model for a long-term relationship, until her best friends, Kendall and Melanie, split up and all three women must reevaluate their lives and their relationships. (978-1-60282-784-4)

Every Second Counts by D. Jackson Leigh. Every second counts in Bridgette LeRoy's desperate mission to protect her heart and stop Marc Ryder's suicidal return to riding rodeo bulls. (978-1-60282-785-1)

Dirty Money by Ashley Bartlett. Vivian Cooper and Reese DiGiovanni just found out that falling in love is hard. It's even harder when you're running for your life. (978-1-60282-786-8)

Sea Glass Inn by Karis Walsh. When Melinda Andrews commissions a series of mosaics by Pamela Whitford for her new inn, she doesn't expect to be more captivated by the artist than by the paintings. (978-1-60282-771-4)

The Awakening: A Sisters of Spirits novel by Yvonne Heidt. Sunny Skye has interacted with spirits her entire life, but when she runs into Officer Jordan Lawson during a ghost investigation, she discovers more than just facts in a missing girl's cold case file. (978-1-60282-772-1)

Murphy's Law by Yolanda Wallace. No matter how high you climb, you can't escape your past. (978-1-60282-773-8)

Blacker Than Blue by Rebekah Weatherspoon. Threatened with losing her first love to a powerful demon, vampire Cleo Jones is willing to break the ultimate law of the undead to rebuild the family she has lost. (978-1-60282-774-5)

Another 365 Days by KE Payne. Clemmie Atkins is back, and her life is more complicated than ever! Still madly in love with her girlfriend, Clemmie suddenly finds her life turned upside down with distractions, confessions, and the return of a familiar face... (978-1-60282-775-2)

Silver Collar by Gill McKnight. Werewolf Luc Garoul is outlawed and out of control, but can her family track her down before a sinister predator gets there first? Fourth in the Garoul series. (978-1-60282-764-6)

The Dragon Tree Legacy by Ali Vali. For Aubrey Tarver time hasn't dulled the pain of losing her first love Wiley Gremillion, but she has to set that aside when her choices put her life and her family's lives in real danger. (978-1-60282-765-3)

The Midnight Room by Ronica Black. After a chance encounter with the mysterious and brooding Lillian Gray in the "midnight room" of The Griffin, a local lesbian bar, confident and gorgeous Audrey McCarthy learns that her bad-girl behavior isn't bulletproof. (978-1-60282-766-0)

Dirty Sex by Ashley Bartlett. Vivian Cooper and twins Reese and Ryan DiGiovanni stole a lot of money and the guy they took it from wants it back. Like now. (978-1-60282-767-7)

The Storm by Shelley Thrasher. Rural East Texas. 1918. War-weary Jaq Bergeron and marriage-scarred musician Molly Russell try to salvage love from the devastation of the war abroad and natural disasters at home. (978-1-60282-780-6)

Crossroads by Radclyffe. Dr. Hollis Monroe specializes in short-term relationships but when she meets pregnant mother-to-be Annie Colfax, fate brings them together at a crossroads that will change their lives forever. (978-1-60282-756-1)

Beyond Innocence by Carsen Taite. When a life is on the line, love has to wait. Doesn't it? (978-1-60282-757-8)

Heart Block by Melissa Brayden. Socialite Emory Owen and struggling single mom Sarah Matamoros are perfectly suited for each other but face a difficult time when trying to merge their contrasting worlds and the people in them. If love truly exists, can it find a way? (978-1-60282-758-5)

Pride and Joy by M.L. Rice. Perfect Bryce Montgomery is her parents' pride and joy, but when they discover that their daughter is a lesbian, her world changes forever. (978-1-60282-759-2)

Ladyfish by Andrea Bramhall. Finn's escape to the Florida Keys leads her straight into the arms of scuba diving instructor Oz as she fights for her freedom, their blossoming love...and her life! (978-1-60282-747-9)

Spanish Heart by Rachel Spangler. While on a mission to find herself in Spain, Ren Molson runs the risk of losing her heart to her tour guide, Lina Montero. (978-1-60282-748-6)

Love Match by Ali Vali. When Parker "Kong" King, the number one tennis player in the world, meets commercial pilot Captain Sydney Parish, sparks fly—but not from attraction. They have the summer to see if they have a love match. (978-1-60282-749-3)

One Touch by L.T. Marie. A romance writer and a travel agent come together at their high school reunion, only to find out that the memory of that one touch never fades. (978-1-60282-750-9)

The Raid by Lee Lynch. Before Stonewall, having a drink with friends or your girl could mean jail. Would these women and men still have family, a job, a place to live after...The Raid? (978-1-60282-753-0)

The You Know Who Girls: Freshman Year by Annameekee Hesik. As they begin freshman year, Abbey Brooks and her best friend, Kate, pinkie swear they'll keep away from the lesbians in Gila High, but Abbey already suspects she's one of those you-know-who girls herself and slowly learns who her true friends really are. (978-1-60282-754-7)

Month of Sundays by Yolanda Wallace. Love doesn't always happen overnight; sometimes it takes a month of Sundays. (978-1-60282-739-4)

Jacob's War by C.P. Rowlands. ATF Special Agent Allison Jacob's task force is in the middle of an all-out war, from the streets to the boardrooms of America. Small business owner Katie Blackburn is the latest victim who accidentally breaks it wide open, but she may break AJ's heart at the same time. (978-1-60282-740-0)

The Pyramid Waltz by Barbara Ann Wright. Princess Katya Nar Umbriel wants a perfect romance, but her Fiendish nature and duties to the crown mean she can never tell the truth—until she meets Starbride, a woman who gets to the heart of every secret, even if it will be the death of her. (978-1-60282-741-7)

The Secret of Othello by Sam Cameron. Florida teen detectives Steven and Denny risk their lives to search for a sunken NASA satellite—but under the waves, no one can hear you scream... (978-1-60282-742-4)

Finding Bluefield by Elan Barnehama. Set in the backdrop of Virginia and New York and spanning the years 1960–1982, *Finding Bluefield* chronicles the lives of Nicky Stewart, Barbara Philips, and their son, Paul, as they struggle to define themselves as a family. (978-1-60282-744-8)